To Ray

with the affectionate
best wishes of his
godfather

Compton Mackenzie

Christmas 1957

BEN NEVIS GOES EAST

BY COMPTON MACKENZIE

BEN NEVIS
GOES EAST

By

Compton Mackenzie

Cmpk Ruckinyu

1954

CHATTO & WINDUS

LONDON

PUBLISHED BY

Chatto and Windus Ltd

LONDON

∗

Clarke, Irwin & Co. Ltd

TORONTO

PRINTED IN GREAT BRITAIN
BY T. AND A. CONSTABLE LTD, EDINBURGH

ALL RIGHTS RESERVED

To
LENNOX MILNE
and
MORAY McLAREN
affectionately

Edinburgh
March 28th, 1954

CONTENTS

Chapter 1

THE DISTURBING LETTER

IT was a November morning, some months after Donald MacDonald 23rd of Ben Nevis added that notable chapter to the long and martial history of mighty Clan Donald when he repelled the invasion of his country by the National Union of Hikers. Mrs MacDonald was conferring with Mrs Parsall, her housekeeper, in that room at Glenbogle Castle which, though it might still be called the Yellow Drawing-Room, she had turned into a cosy retreat for herself that was for ever England.

"I'm glad Mrs Ablewhite's holiday has done her so much good," the Lady of Ben Nevis said to her housekeeper.

"Yes, indeed, madam, and she really needed it. The way her dinner was spoilt that night of the Gathering seemed to regularly prey upon her, as they say!"

"And she is *such* a good cook."

"Yes, indeed, madam. I don't know where I should find such another in these days."

At this moment the quiet air of Mrs MacDonald's chintz sanctum was disturbed by a sound that a stranger might have been excused for comparing to the noise of the lions in the Zoo roaring impatiently in the half-hour before their feeding-time.

"That will be Ben Nevis, madam," said the housekeeper, with the faintest hint of a frown above her austere and respectable nose.

"I think it must be," Mrs MacDonald agreed.

A few seconds later the door of the Yellow Drawing-Room burst open and Mac 'ic Eachainn himself charged in, waving a letter.

"Trixie, I want to read you a letter. Good-morning, Mrs Parsall. It's a letter from India, Trixie."

"Nothing has happened to Hector?" Mrs MacDonald asked, her usually steady contralto quavering in momentary apprehension.

"Well, it depends what you call 'happened'," the Chieftain barked. "I mean, he hasn't had his leg ripped up by a pig or anything like that."

Mrs Parsall by now had reached the door.

"There's nothing more you want to talk to me about, madam?"

Mrs MacDonald shook her head.

"Not that the poor soul would have had a chance to say anything," Mrs Parsall observed to Mrs Ablewhite when she reached the housekeeper's room. "He was in one of his bubbles."

Mrs Ablewhite nodded sagely.

Upstairs the Chieftain was bubbling so hard over the letter from India that his wife insisted upon reading it to herself.

The sheet of writing-paper carried the crest of the Duke of Clarence's Own Clanranald Highlanders—the Clanranald bear beneath a ducal coronet with the regimental motto '*Air Adhart*'—in English 'Forward'. The word 'secret' in red ink had been scratched out and 'confidential' substituted.

> *North Cantonment,*
> *Tallulaghabad*
> *October 9.*

Dear Ben Nevis,

After a great deal of anxious thought I feel that as his commanding officer it is my duty to write to you about your boy Hector because I should consider myself lacking in my duty if I did not let you know that he may presently find himself committed to a marriage of which I am sure neither you nor Mrs MacDonald would approve.

I have always regarded your boy Hector as one of my most promising subalterns and provided war comes within the next few years (which of course we all of us hope it won't) I believe he will gain rapid promotion. It would be a great pity if when war does come your boy Hector should find himself tied to a most unsuitable wife, because nothing impedes promotion so much. The lady in question is a Mrs Winstanley who recently divorced her husband the manager of the British and Oriental Bank in Jumbulpore. Another story says that he divorced her, and my wife is having enquiries made about this in England. Mrs Winstanley is a young woman of twenty-six, although I should add that my wife insists she is certainly at least thirty, in which case she'd be five years older than your boy Hector. She is also having enquiries made about this in Mrs Winstanley's home town which according to her story is Canterbury. There is, however, a strong rumour that she is the daughter of a clerk in the office of a Calcutta jute firm and that her mother was as we say here 'of the country' or, to speak bluntly, that her mother was Anglo-Indian. Certainly Mrs Winstanley is dark and unquestionably extremely good-looking. I understand from one or two of Hector's brother officers that during the recent short spell of leave he had in Scotland he suffered a disappointment in an affair of the heart. You know what Kipling says. I can't remember the exact quotation, but it's something about falling in love with somebody else on the rebound. Anyway, there's no doubt at all that he is completely infatuated by the charms of this Mrs Winstanley which I will say frankly are considerable, though my wife cannot understand her attraction for men.

It may of course be only one of those flirtations which the Indian climate seems to encourage, but I have been assured that Hector is determined to marry her and that the only thing that deters her from accepting him at once is some complication about this business of a decree nisi which I've never really understood.

Anyway, I should feel much happier if you could see your way to come out to Tallulaghabad, which is quite a pleasant station in winter though rather a terror between May and September. I feel that if Mrs Winstanley could be made to realise that a match between her and Hector would not be approved of by his family she would look elsewhere. Fortunately from what I hear she can look in several directions, and indeed already has two or three other possibles in tow.

You could fly out, and my wife and I would be delighted to put *you up. I am sorry to worry you with such a disturbing letter, but I feel you might rightly blame me if I let things go too far without warning you of possible eventualities. As I say it may be only a flirtation but a stitch in time saves nine, as my dear old Nannie used to say.*

Please remember me most kindly to Mrs MacDonald.

Yours sincerely,

Alastair Rose-Ross

"Oh dear, oh dear," Mrs MacDonald murmured with a profound sigh when she had finished the Colonel's epistle. "This is all most distressing. I wonder what is the wisest thing to do now."

"Did you notice what Rose-Ross said about flying out, Trixie?" the Chieftain asked. "I wonder he doesn't suggest I should turn head over heels in the dining-room of the New Club. I always said Rose-Ross was a bit of a nincompoop."

"I don't agree with you at all, Donald. I think this is an extremely considerate letter."

"What, suggesting that I should fly out to India? I never heard a more peprosterous suggestion in my life."

"Never mind about the way you go to India, Donald. The point is that you will certainly have to go. That is obvious."

"Oh, you think it is?"

"I do."

"But suppose it all turns out to be a storm in a teapot, Trixie?"

"You can't afford to suppose that," she answered firmly. "You can't have Hector coming home from India with somebody else's divorced wife. Imagine what Colonel Lindsay-Wolseley would say. He knows India."

"It's all he does know then. I haven't forgotten the way he ran out on me when I decided to take drastic action about those hikers. I said, 'You talk a lot about the way you Puffers kept the North-West Frontier quiet, Lindsay-Wolseley,' and what do you think he said to me? He said, 'I suppose you mean Piffers, Ben Nevis.' He was quite annoyed with me for calling them Puffers. These soldiers are as touchy as old women. But he knew he was in the wrong. That's why he's been trying to annoy me by putting round this vile rumour that the Loch Ness Monster is an optical delusion."

"Donald, must the Loch Ness Monster be brought into this? Please give your attention to the very grave problem Colonel Rose-Ross has brought to your notice. What are you going to do about it?"

"I'm going to see Hugh. If he'll come out with me to India we'll sail at once."

"But supposing Hugh Cameron won't go?"

"I'm sure that Hugh will come. Hugh holds fast by the old clan loyalties."

While Donald MacDonald of Ben Nevis in Glenbogle Castle was thus confidently disposing of his movements, Hugh Cameron of Kilwhillie, with Bonzo his black retriever, was taking a pensive stroll along the banks of Loch Whillie and, although he was not a man who approved of displaying the least emotion, he could not help stopping to admire the reflection of Ben Quilt in the unruffled water on this still November morning, the bracken on the lower slopes of the most graceful ben in the West, rich as Titian's auburn after the rain. As he tugged gently at his long drooping moustaches the laird of Kilwhillie recalled the figure of some philosophic mandarin in a Chinese screen. He was in a state of equanimity. The new Austin which the sale of Knocknacolly Lodge to those rich American friends of Ben Nevis had made a possible purchase had been his for six weeks now. Neil Mackillop, his factor, had not argued with him about the new garage he was proposing to build. His sister Georgie's annual visit was over; she and her Pekes had gone home to Wimbledon. Morag Fraser his housekeeper was back from Beauly, where she had been looking after an elderly aunt from whom she had expectations. The long winter stretched agreeably before his fancy now that he had been able to afford some repairs and improvements to Kilwhillie House, which he had been unable to manage lately owing to the weight of taxation. Yes, a long undraughty winter . . . an occasional drive in to Inverness for a well-hung grouse with a bottle of port at the Club . . . an occasional drive to lunch with old friends . . . an occasional night at Glenbogle with Donald . . . *Blackwood's*, *The Field*, *Country Life* . . . he might even buy what they called a wire-less set . . . his cousin John had one at Invercoddle . . . of course the Macleans always did go in for novelties . . . still, this wireless business had been going now for over ten years and looked like being a permanency . . . in the present state of the world and with *The Scotsman* not arriving until next day it might be a good notion to listen to the news. Quite sound people made a habit of listening to the news on the wireless nowadays.

At this moment the laird caught sight of his factor's bulk approaching him. He frowned slightly. He was not inclined to have this tranquil mood disturbed by Neil Mackillop's loud, high, metallic voice.

"Good-morning, Neil. Nothing the matter, I hope?"

"Not at all. But there's been a telephone message from Glenbogle to say that Ben Nevis is coming to lunch with you. Morag was a bit put about because she was meaning to go in to Fort William to one of these cinemas."

"Good god," Kilwhillie exclaimed. "I hope she's not going to make a habit of that sort of thing."

"It seems she went in to Inverness once or twice when she was with her aunt at Beauly. Och, the women like them. The *cailleach* is always on at me to take her to what they call the pictures."

"I'm surprised to hear that Mrs Mackillop likes the cinema. I've only once been to a cinema myself and I simply couldn't understand what it was all about. By the way, Neil, I am thinking seriously of getting what they call a wireless set."

"Och, it'll be no kind of an amusement for you at all, Kilwhillie. I can't hear myself speak when the *cailleach* turns it on and Herself says she can't hear the wireless because I'm talking so loud."

"I shall only listen to the news," said the laird severely.

"Ach, you won't get any news at all, Kilwhillie. There's more news in the *Obaig Times* once a week than there is on the wireless in a whole year."

When Kilwhillie and his factor were arguing about the merits of wireless, Ben Nevis in his pre-1914 Daimler, once described as a boudoir on the back of an elephant, was being driven down majestic Glenbogle in due course to be driven up equally majestic Glenbore to his neighbour's ancient grim grey house.

Kilwhillie awaited his arrival in the drawing-room that was crowded with the bric-à-brac accumulated by his father and grandfather through the nineteenth century; when Ben Nevis surged in, the lustred candlesticks tinkled, one could have fancied apprehensively.

"I told Toker to ring through to say I was coming. I'm so tremendously excited about this little trip of ours, Hugh, that I couldn't have borne it if you'd taken it into your head to go out. I should have burst."

"This little trip of ours, Donald? What little trip?"

"We ought to be able to sail next week."

"Not in Jack Rawstorne's yacht," Kilwhillie snapped. "Nothing will induce me to go anywhere on the *Banshee* in November. Nothing."

"Not the *Banshee*," the Chieftain guffawed loudly. "The *Banshee* might have been all right for old Christopher Columbus to go to India in, but it wouldn't suit us, Hugh."

"To go where?" Kilwhillie gulped incredulously. "Did you say 'go to India?'"

"Yes, in the good ship *Taj Mahal* of the I.B.C. line sailing to Bombay on November 20th according to the advertisements in *The Times*. I'm awfully excited about it. I haven't been so far away from Scotland since I was with the Scouts in South Africa. I'm longing to see Lindsay-Wolseley's face when we come back with tigers and those things with crinkly horns whose name I never can remember. We'll go to Edinburgh the day after to-morrow and fit ourselves out."

"Look here, Donald, is this an elaborate joke of yours?" the Cameron laird asked earnestly.

"Joke? It won't be a joke at all if young Hector comes back here with this Mrs Winstanley. Trixie's frightfully worried. But you and I will be able to make him see sense. And if he won't see sense, by Jove, I'll cut off his allowance which would mean selling his ponies. You can't play polo on the pay of a subaltern. I'm going to be absolutely firm, Hugh. After all, Hector will be the 24th of Ben Nevis one day, and we can't have Glenbogle swarming with a lot of little piccaninnies. Look here, you'd better read this letter from Hector's colonel and then you'll see why you and I have to go to India as soon as possible."

Kilwhillie read what Colonel Rose-Ross had written, his brow wrinkling with distaste from time to time, one of his moustaches squeezed so tightly as to give the impression that he was wringing from it moisture engendered by the story of Hector and Mrs Winstanley.

"Yes, it certainly sounds a most unpleasant business," he muttered at last. "Most unpleasant. I think it would be wise if you took his colonel's advice and did fly out."

"Fly out?" Ben Nevis echoed, if a repetition six times as loud as the original can be called an echo. "You're not seriously proposing that I should climb into one of these ghastly contraptions and go buzzing half across the world in it? You really are an extraordinary chap, Hugh. Sometimes, you know, I wonder if you quite realise what you're saying."

"It's no more extraordinary for me to suggest you should fly out to India than for you to suggest that I should go there in a boat," Kilwhillie shuddered. "You know that I dislike being on the sea more than anything else in the world."

"I know you're not a very good sailor."

"I'm a very bad sailor," Kilwhillie interrupted to affirm,

the tone of his voice coming as near to passionate utterance as it had ever been known to come.

"Yes, well, these wise men of Gotham have invented a pill. 'Neversick' they call it. You just take one when you're feeling squeamish and before you know where you are you're running up the rigging like a regular Nelson. I saw it in an advertisement."

"I don't believe in advertisements," said the laird of Kilwhillie coldly.

"But anyway, Hugh, you won't feel seasick on the *Taj Mahal*. She's over 10,000 tons."

"I am not coming, Donald."

"That's what Trixie said," Ben Nevis sighed. "But I said she was wrong. I said I jolly well knew that the old clan spirit wasn't dead in Kilwhillie. Dash it, Hugh, we've fought back to back for five hundred years and more. If we hadn't, Glenbore and Glenbogle would have been over-run by Campbells and Macintoshes and hikers. Look here, Hugh, you can't desert me at this moment. I shall want your advice. I rely on you. Rose-Ross means well, but in my humble opinion he's fundamentally a duffer. You mark my words, they'll give him a brigade as soon as we have another war. We shall be able to settle Hector's business as soon as we arrive and then we'll enjoy ourselves. I thought we'd go and stay with the Maharaja of—I can't remember his exact name at the moment, but it begins with 'Bang'. Or is it 'Bung'? No, it can't be 'Bung' because he used to be called 'Banjo' at Harrow. Anyway, he's a capital chap and he'll give us some great sport. He was in the Harrow Eleven."

"If you think I'm going all the way to India to play that extremely boring game cricket, you're wrong, Donald."

"I don't mean cricket. I mean shooting tigers and those things with crinkly horns. And then there's old Finchampton, the Viceroy. He was at Harrow with me too. Oh, we shall have a jolly good time, Hugh."

Why on that calm morning early in November with the

B

long undraughty winter stretching agreeably before him he should have consented to accompany Ben Nevis to India would puzzle Hugh Cameron for a long time. It meant separation from Bonzo. It meant leaving Morag Fraser to become a cinema addict. It meant postponing the improvements he had planned to make at Kilwhillie with the money he had acquired from the sale of Knocknacolly. It meant laying up his new Austin. It meant divesting himself of the kilt and living for the next three months in trousers. It meant a complete upheaval in his orderly life. Yet none of these deterrents had availed against Donald's appeal.

And to sail from Liverpool! The very name of the port curdled his inside!

Chapter 2

CLAN LOYALTIES

B EN NEVIS got back to Glenbogle that afternoon in a
mood of expansive and explosive geniality.

"I don't know why you thought Hugh wouldn't come,
Trixie," he said to his wife, who was presiding over the tea-
table like the Demeter of Cnidos. "He jumped at the idea.
Well, I knew all those Burmese gongs and carved Indian
bellows and brass tables and ebony elephants and what not
his grandfather brought back with him from the East must
have made old Hugh as keen as mustard to see where they
all came from. I suggested he should practise with that
hookah he's got. I think it would appeal to the Maharaja
of Bang . . . what is his name, Trixie? Don't you remember?
He was at Harrow with me and you met him at the
Finchamptons when you dragged me down to London on
one of your appalling visits to that horrible place? I couldn't
go to lunch, but *you* met him."

"You mean the Maharaja of Bangapatam."

"That's it. I wish I had your memory for names, Trixie.
Did you ever hear of a thing they call Pelmanism? The idea
is that you remember something else and then you can
remember by remembering something else what you really
wanted to remember. Now I shall remember 'Pat-a-cake-
pan the baker's man', and then I shall remember Banga . . .
Banga . . . it can't be Bangapancake, or can it?"

"Bangapatam," said Mrs MacDonald patiently.

"Yes, of course!" The Chieftain muttered over to himself
once or twice the elusive name. "Yes, Hugh's as keen as
mustard," he went on. "He shied a bit at having to give up
the kilt. He seemed to have old-maidish notions about
getting a chill on the stomach. I said, 'The answer to that,
Hugh, is to wear a flannel or woollen stomach-protector,

and anyway you can always wear the kilt in the evening when we stay with the Maharaja of Bang . . .' now, don't tell me, Trixie . . . of Bangapatam. Got it," he shouted triumphantly. "You see, there really is something in this Pelmanism business. The other thing that worried Hugh was leaving that dog of his. 'Well,' I said, 'you'd look jolly foolish if old Bonzo went mad and bit you.' And of course he saw my point."

"It's a pity in a way that you can't take Catriona or Mary with you," said Mrs MacDonald, who was beginning to wonder if either of her two hefty daughters would ever find an eligible young man to propose marriage."

"Yes, well, I don't think I could take one without the other," said their father. "And I couldn't very well ask Hugh to spend all his time chaperoning them. Of course, if you were coming out it would be different, but you hate hot weather, don't you?"

"I shall only come out to India if Hector refuses to listen to you. I would do anything to stop this dreadful marriage," Mrs MacDonald declared with unwonted emphasis.

"I wondered whether I should take Toker with me, but Hugh said we should both need bearers. I didn't know what he was talking about at first. 'Good lord, Hugh,' I said, 'the heat won't be as bad as all that. We shall be able to walk about without being carried about like a couple of infants.' And then he explained that a bearer is what we call a valet really. So when I write to Hector I shall tell him to look out for a couple of good bearers and send them to meet us at Bombay when we arrive. I stopped at Kenspeckle and telegraphed to the I.B.C. steamship people for a couple of cabins on the *Taj Mahal*. Hugh and I are going to Edinburgh the day after to-morrow. We'll stay at the New Club, but Hugh thinks we may have to go down to that frightful place London for a few days. I'll stay at Brown's if I do and eat at White's. I've just been working out it has cost me about a hundred guineas each of the times I've been in to White's since I became a member soon after going down from Cambridge. So I must try and reduce the average. Hugh says he feels the same about the Guards, but I pointed out to him that he got jolly good value from the Guards Club when he was in the Brigade. I may have to go to a tailor chap in Conduit Street for a pair of jodhpurs. I doubt if old Simpkins in Edinburgh will be able to make them."

"What are jodhpurs?" Mrs MacDonald asked.

"Well, they're a kind of cross between riding-breeches and tights, if you know what I mean."

"Yes, I know now what they are. General Mackenzie's little granddaughters wear them."

"Really? Makes 'em look a bit shrimpish, doesn't it? Well, perhaps I'll take my old Bedford cord breeches out with me and get cooler ones made out there."

"You'll have to make up your mind very soon what clothes you are going to take with you if you propose to start the day after to-morrow, Donald."

The Chieftain rushed from the Yellow Drawing-Room to shout exuberant orders all over the Castle.

"How quiet it all sounds, Mr Toker," Mrs Parsall observed to the butler when the great pre-war Daimler with Ben Nevis and Kilwhillie inside and their trunks bestowed on top was on the way to Inverness two days later.

"Yes, it has been a bit fidgety yesterday and this morning," the butler agreed.

"Fidgety, Mr Toker?" Mrs Parsall exclaimed. "An earthquake would have seemed like a rest cure beside Glenbogle these two days. Mrs MacDonald has gone up to lay down. She's quite exhausted, poor soul."

In the Daimler, Ben Nevis and Kilwhillie were critically eyeing one another's trousers.

"You look awfully funny in trousers, Hugh," said Ben Nevis.

"I don't look any funnier than you do, and I can't think why you wanted to drive all the way to Inverness when I could have met you so easily at Fort William," Kilwhillie said fretfully.

"I wanted to get this gun I heard Macfarlane was offering."

"What gun?"

"This gun for shooting tigers and all that sort of thing."

"What is it?"

"I don't remember exactly what it is. Express something or other. But I wish you wouldn't talk so much, Hugh, while we're driving beside the Loch."

From the Daimler Ben Nevis was gazing out across Loch Ness.

"Too late in the season, Hugh, I'm afraid, for the dear old Monster," he commented. "But I must say I should have liked to have a last glimpse of our old friend. Stop a minute, Johnnie, just in case," he told his driver.

The waters of the great loch were cold and grey in the light of the November afternoon: the air through the open window of the Daimler came chill.

"May be you'll be seeing a sea-serpent before you get to India, Ben Nevis," said Johnnie Macpherson sardonically.

"By Jove, so I may, Johnnie," the Chieftain agreed enthusiastically. "And you know, Hugh, Johnnie's right," he continued when the Daimler was again on the way to Inverness. "You'll hear people argue that there are no such creatures as sea-serpents. But in my humble opinion some people will argue anything. I heard a fellow arguing the other day that we ought to make a national park of the West Highlands. 'And I suppose you'd like to put me behind a turnstile and charge the public sixpence for looking at me,' I said. Oh, I say, Hugh, I made a jolly good joke at the last Council meeting. I haven't told you about it. You know that Bolshie minister from Skye who always makes me see red at Council meetings."

"That's what he's trying to do, isn't it?" Kilwhillie observed drily.

This sally was greeted with exuberant appreciation.

"Jolly good, Hugh. That's almost as good a joke as mine when I said to the Reverend Duncan MacLachlan, 'I do wish you wouldn't wash your dirty Lenin at Council meetings, Mr MacLachlan."

"I don't think a pun's a very good joke," Kilwhillie commented distastefully. "Mine wasn't a pun."

"What was your joke, then, Hugh?"

"I don't think it has any particular name. It was just a simple joke. It wasn't quite an epigram."

"I know that. Good lord, you don't make jokes on tombstones."

"As a matter of fact, people do sometimes."

"Do they?" the Chieftain asked incredulously.

"There's a collection of amusing epitaphs in one of the books at Kilwhillie."

"Ah, in a book," the Chieftain allowed. "Well, people will put anything in a book. I don't read much, Hugh. But I've read enough to know that. I'll tell you what I am going to do when we get to Edinburgh, Hugh. I'm going to buy a book about India at a bookshop, and if I can I shall read it on board. I say, Hugh, do you realise that this is going to be a bit of an adventure for us both?"

"I'm only thinking about the voyage," his companion replied gloomily.

When they reached Inverness Kilwhillie announced that he would wait for his companion in the Porridge Hotel.

"But I think you ought to buy a rifle too, if Macfarlane has one."

"I am not going tiger-shooting," Kilwhillie declared.

Ben Nevis sighed gustily.

"You'll get old before your time, Hugh, if you aren't careful," he protested. "I should have thought you'd have jumped at the idea of hanging two or three tiger skins among all those brass trays, and I'm sure your factor would like one."

"Neil Mackillop has quite enough to do filling up forms without bothering about tigers," said Kilwhillie testily.

Leaving the Chieftain to deal with the problem of his armoury, the Cameron laird went in to the hotel.

Maclean, the porter, greeted him.

"Is it true what they're saying, Kilwhillie?"

"Is what true? They'll say anything in Inverness."

"That you and Ben Nevis are off to India on a jaunt. The Colonel was asking me about it just now."

"We are going to India, yes," Kilwhillie admitted. "But not on a jaunt."

At that moment Colonel Lindsay-Wolseley of Tummie rose from a chair in the lounge to greet his neighbour.

"So you and Ben Nevis are going East, eh?" he said, and his sallow complexion was faintly flushed by the prospect before his friends. "By Jove, you're going to enjoy this jaunt."

"I wish everybody wouldn't call it a jaunt," said Kilwhillie. "I've agreed to accompany Donald Ben Nevis to Tallulaghabad on a family business."

"Yes, I heard from Morton . . . he's a Gurkha, you know. Commands the 12th . . . that young Hector's got himself tied up with a woman who was in a rather queer kind of a divorce case."

Kilwhillie looked at the Colonel in amazement. That a man who had impressed himself upon the whole county as the embodiment of soldierly reserve should be gossiping like some member of the Women's Rural Institute shocked him deeply.

"Of course, it may be only bazaar talk," the Colonel went on.

Kilwhillie clutched his moustache. For the Colonel actually to admit that he had been talking about a neighbouring Chieftain's family affairs at a bazaar appalled him.

"Still, I expect Rose-Ross will be relieved to have Ben Nevis on the spot. It's a great responsibility for a commanding officer when one of his subalterns takes the bit between his teeth, what? I had a subaltern once who went home on leave and came back married to an actress nine years older than himself. If we'd still been in Peshawar it wouldn't have mattered *so* much. But we'd been ordered up the Khyber where this magenta woman looked dreadfully conspicuous. Look here, we must have a chota peg to drink bon voyage."

"What is it, sherbet or something?" Kilwhillie asked. "I'd rather have a small whisky."

"A chota peg *is* a small whisky," the Colonel chuckled as he beckoned to the waiter. "What ship are you sailing in?"

"I believe it's called the *Taj Mahal*."

"Ah, one of the old I.B.C. packets. I know her well. I wonder if Captain Bunting is still with her. Capital chap. Coolest hand at liar dice I ever met. Remember me to him if he's still her captain."

"I don't expect I shall be about much during the voyage," said Kilwhillie. "I think you'd better send any messages you have for the Captain by Donald Ben Nevis."

"Ah, here are our whiskies. Well, my dear fellow, I envy you," said the Colonel, raising his glass. "By Jove, I wish I were going out with Ben Nevis."

"I wish you were too," Kilwhillie said, almost fervidly.

The slightly strained relations between Mac 'ic Eachainn and the laird of Tummie after the refusal of the latter to support his attack on the hikers on Drumcockie Moor last Twelfth of August had been gradually relaxed, and when Ben Nevis came into the lounge of the Porridge Hotel carrying his new rifle in a leather case they greeted one another cordially enough.

"Well, I envy you, Ben Nevis," said the Colonel. "Yes, first with the old Forty Thieves—40th Pathans, you know —for a year and then with the Frontier Force Rifles. It was a great life. Often wish I was back with the Piffers. That's what we call the old Punjab Frontier Force."

"Yes, and don't you call them Puffers, Hugh," said Ben Nevis.

"Why should I call them Puffers?" Kilwhillie asked in some bewilderment.

"Well, it's the sort of thing you might do. You never know."

"I think you'd better have a chota peg with me, Donald," his friend suggested.

It was the turn of Mac 'ic Eachainn to look puzzled.

"A small whisky."

"Well, slahnjervaw, Hugh, to our expedition," said the Chieftain raising his glass. "Good lord," he exclaimed, "there isn't enough whisky in that to choke a fly. What's the Indian for a large whisky, Wolseley? I'll find that more useful to remember than choker peg."

"Burra peg."

"Waiter," Mac 'ic Eachainn roared.

An old lady who had been nodding in an adjacent chair woke up with such a start that her spectacles fell into her lap. A minister looked over the top of *The Glasgow Observer* to gape at Ben Nevis. A toy poodle yapped, and a small child descending the main stairs slipped down a couple of them. The waiter hurried across the lounge.

"Three barrow pegs," said the Chieftain.

"Sir?"

"Three large whiskies. You try and remember that word, Hugh. I don't want to start ordering choker pegs when what we want are barrow pegs. How many tigers did you kill when you were in India, Wolseley?"

"I only bagged a couple. Never had much chance to get away from the Frontier. You won't get any tigers round Tallulaghabad, Ben Nevis."

"Won't I?"

"Wonderful duck, though."

"Dash it, I can't shoot duck with an Express rifle," Ben Nevis protested. "Do you know the Maharaja of Bang . . . Bang . . . Bang . . . don't tell me, Hugh . . ."

"I remember the Raja of Bong in the *Country Girl* when I was at Winchester," said Kilwhillie.

"My dear Hugh, don't go dragging a lot of other rajas into it. You'll get me into a frightful muddle. Bang . . . Bang . . ."

"I beg pardon, sir?" said the waiter, who was arriving with the three burra pegs at that moment.

"Nothing, nothing. I was trying to remember something." He turned to Kilwhillie. "What does pat-a-cake remind you of, Hugh?"

"It doesn't remind me of anything."

"Well, it ought to," Ben Nevis declared firmly.

"I really cannot see why, Donald."

"Because it's Pelmanism. You ought to go in for that, Hugh."

The Colonel intervened.

"Isn't pat-a-cake-pan the baker's man an old nursery rhyme?"

Ben Nevis shook his head reproachfully.

"How can I remember the Maharaja of Bangapatam when you start talking about bakers, Wolseley? But I have remembered his name," the Chieftain went on in surprise. "Good lord, what a wonderful thing this Pelmanism is!"

"Oh, I know old Bangapatam," said the Colonel. "He's a great chap. You'll get a tiger if you go and stay with him. Well, you're going to enjoy yourselves in Tallulaghabad. You'll arrive just at the right time of year. By Jove, I do wish I were going with you. Best years of my life. What wouldn't I give to be getting my spoon into a mango at this moment!"

"Getting your spoon into a mangold?" Ben Nevis exclaimed in amazement. "Did you say 'mangold', Worsley . . . Wolseley, I mean?"

The Colonel laughed heartily, and even Kilwhillie had to smile very briefly.

"No, no, mango," the Colonel said. "It's the great Indian fruit."

"Well, why do they call it mangold if it's a fruit?" Ben Nevis demanded. "A root isn't a fruit."

The Chieftain's indignation was diverted at that moment by the entry of Maclean the porter to say that his chauffeur was suggesting that if he and Kilwhillie intended to catch the Edinburgh train it was high time they came along to the station. Five minutes later MacDonald and Cameron were sitting opposite one another in a first-class carriage looking pensively out at the northern landscape in the fading light of the grey November afternoon.

"I don't know why Hector wanted to get tied up with this woman," said Ben Nevis presently.

"And I certainly don't," his friend agreed.

"I feel we have a lot to answer for, Hugh."

"I don't see how we can be held responsible for Hugh's infatuation."

"No, you don't see what I mean. I was thinking about the clearances."

"What have the clearances got to do with the problem of an unsuitable match?"

"I was thinking how depressing it must have been for our people when we made them emigrate. I've always argued that my great-grandfather was right when he cleared Glen Bristle, but I'm beginning to wonder now if he was."

"You're not getting converted to Scottish Nationalism, are you?" Kilwhillie asked suspiciously.

"Good lord, no. All the same, when one's leaving Scotland like this one begins to appreciate it, if you know what I mean. And I appreciate very much what you're doing for me, Hugh. I'm afraid you'll miss dear old Glenbore."

The Chieftain blew a fanfare on his great beak.

"Johnnie will be well on the way home by now," he went on. "I have two flasks of Glenbogle's Pride in my dressing-case. I think we want a dram. These trousers make me feel very tired."

The two Highlanders drank to one another. Then they drank to the land of bens and glens and heroes. Then they drank to one another again and finally they emptied the flasks with a toast to their happy return.

Some minutes later both of them were sleeping as the train went southward into the darkness. They might have served a Victorian painter as models for an Academy picture entitled 'The Emigrants' Dream of Home'.

Chapter 3

EASTWARD HO!

WHEN a week later Ben Nevis and Kilwhillie entered the train at Euston that was to take them to Liverpool the Cameron laird looked five years older than when still a year and a half away from fifty he left Lochaber. On the other hand Mac 'ic Eachainn had been rejuvenated by a week of intensive shopping in Edinburgh and London, and although he was now in his sixty-second year he did not look any older than fifty-five.

"I didn't mind that ghastly place London as much as usual," he told his companion. "But I cannot understand why Brown's have doors in two streets. I never know which street I'm in when I go out. I suppose you aren't old enough to remember the Long Bar at the Criterion, Hugh?"

"I feel old enough to remember the Flood," Kilwhillie muttered languidly.

"I hope you didn't feel seasick in the Ark," Ben Nevis woofed.

An expression of weary distaste made Kilwhillie's moustaches twitch faintly.

"Well, at the Long Bar," Ben Nevis went on, "at the Cri as we used to call it at Trinity, you went in from Piccadilly and you went out in Jermyn Street. No, I'm wrong. It wasn't Jermyn Street. It was Panton Street. Or was it?"

"Does it matter much?" Kilwhillie asked coldly. "The place is now extinct apparently."

"No, it doesn't matter so much as all that except that I always like to get my facts correct. We'll arrive at Liverpool by two."

"I wish we were going to arrive at Fort William at any time," said Kilwhillie. "Any time at all," he repeated.

Ben Nevis leaned over to admonish his companion.

"Look here, Hugh, I wish you wouldn't be so gloomy. It depresses me. You and I are going out to India because we want to rescue young Hector from the charms of a . . . of a . . . dash it, I've forgotten what the word is. It begins with H."

"If you're thinking of the same word as I am you're spelling it wrong. It begins with W."

"Harpy!" Ben Nevis shouted triumphantly.

"Oh, harpy. I thought you were thinking of another word."

"When we've rescued him," Ben Nevis went on, "we want to enjoy ourselves. After all, Hugh, one doesn't go to India every day."

"No, thank Heaven," his companion agreed with warmth.

"Even if you're seasick every single day between here and Bombay, you won't be sick *in* Bombay if you see what I mean, and when we get home again after breaking off this peprosterous business we shall feel we've done the right thing and at the same time we shall have enjoyed ourselves."

"You'll have enjoyed yourself, Donald. I shan't."

"Don't you want to see the East?"

"Not a bit," Kilwhillie replied firmly. "Edinburgh is as far east as I want to go and I don't particularly want to go to Edinburgh."

"Well, it's too late to change your mind now."

"Look here, Donald, I agreed to accompany you on this expedition because of our long friendship, but I object, I object strongly to this uncomfortable expedition being regarded as a pleasure trip. Not only have I to face the prospect of spending about three weeks at sea in order to reach India, but I have to remember that in order to get away from the beastly place I shall have to spend about another three weeks at sea."

"Yes, but with these Neversick tablets I saw in an advertisement you're going to be perfectly all right, Hugh.

Did I show you that cable from Rose-Ross saying how delighted he was that we were coming out?"

"Yes, you showed it to me three times."

Kilwhillie opened his copy of yesterday's *Scotsman* and sat hunched in the corner of the compartment. Ben Nevis, with a touch of bravado, produced the book about India he had bought in Edinburgh and began to read it.

Presently the Chieftain laid it down on the mat beside him and sighed deeply.

"Good lord, Hugh, we shall never be able to learn Indian."

"I haven't the slightest intention of trying to learn the language," the Cameron laird avowed.

"Well, you couldn't if you did. This book I bought in that extraordinary shop in Edinburgh which was absolutely crammed with books . . . it seems that there are a lot of extraordinary people quite prepared to waste any amount of money on books . . . yes, well, this book I bought says that there are over fifty different languages in India. Think of learning fifty different languages."

"I don't suppose anybody would be foolish enough to try," Kilwhillie said.

"No, but anybody who wanted to learn a language would have to make up his mind which language he wanted to learn. But look here, Hugh, I don't want to start an argument while this train is making such a noise."

"And I certainly don't," Kilwhillie agreed, burying himself again in yesterday's *Scotsman*, which a moment or two later was almost blown out of his hands by the wind rushing into the compartment because Ben Nevis had lowered the window.

"It looks as if we shall have a bit of a breeze from the nor'-west on board," said the Chieftain.

"Need we have the breeze in our compartment now?"

"I was trying to find out whether the wind was nor'-west or sou'-west."

"Well, you know now," said Kilwhillie fretfully. "So perhaps you'll put the window up again."

Mac 'ic Eachainn obliged his friend, who observed, "It hasn't taken you long to read that book, Donald."

"Oh, I haven't read it all yet, Hugh. I'm keeping it in case I'm kept awake by foghorns. A fellow I was talking to in White's told me he started to read a book once when he couldn't sleep on account of foghorns and it started him on the habit of reading books, and now he reads two or three every year—sometimes more if frost interferes with hunting."

A dining-car steward opened the door of the compartment to enquire whether they would take the first or second lunch.

"We'll go along at twelve," said Ben Nevis, putting out his hand for the tickets. "I think that's a wise move," he continued when the attendant had passed on. "You'll be able to digest your lunch before we get to Liverpool and if you take one of these Neversick tablets before we leave the train it ought to be working by the time we go on board. No, I'm wrong, you have to take one green tablet an hour before you eat, the directions say," Ben Nevis went on, looking at the little cardboard box he had taken from his pocket. "And then one yellow tablet half an hour after you've finished eating."

"I don't believe in quack medicines," Kilwhillie insisted. "I've made up my mind to feel seasick for the next three weeks and I merely wish to be left alone till we reach Bombay without having to remember whether I took a green pill when it ought to have been some other colour. And now do you mind if we drop this discussion of seasickness? I still have three hours of not feeling seasick and I want to make the most of them."

Kilwhillie retired behind *The Scotsman*. Ben Nevis looked out of the window at the dreary November landscape.

At last the door of the compartment was opened for the attendant to announce that the first lunch was now being served, and the two travellers made their way along the corridor to the dining-car.

Kilwhillie eyed the plate of soup in front of him without enthusiasm.

"Waiter," he said presently. "If this is thick soup I'd rather have clear, but if this *is* clear soup I should prefer thick."

"That is thick soup," said the attendant.

"Then bring me some clear soup."

"I'm afraid there's no clear soup on to-day's menew, sir."

"Oh, very well," said Kilwhillie in a tone of icy resignation.

This deliberate stoicism was interrupted by a sudden exclamation.

"Good lord!" Ben Nevis was ejaculating. "What an extraordinary thing! I say, Hugh, look at that fellow's case on the table opposite us."

"It's a perfectly ordinary attaché-case," Kilwhillie commented.

"But look at the name, Hugh." Then leaning over the table he tried to whisper but in effect croaked, "Winstanley."

"It's a perfectly ordinary name."

"But it's the name of this gal that's trying to hook young Hector."

"I don't see what that's got to do with the fellow at the other table."

"I'm not so sure. He's going to India, isn't he? This is a boat train, don't forget."

"I'm not likely to forget that," the Cameron laird murmured almost poignantly.

"Look here, Hugh, let's move across and sit at his table."

And before his friend could stop him Ben Nevis had surged over to the other side of the dining-car."

"Good-morning, sir," he said. "Do you mind if my friend and I sit over here. It's rather draughty on the other side of the car? You're sailing in the *Taj Mahal*, I suppose?"

The stranger, a tall spare man with hair grey at the temples, a small grizzled moustache, a narrow tanned face and dusty blue eyes, nodded curtly.

"Are you soldiering out in India?" Ben Nevis asked.

"No, I'm in the British and Oriental Bank."

Ben Nevis kicked at Kilwhillie triumphantly under the table.

"Really? I have a letter of credit on the British and Oriental. Do you know if there's a branch at Tallulaghabad?"

Mr Winstanley frowned for a moment before he replied.

"No, we haven't a branch there."

"I say, I ought to introduce myself. My name is Mac-Donald. Donald MacDonald of Ben Nevis, and this is my friend Hugh Cameron of Kilwhillie."

"You're sailing in the *Taj Mahal*?"

"Yes, my friend Hugh Cameron and I thought we should like to have a look at India, and as my boy Hector is stationed now at Tallulaghabad with the Clanranalds we thought we'd make that an excuse for this little jaunt."

Kilwhillie frowned.

"Jaunt is hardly the word, Donald," he objected.

"I agree with you, Mr Cameron," said their new acquaintance. "India is no jaunt. Well, the *Taj Mahal* is not a bad old packet and we shan't be too hot in the Red Sea at this time of year. My name is Winstanley. I'm in charge of our bank at Jumbulpore."

Having said so much, Mr Winstanley seemed disinclined to say much more and replied to the questions of Ben Nevis as far as possible in monosyllables.

"A cold fish, Hugh," the Chieftain observed when he and Hugh Cameron were back in their compartment.

"Many people dislike talking in railway carriages," Kilwhillie said. "I rather dislike it myself. It's such a strain on the voice."

"I see we shall have to be jolly careful in the way we handle this business, Hugh. In my opinion this fellow Winstanley must have been an impossible sort of husband. I mean to say no woman likes to sit opposite a fellow at breakfast who says nothing but 'yes' and 'no'. I wish I knew for certain whether he divorced her or she divorced him."

Ben Nevis was not to find the answer to this until the night before the *Taj Mahal* reached Gibraltar, when the persistent hooting of the ship's siren brought him out from his cabin at three a.m., his book about India having been unsuccessful as a soporific. As he strode along the boat-deck the figure of Mr Winstanley appeared out of the fog.

"Hullo, can't you sleep either?" he exclaimed in tones of rumbustious sympathy. "What we want is some hot buttered toast. Let's go down to the smoking-room and get hold of the night-watchman. I'm told he can make wonderful hot buttered toast."

Presently Ben Nevis and Mr Winstanley were sitting in the comfortably shabby and pleasantly old-fashioned smoking-room of the *Taj Mahal* with a large plate of hot buttered toast between them.

"And would you like two nice cups of cocoa?" the night-watchman suggested. "There's nothing like a nice cup of cocoa to give you a good sleep."

"I don't believe I've had cocoa since I was at my prep school," said Ben Nevis. "It sounds rather a good notion. Let's have some, watchman."

Cocoa is reputed to be a recognised stimulant of conversation among women undergraduates, and without doubt it acted similarly on Mr Winstanley.

"My late wife always used to brew cocoa for me when I came back from the bank after a rush of work in the evening."

"Really?" Ben Nevis exclaimed. "I thought everybody stopped work in a bank early in the afternoon. My bank in Inverness always does." The Chieftain himself was playing for time, trying to make up his mind how he should frame his next question.

"How did you lose your wife?" he asked at last in the

tone of a B.B.C. announcer giving the news of a railway accident.

"It was a divorce."

Ben Nevis was only just able to stop himself from saying, "Yes, I know that, but did you divorce her or did she divorce you?" It was essential to know this for certain before he tackled Hector. He might drive the boy into a hasty marriage if he upset him by presuming that Mrs Winstanley was the guilty party. He decided to keep quiet and let Mr Winstanley, under the influence of cocoa, go on talking.

"Yes," said Mr Winstanley gloomily, "our marriage began to break up three years ago. Mind you, it wasn't entirely Angela's fault. Sorry! Angela is the name of my wife."

"Angela? But that's not an Indian name," Ben Nevis commented.

"Indian name? My wife isn't Indian."

"No, of course not," Ben Nevis woofed. "I don't know why I got it into my head that she was Indian. I suppose my mind has been running so much on India since Hugh Cameron and I set out on this little jaunt."

"As a matter of fact I've just been down to see her grandmother in Canterbury. Her father and mother are both dead. He was with Campbell, Campbell, Campbell and Co."

"Poor fellow," said the MacDonald chieftain. "How frightful for him!"

"They had one of the biggest jute businesses in Calcutta," Mr Winstanley exclaimed in surprise.

"They would have," said Ben Nevis sagely. "Anything that rhymes with loot, and the Campbells will be there."

"Angela's grandmother is the widow of one of the assistant organists at the Cathedral. His name was Peppercorn. He set Tennyson's poem *Crossing the Bar* to music. It was a very popular drawing-room song once upon a time. Unfortunately I'm not at all musical and my wife definitely is. My late wife, that is, though I believe I'm technically still married to her until the decree nisi is made absolute."

An extra loud blast on the ship's siren emboldened Ben Nevis to put his next question.

"I don't want to pry into your private affairs, Mr Winstanley, but may I ask if Mrs Winstanley—er—divorced you or did you—er—feel called upon to take proceedings, as they say, against her?"

"Oh, she divorced me," said Mr Winstanley with a bitter laugh. "I provided her with the so-called evidence," he added.

"Ah, I see. What they call collision, eh? Isn't that rather a tricky business?"

"But the trouble is that Angela insists on staying on in India. In fact, she's now at Tallulaghabad. I've been urging Mrs Peppercorn, her grandmother, to get her back to Canterbury. India is no place for a woman divorced from her husband. Every station is a hotbed of scandal and suggestive gossip. Angela is a child of nature and she cannot realise that people talk. I tell you, Mr MacDonald, I dread the stories I'm going to hear when I get back to Jumbulpore. I suppose in a way it was feeble of me to consent to this divorce. But the feeling that his wife is bored saps a man. I was twenty years older than Angela—and she always seemed to be reproaching me because I wasn't a soldier or a Civilian."

"But you must be one or the other," Ben Nevis protested.

"I meant in the Indian Civil Service. They talk about caste among the Indians, but believe me caste is much more perniciously rigid in the British Raj. The men are all right, but the women are the very devil. So my wife grew discontented and I dare say I was irritated and . . . oh, well, there it is, we agreed to part. Really, you must forgive me, Mr MacDonald, for drivelling on about my private affairs like this. But I couldn't sleep and this cocoa seems to have made me talkative."

It cost Ben Nevis three turns round the boat-deck to muster up the self-denial that would prevent his going down to Kilwhillie's cabin and bursting in with the news that Mr Winstanley was in fact Mrs Winstanley's husband. However, he managed to refrain.

Next morning, although the sky was a limpid azure and the sea calm, Hugh Cameron was still in his cabin when the *Taj Mahal* reached Gibraltar.

"Look here, Hugh," Ben Nevis protested, "you really must get dressed and come up on deck. You must see Gibraltar."

"I don't want to see Gibraltar," Kilwhillie declared obstinately. "I know exactly what Gibraltar looks like."

"Yes, but people won't understand."

"Won't understand what?"

"Not wanting to look at Gibraltar."

"I'm really not prepared to make myself uncomfortable in order to gratify popular sentiment."

"The sea's like a mill pond, Hugh. You'll be able to have your first lunch in the saloon. It's a wonderful morning after the fog. Did you hear the foghorns last night?"

"I'm not deaf."

"I dreamt I was on an elephant or I may have dreamt that I was actually an elephant myself and it was trumpeting —or I was—at a tiger, and then I woke up and couldn't get to sleep again on account of the ship's siren. So I walked about on the boat-deck and got into conversation with Winstanley, and I was right. He is Mrs Winstanley's husband, or rather he was before they were divorced. And his wife isn't an Indian at all. Her name is Angela and her father, poor chap, was in a firm called Campbell, Campbell, Campbell and Co. He must have had a frightful life. I'm not surprised he's dead. You know, I was quite sorry for Winstanley. He didn't really want to be divorced at all, but he felt his wife ought to go back and live with Mrs Peppercorn in Canterbury. He told me all this over the cocoa."

"Cocoa?"

"Yes, the night-watchman brewed cocoa."

"Donald," his friend interrupted with a shudder, "I

know it's calm, but if you go on talking about cocoa I shall feel seasick again."

"I wish I'd met Winstanley earlier," Ben Nevis went on. "We could have gone down to Canterbury and seen Mrs Peppercorn."

"Why on earth should we go and visit a woman called Peppercorn?" Kilwhillie asked.

"She's Angela's grandmother. I say, Hugh, do you notice the way I call her Angela? Hector is going to like that. I feel as if I'd known her for years."

"I think you're going the right way to encourage Hector in this ridiculous affair. It's essential you should remain on the most formal terms with Mrs Winstanley. The reason you are dragging me out to India is to break off this match, not to help it along."

"Oh, of course. But I must say I'm relieved to find that things aren't nearly so bad as Rose-Ross made them seem in his letter. But look here, Hugh, I do think you ought to get up and look at Gibraltar."

"I will not get up and look at Gibraltar. I've told you, Donald, that I know exactly what Gibraltar looks like."

However, when Ben Nevis had left the cabin Kilwhillie decided that he would get up.

And the Mediterranean remained so placid for the next three days that when the *Taj Mahal* dropped anchor at Port Said he was on deck to see the gulli-gulli man arrive to conjure with his chickens.

"Ha, ha! Jolly good," Ben Nevis guffawed to the passengers standing round to watch the gulli-gulli man's antics. And when Kilwhillie found a chicken in the inside pocket of his coat the Chieftain's hilarity was extreme.

"He's awfully fond of dogs," he explained to the circle of onlookers. "But he simply loathes chickens. Ha-ha-ha!"

Suddenly Ben Nevis began to wriggle.

"Please, mistah, please you have my little sickens, please."

With this the gulli-gulli man stepped forward and thrusting his hand inside the Chieftain's waistcoat he took out three cheeping chickens which he placed on the deck. "Good lord," Ben Nevis exclaimed.

"I think this fellow's rather clever," Kilwhillie observed to his friend.

Ben Nevis was still talking about those chickens when the *Taj Mahal* reached Aden.

Chapter 4

IN TALLULAGHABAD

WHILE the *Taj Mahal* was eastward bound across the Arabian Sea Colonel Rose-Ross and his wife talked much about the approaching visit of Ben Nevis.

"The Brigadier suggested that we should all dine at Flagstaff House," said the Colonel.

"That's very thoughtful of him, dear, and of course we shall have a dinner party here on the night after they arrive," said Mrs Rose-Ross.

"I can't help wishing Ben Nevis had flown out when I first wrote to him," the Colonel went on. "I hear young Hector spends every moment of his spare time with this Mrs Winstanley. It's most worrying."

"Yes, and it's so extraordinary that what she says about coming from Canterbury is apparently true."

"And also that she divorced her husband," the Colonel added. "I wish I hadn't given Ben Nevis the impression that she was chichi. Mind you, I still think it would be a most imprudent match for young Hector MacDonald, but obviously the woman herself is in a much stronger position than we thought at first. I wish Ben Nevis had brought out his wife with him instead of Hugh Cameron. I don't know Cameron well, but he has always struck me as rather a feeble sort of chap, though I believe he was quite a good soldier. Oh dear, I shall be glad when all this unpleasant business is over. It's beginning to get me down."

"I hear she's going about a good deal with that dreadful creature who runs the brewery. Paula Cartright told me she saw them riding together yesterday."

"Oh, John Tucker isn't a bad fellow. I only wish Mrs Winstanley would run about with him to some purpose."

"Alastair!" Mrs Rose-Ross exclaimed. She was a dislustred blonde with a tight, small, prudish mouth and eyes like faded forget-me-nots.

"I mean I wish she'd get married to him when this decree nisi business, which I never can understand, is finished. John Tucker would make her a perfectly good husband and he has plenty of money."

"Which we're never allowed to forget," said Mrs Rose-Ross acidly.

"He's a very hospitable fellow, Myra."

"Well, if a brewer can't give his guests plenty to drink, who can?"

At that moment the khitmatgar came in to take away the coffee, and Mrs Rose-Ross gave him some directions in kitchen Urdu the meaning of which by a miraculous feat of divination the dignified Muslim butler grasped with apparent ease.

"I cannot think what made Mrs Winstanley come to Tallulaghabad," Mrs Rose-Ross continued when the khitmatgar had retired. "She went to England over her divorce. Why didn't she stay there? Why did she come back to India? Well, her father's people may come from Canterbury, but who was her mother? I'm quite sure *she* didn't come from Canterbury. After all, Jumbulpore is only a night's journey from Tallulaghabad and you would think that a woman with any sense of decency would want to be as far away as possible from the husband she had divorced. And I cannot see what her attraction is for men."

"Well, of course, my dear, as you should know, I've never been attracted by brunettes," the Colonel began prudently. "But I can imagine that if a man *was* attracted by dark women he'd find Mrs Winstanley quite a . . . quite a . . ."

"Quite a what, Alastair?" Mrs Rose-Ross asked, raising her light eyebrows.

"Oh, quite attractive, that's all, my dear," said the Colonel quickly.

"My dear mother always used to say that there was something fundamentally coarse in all men. And I'm afraid that my own experience has proved her to be only too right," Mrs Rose-Ross sniffed.

While the Colonel and his wife were discussing matters over their coffee Mrs Winstanley herself was playing on her piano, which had been salvaged from the wreck of her marriage, nocturnes of Chopin. The *rubato* may have been excessive but the effect of the romantic music in the rose-shaded drawing-room of the small bungalow on that starry Punjab night would have been alluring even if it were being played by a less beautiful young woman than Angela Winstanley. The problem of her attraction for men which so much puzzled Mrs Rose-Ross was as simple as a crossword puzzle in the children's corner of a popular newspaper.

She was fragile-seeming as a figurine of ivory, with soft dark-brown hair and a small oval face in which two deep almond eyes flashed or melted, or hardened almost to ebony, at will. Her upper lip was a fine bow, her under lip the petal of a rose. Her hands without rings and her ankles competed in slim shapeliness. She was wearing a clinging black dress, and a ruby pendant from a thin chain of white gold rested upon the curve of her breast as she played those nocturnes of which she herself seemed the embodiment.

Angela Winstanley had been playing to herself for almost a quarter of an hour when the door of her rose-shaded drawing-room opened and a tall Muslim khitmatgar announced "MacDonald Sahib."

"Hector, how quick you've been," she exclaimed, rising from the piano to greet the kilted form of Lieutenant Hector MacDonald, Younger, of Ben Nevis, in the mess kit of the Clanranald Highlanders.

"I came away as soon as dinner was over. The Colonel was dining at home to-night. So I didn't have to hang around while he was grumbling at the Government over his coffee."

"Come and sit down by me," she said, leading the way to a sofa covered with worn chintz.

The twenty-five-year-old subaltern was neither so florid

nor so weather-beaten as his father, and his big aquiline nose as yet lacked the rich deep hues of amaranth and damson which could flood his father's, but he was in all outward essentials the fine figure of a young man that would uphold the renown of an ancient line and make a worthy successor to the monarchy of Glenbogle.

"Cigarette, Hector?" Mrs Winstanley asked as he sat down in one corner of the sofa, and with his blue eyes, choleric usually but now softened by infatuation to a bovine mildness, gazed at his hostess seated in the other corner.

"No, thanks," he said. "I've been smoking too much lately. I suppose it's what's called anxiety. However, I think I've got hold of a couple of good bearers. I'm sending them to Bombay to meet my father and Hugh Cameron. I've got a rather sturdy Pathan for my father. Sher Khan he's called, and for Hugh Cameron I've got a Dogra—a little chap very quiet and neat they tell me, Balu Ram he's called. But it's not bearers that's making me so anxious. Look here, Angela, I wish you'd give me an answer."

"An answer to what, Hector?"

"Oh, I say, look here," he protested. "Will you marry me?"

"Listen, Hector, I can't give you the answer to that question until the decree nisi is made absolute. I've told you that repeatedly. I don't want to find myself married all over again to poor Herbert, and this creature called a King's Proctor would love nothing better than to upset the whole business. My lawyer warned me particularly about him."

"But I don't see how this King's Proctor chap can do anything about a private arrangement between you and me. He won't know anything about it. I want to be able to tell my father when he arrives that you and I are definitely engaged. I'm pretty sure that my Colonel is getting him out here to upset matters. It's that confounded wife of his who thinks it's her mission in life to interfere with the private lives of his subalterns."

"Exactly. And she'd take a delight in upsetting my

private life. Please be sensible, Hector. Remember how careful I am being. Why do you suppose I have Maisie Lambert with me?"

"I'm sure I don't know," Hector muttered. "She's one of the most boring females I ever met."

"I wish you wouldn't be so unkind about Maisie. That man in Bulger's treated her disgracefully. And she's never got over it."

"That fellow Ripwood in Bulger's treated everybody pretty foully. He sold young Colin Macrae of Ours a pony that sat down in the middle of the opening chukka when we were playing the 3/22nd Punjabis in the first round of the Junior Cup. Nobody in Bulger's had a good word to say for him. He's an absolute stumer."

"Ah, well, Hector, we poor women don't always choose the right man."

"I know, I know," Hector murmured with what he hoped was enough emotional sympathy in his voice to justify him in grasping Angela's small hand in his red freckled fist.

She drew her hand away.

"Hector, please. You're forgetting your solemn promise. And I don't want Maisie to think you're just like every other man."

"I don't care what Maisie thinks," he barked, and one might have fancied that it was the rumbustious voice of Mac 'ic Eachainn himself.

"Not so loud, Hector, please! Maisie will hear you. She's sewing in the dining-room."

Maisie Lambert must have heard Hector's exclamation; she came into the drawing-room almost immediately.

"Mr MacDonald! What a pleasant surprise!"

"Did you think a tiger had broken into the bungalow, Maisie?" Angela Winstanley laughed.

Miss Maisie Lambert was the daughter of an official in the Public Works Department. She was still a pretty little thing, but already she had that look of imperfectly dusted porcelain which the complexion of a fair English girl is apt to

acquire in the Indian climate, and her engagement to
Captain Gerald Ripwood of Bulger's Horse (the 9th
Baluchistan Lancers) had etched a few premature lines
upon her face.

"Oh, no, Angela, I didn't think it was a tiger," she said
seriously. "I thought it was Mr Tucker." Angela darted a
warning look at her friend and chaperon.

"Tucker?" Hector growled. "Does he come here often in
the evening?"

"Oh, no, Mr MacDonald," Maisie replied hastily. "But
he called this afternoon to bring back Angela's riding-
whip."

"Yes," said Hector sulkily, "Mrs Cartwright told me
she'd seen you riding with him yesterday."

"You seem to disapprove of my going for a ride with Mr
Tucker," said Angela coldly. "I wonder what makes you
think that you are entitled to disapprove."

"Oh, I'm sure Mr MacDonald doesn't think at all,
Angela," Maisie Lambert put in, with the kindliest
intention.

"I find that quite easy to believe," said Angela Winstanley.

At this moment the khitmatgar came in to announce,
"Tucker Sahib."

The plump little managing director of Golden Lion
Lager, the most popular brand in all India, stood beaming
in the rose-shaded room.

"Why, Mr Tucker, how nice of you to call. And this is
Mr MacDonald . . ."

"Oh, Mr MacDonald and his brother officers are all
good friends of mine," said the little brewer.

Hector who only two days ago had sat for a couple of
hours before dinner in Mr Tucker's house drinking several
of the powerful whiskies and soda for which his hospitality
was renowned could not treat the benevolent visitor with the
discourtesy he would have liked to show. Nevertheless, he
could not be cordial. He had come to Mrs Winstanley's

bungalow in the hope of persuading her to promise him her hand so that he could meet his father a few days hence in a state of firm affiance instead of which he was in the position of apparently competing with the managing-director of Golden Lion Lager.

"I hear your father is expected at any minute now, MacDonald, and that you secured Balu Ram for him as a bearer. You've done well to get him."

"I got him for Hugh Cameron of Kilwhillie. I'm sending that big Pathan, Sher Khan, for my father."

Mr Tucker shook his round little head doubtfully.

"He has the reputation of being rather a tough customer, you know. Still, as long as your dad doesn't bring out too many Highland daggers, Sher Khan probably won't pinch anything, but I'd warn him to keep a sharp lookout if I were you. Oh, yes, and don't let him leave any embroidered waistcoats lying about. Pathans can't resist them. Well, we're all looking forward to meeting your father. And I hope you'll bring him round to Scarborough Towers. It will be a privilege to entertain him and Mr Cameron."

"And what can I offer you now, Mr Tucker?" his hostess asked.

"I won't take anything, thanks. What I came round for was to ask if you and Miss Lambert would care to drive up to Pippla with me to-morrow. It means staying the night because I have some business to do and I don't like that corkscrew road in the dark."

"Why, I think it would be lovely, Mr Tucker. You'd like to go, wouldn't you, Maisie?"

"Oh, I'd love to go, Angela."

"That's fine," said the genial little barrel of a man. "I'll be round with the car by 9.30 sharp and that'll get us up to Parker's Hotel in good time for tiffin. And now I'll be off. I'm so glad you feel like this little run up to Pippla. They tell me the weather's glorious and no sign of any snow yet."

With this Mr Tucker bade the company good-night and retired beaming.

Maisie Lambert presently followed him out of the drawing-room, leaving Hector and Angela together.

"You don't seem at all afraid of what this King's Proctor wallah thinks where John Tucker is concerned," said Hector gloomily. "Good lord, people talk enough in Tallulaghabad, but you can't hear yourself speak for gossip in Pippla."

"It's one thing to drive up to the hills with Mr Tucker, chaperoned by Maisie Lambert. It's quite another thing to let your engagement be announced before you have your decree nisi. Be sensible, Hector."

"Yes, but you won't even say that you'll be engaged when you do get this decree-nisi bundabust cleared up. You know how awkward I find it to talk about love. It's much easier for me to talk about being married. I mean to say, it's a definite step forward if you see what I mean."

"But, Hector, I haven't made up my mind yet. I like you very much, as you know. I'm really very fond of you. Still, marrying is such a definite step and I didn't make a great success of my first marriage. Scotland seems a long way off and it sounds rather cold."

"Pippla can be very cold at this time of year," Hector observed.

"I think that's rather a silly little remark. No, no, don't let's talk any more about the future. I want to meet your father. He may not like me and I couldn't possibly intrude where I wasn't welcome. I'd rather go back and live in Canterbury with my grandmother and put up with the noise of church bells for the rest of my life."

"The only cathedral city I know anything about is Salisbury, and if Canterbury is like Salisbury you'll be bored to death."

"I haven't said that I *am* going to live in Canterbury. Oh, Hector, I do wish you wouldn't keep on about the future. You'll make me sorry that I've let you see so much of me. Do you think it's pleasant to be criticised by Mrs Rose-Ross? However fond I was of you I shouldn't like to spend the rest of my life being criticised by women like Mrs Rose-Ross."

"But the Rosses come from the other side of Inverness-shire, and anyway the Colonel is staying on in the service. I shall chuck it if you marry me. We've got a jolly little lodge beside Loch Hoch and I shall teach you how to fish and all that sort of thing. I'm sure you'll enjoy it."

"We'll see," she said in the tone of a mother trying to check a small boy's persistency. "And now you must go, Hector. I will not be talked about by Mrs Rose-Ross and Mrs Cartwright and Mrs Fraser and that odious Mrs Murray. And now I hear that Brigadier Coppendale's wife is coming out after Christmas and I'm told she's the worst of the lot. I used to grumble at poor old Herbert because we didn't move more in military society. Yes, the men are all right, but the women . . . no, I'm afraid I wasn't cut out to be the wife of a soldier . . ."

"I've told you, Angela. I'll chuck soldiering if you'll marry me."

"I'd sooner marry a minor canon than a soldier, yes, and listen to him singing *Benedicite omnia opera* in his bath every morning," she exclaimed passionately.

"Well, you won't hear me singing operas in my bath," Hector promised fervidly.

"My dear boy, do go back to your quarters. I'm going to bed."

But Angela Winstanley did not go to bed. When Hector MacDonald left her bungalow she called to Maisie Lambert to come and sit with her.

"Angela, I'm terribly sorry I was so stupid about saying I didn't think Mr Tucker was a tiger. I nearly passed out when you gave me that look."

Angela Winstanley put her feet up on the sofa and lit a cigarette.

"Sit down, Maisie, and don't bother any more about it. Maisie, do you think I could be happy with a soldier?"

"I thought I was going to be terribly happy with Gerry

D

Ripwood, my dear, but . . ." Maisie Lambert hesitated . . . "oh, you'll think it awful cheek for me to talk to you like this, especially as you're married. I mean, as you were married and I'm not. But, Angela, as your friend I must say it. Don't, don't let him go too far."

Having said as much, poor Maisie Lambert fell into a titubation from which she did not recover until Angela had told her to give her a chota peg and have one herself. "Unless you'd rather have a brandy-Mac," she added.

"Oh, no, dear. Brandy gives me heartburn."

"The ginger should cancel that."

"Oh, no, dear. . . . I'm always afraid of ginger. Gerry Ripwood gave me two brandy-Macs the night the 12th Gurkhas had their dance and a week later he told me he thought that our engagement had been a mistake. Oh, don't think I'm comparing Gerry Ripwood to Hector Mac-Donald, because he really did behave like a cad. All the same, I do feel that Rudyard Kipling was right when he said it's better to have loved and lost than never to have loved at all."

"It was Tennyson as a matter of fact."

"Yes, of course it was. How silly of me! We learnt it at school with the Miss Wilberforces at Pippla. Oh dear, I hope you're not being unwise in driving up to Pippla to-morrow with Mr Tucker. I mean to say, I think Mr Mac-Donald didn't like it at all."

"That doesn't worry me a great deal, Maisie."

"Oh, well, as long as you feel it's all right I'd love the drive. And Mr Tucker is extremely kind."

Angela Winstanley finished her chota peg and lit another cigarette.

"Put another log on the fire, Maisie," she said, and while her friend was stirring it to a blaze she looked thoughtfully at her ringless left hand.

"I don't really want to be married again at all," she said thoughtfully. "And I wouldn't if I could draw the winner in the Calcutta Sweep," she added.

"Oh, I think it's nice to be married," Maisie Lambert sighed.

"How do you know? You haven't had experience of the happy state."

"Oh, but I . . . no, no, well, of course, that's true. I haven't," Maisie ended a little lamely after the enthusiastic monosyllabic ejaculation with which she had started her reply.

"Of course, Hector MacDonald will be well off one day," Angela went on. "As far as I can make out his father has a huge property in Scotland. I could certainly make him give up the Army, but could I stand him round about me for the rest of my life? All the same, I'm not going to let Mrs Rose-Ross and Mrs Cartwright and the rest of these stuck-up memsahibs think that I can't marry Hector if I want to. *If* I want to," she repeated. "Do you think I don't know why Hector's father is coming out here? He's coming out here to threaten he'll cut Hector off unless he stops running after me. Well, we'll see who's cleverest, me or Mrs Rose-Ross. But, oh, I wish I was the least little bit in love. Then I really would give them all a run for their money. Come on, Maisie. Bed. We mustn't keep John Tucker waiting to-morrow morning."

Chapter 5

GOVERNMENT HOUSE

IT was the day before the good ship *Taj Mahal* was due to berth in the harbour of Bombay. To what would have been the amazement of his friends in Inverness-shire, Hugh Cameron of Kilwhillie was to be seen stepping round the main deck at a brisk pace beside his friend Donald Mac-Donald of Ben Nevis. Quoit players, concentrated upon the interminable repetition of the dullest game hitherto devised to while away time, did not deflect Kilwhillie from his steady pace. Children diving in front of him to rescue balls from bouncing overboard could not confound his sense of direction. He avoided deck-chairs with the ease of an accomplished football player. His eyes were bright, or at any rate much nearer to being bright than they had ever been seen in the land of bens and glens and heroes. His moustaches seemed to float as effortlessly as the wings of a fulmar petrel in the light breeze that hardly pectinated the pale blue sea.

"What are you singing, Hugh?" asked Ben Nevis, whose great eagle's beak was peeling under the influence of more sunshine in three weeks than he had experienced since the South African War.

"I wasn't singing," said Kilwhillie. "I may have been humming to myself."

"Well, what were you humming?"

"I was humming 'On the road to Mandalay, where the flying-fishes play'."

"Oh, yes, the song that fellow was singing at the concert last night." The Chieftain looked round at his friend. "I don't ever remember hearing you hum, Hugh. You must be feeling very well."

"I'm feeling as fit as a fiddle. But, mind you, Donald,

that doesn't mean I'm going to be lured on board the *Banshee* when we get home for one of those ghastly cruises in the Minch."

"Well, if you feel as fit as a fiddle, Hugh, I feel as fit as a double-bass."

Ben Nevis guffawed so loudly at his own joke that a quoit player about to play overshot his aim by several yards and looked at him reproachfully.

"Rather a vigorous shot, Major, what?" the Chieftain barked as he strode on along the deck. "Yes, it's been a wonderful voyage," he continued, "and in my opinion we're going to have a wonderful time in India. Mind you, I like poor Winstanley, but in my humble opinion he was the wrong chap for Angela."

"Donald, I think you make a mistake in always alluding to Mrs Winstanley as Angela."

"But I only do it to you," the Chieftain protested.

"Yes, but before you know where you are you'll be calling her Angela in front of Hector, which would obviously be fatal."

"How do you mean, fatal?"

"It would obviously encourage Hector to suppose that you could imagine her as a daughter-in-law."

"Well, from what Winstanley tells me about her I think Rose-Ross has been exaggerating. She may be a perfectly good wife for Hector. The boy has a lot of sound common sense."

"Has he?"

"He's like me. I consider I have more common sense than anybody on the County Council. If I'd been made Convener of the Roads Committee we should have had a proper road up Glenbogle years ago. And I'd have jolly well seen you had a good road up Glenbore too. I think you're taking a very prejudiced line about Angela . . . about Mrs Winstanley. After all, her husband must know more about her than Rose-Ross."

"Her ex-husband," Kilwhillie reminded his friend coldly.

"Have you told Mr Winstanley that Hector is proposing to marry his ex-wife when the decree nisi is made absolute?"

"Of course not," Ben Nevis spluttered.

"But you told him that Hector had met Mrs Winstanley?" Kilwhillie pressed.

"I may have mentioned that he had met a certain Mrs Winstanley and wondered if it could be the same Mrs Winstanley."

"It's clear to me," said Hugh Cameron, "that as soon as we reach Bombay I must telegraph to Beatrice and urge her to come out to India immediately."

"Telegraph to Trixie?" the Chieftain exclaimed.

"I gave up the quiet winter I had planned for myself," Hugh Cameron went on severely, "in order to help you get Hector out of this deplorable entanglement. Beatrice was good enough to express to me her full confidence in me. I should not be doing my duty as a friend of hers and a friend of yours if I stood by and let your impulsiveness get the better of you. I am not so easily cajoled as you are, Donald."

"Cajoled?"

"Yes, cajoled. If you are capable of allowing yourself to be influenced by Mr Winstanley, what is going to happen when you meet Mrs Winstanley herself? Are you prepared to accept a marriage between the divorced wife of an Indian bank-manager whose maiden name apparently was Peppercorn and your heir?"

"No, of course, I'm not."

"Very well, then, it is your duty to adopt an attitude of extreme reserve. And I tell you, Donald, that if I detect the slightest departure from this attitude of extreme reserve I shall telegraph to Beatrice that her presence in Tallulaghabad is imperative."

"Do you know what I'm going to do when we get home, Hugh?"

"Give up eating hot buttered toast and drinking cocoa in the small hours, I hope," said Kilwhillie.

"I'm going to suggest to the Inverness-shire Unionist Association to adopt you as their candidate at the next election. I never knew you could talk like that, Hugh. And look here, if you do get into Parliament, you must take a strong line about this abominable hydro-electric scheme in Strathdiddle. We shan't have a salmon left if these ruffians are allowed to interfere with every river in the Highlands."

At this moment the Chieftain's plans for his neighbour's political future were interrupted by a steward bringing him a wireless message. The Chieftain opened and read it.

"Sir Henry Harbottle wants us to spend a night at Government House before we go on to Tallulaghabad," he announced. "He says his A.D.C. will meet the boat and take us along. I call that very civil of him. I think we'll accept this invitation, Hugh. I suppose Finchampton let him know we were arriving in Bombay. I sent Finchampton a note by air-postage before we left London."

"I should have preferred to go right on to Tallulaghabad," said Hugh Cameron. "We want that unpleasant business over as soon as possible. However, I suppose one night won't make much difference."

That last evening of the voyage Ben Nevis and Kilwhillie with other chosen guests gathered in the Captain's cabin before dinner. These occasions on board ship always possess a kind of Horatian melancholy. The intimacies fostered by daylong association for three weeks of slow sea days are on the verge of being broken up, and although all are busy exchanging addresses and making resolutions to meet again, all know full well in their hearts that these planned reunions are written in blue water and will never be accomplished. It is too late to introduce the various fellow-passengers with whom Ben Nevis has been consorting since the *Taj Mahal* sailed down the Mersey. Neither he nor we shall meet them again in Glenbogle in spite of the invitations to come and stay there with him whenever they find themselves within reach of Inverness-shire. Even Hugh Cameron's reserve has been bored through by five gimlets and at least two of the guests have been invited to visit him at Kilwhillie.

"Well, ladies and gentlemen," said the Chieftain, raising his glass, "I want you all to drink the health of our good friend Captain Bunting, who is a fine seaman, a grand host and a great gentleman. The good old *Taj Mahal* is what my sailor son Murdoch calls a happy ship. Yes, just before I left Scotland I had a letter from him in the destroyer he's just joined. '*Atrocious* is a happy ship,' he wrote. And by Jove, I want to say here and now, here and now, ladies and gentlemen, that the *Taj Mahal* is a happy ship. I have made many new friends and I hope that in the future one and all of these new friends will consider me an old friend and visit me at Glenbogle where I promise them in the words of our dear old Gaelic 'keeut mealy fahltcher,' which for the benefit of those who do not know our ancient language means a hundred thousand welcomes. Captain Bunting is not a Highlander, but when I say that his hospitality has been Highland I'm sure you will understand that I am paying him the highest compliment in my power. And so when I ask you to raise your glasses to him and drink slahnjervaw, which means great health in our dear old Gaelic, I'm sure you will do it with right good will. Captain Bunting!"

The Captain's health was then drunk with loud plaudits.

"What a beautiful speech, Mr Ben Nevis," said a nice old lady who was on the way out to spend the winter with her son, a Civilian of worth and weight. "Yes, I know you've told me I ought to call you 'Ben Nevis', but I still feel I'm being too familiar. And when you and Mr Kilwhillie do come to Delhi I do hope you will give my son and me the pleasure of dining with us."

Soon after this the company went down to dinner.

Later on in the smoking-room Kilwhillie observed with a frown that the Chieftain had got into a corner with Mr Winstanley. The effect of the five gimlets in the Captain's cabin had by now long worn off and he did not feel the least desire to be even coldly agreeable to Mr Winstanley.

"Don't you think you ought to turn in early, Donald?" he suggested. "I'm told it's a long and boring business before one gets away from the dock."

"You'd better have a jockendorrus, Hugh."

"I don't want a jockendorrus. I'm going to bed, and I think you ought to go to bed too, Donald."

"Mr Cameron is right," Mr Winstanley put in. "You'll have a tiring morning. So many formalities nowadays. Will your bearers be meeting you?"

"I really don't know," said Ben Nevis. "But we're staying at Government House to-morrow night and I expect there'll be an A.D.C. to meet us."

"Oh, then you won't have any bother at all."

"You hear what Winstanley says, Hugh? There's no reason at all to do a bunk." Ben Nevis laughed at his nautical joke and called for the steward. "Three large choker burrows, George."

The steward had learnt by now what Ben Nevis meant by choker burrows.

"I don't want a whisky," said Kilwhillie irritably. "I'm going to bed. Good-night, Mr Winstanley. Good-night, Donald."

"Your friend is rather standoffish," Mr Winstanley observed when Hugh Cameron left the smoking-room. "He'll be in his element in India."

"He doesn't mean to be," Ben Nevis assured his companion. "But he's a bachelor, you know, and he's got into this frightful habit of enjoying being alone. Mind you, I don't want him to get married. In fact, it would be a great blow to me if he did get married. But I think he ought to get married."

"I used to think that," said Mr Winstanley gloomily. "But I made a big mistake. No confirmed bachelor should marry a girl twenty years younger than himself. He can't adjust himself."

"You know what I'd do if I were a bachelor," said Ben Nevis sagely. "I'd marry a widow of my own age. Well, she'd go into it with her eyes open, if you see what I mean. And what's more she'd know the ropes. From what you've told me about Mrs Winstanley I gather she didn't know these ropes. Well, I suppose I shall be meeting Mrs Winstanley in Tallulaghabad."

"You're bound to."

"Would you like me to give her any message from you?"

"That's the last thing I should like. Indeed, I would much rather you said nothing about having met me. We have passed out of each other's lives."

"Yes, I see what you mean," the Chieftain said, nodding his head gravely.

"But if you get an opportunity I *would* be grateful if you'd do your best to persuade her to leave India. India is no place for a young woman who has divorced her husband."

"You mean — er — the climate?" Ben Nevis asked earnestly.

"No, no, I mean the gossip."

"Ah."

"People have said that Angela's mother was of the country, and if she stays on in India that will make the story seem all too probable. And if you know how poisonous the memsahibs can be about Anglo-Indians you'd understand my anxiety that Angela should get away to England."

"But was Mrs Winstanley's mother Anglo-Indian?"

"Honestly, Mr MacDonald, I do not know. All I know is that her maiden name was Cameron before she married Peppercorn, who as I told you was with Campbell, Campbell, Campbell and Co. A very decent chap. I wish he was still alive."

"Good lord, Cameron!" Ben Nevis exclaimed. "I wonder if he came from Lochaber."

"My wife's grandfather came from Dundee, I believe. He was with another of the big jute firms in Calcutta —Macintosh and Macintosh. I never heard his wife's name."

"Campbell, Campbell, Campbell and Co., Macintosh

and Macintosh," Ben Nevis muttered to himself. "Extra-ordinary, in fact absolutely appalling. George! Two more choker burrows," he said when the steward took his order.

"Not for me, please," said Mr Winstanley. "And you'll excuse my correcting your Urdu, but a large whisky is a burra peg. A small whisky is a chota peg."

"Yes, but George knows what I mean," said Ben Nevis.

"No doubt, but you don't want a waiter who doesn't know to bring you a small whisky."

"Good lord, I certainly don't. So choker doesn't come into it? I must remember that. Did you ever go in for Pelmanism, Winstanley?"

"No, I never did."

"It's a wonderful system for remembering what you want to remember by remembering something absolutely different. For instance, if I wanted to remember your name I should remember 'Lose Livingstone': you see the idea?"

"But why is it easier to remember Lose Livingstone than Winstanley?"

"Ah, that's the point. It's much easier to remember some-thing you don't want to remember than to remember some-thing you do want to remember."

The bank-manager looked as sceptical as if he were listening to an insolvent customer trying to justify an over-draft.

"But Mr Cameron was right," he said. "You ought to turn in early to-night. In the flurry of arrival I may not have a chance to say 'good-bye'. So I'll say 'good-bye' now. Thank you for listening to my troubles so patiently. I've appreciated your sympathy. And you won't say anything to my wife—to my late wife—about having met me? I don't suppose you'll be coming to Jumbulpore, but if you do I'd be delighted to show you round. We have, that is to say I have, quite a jolly bungalow."

Next morning when the *Taj Mahal* docked in Bombay a slim good-looking young man came on board and introduced himself as Charles Henderson, A.D.C. to His Excellency the Governor.

"We'll soon have your luggage cleared, sir," he assured Ben Nevis. "By the way, what about your bearer?"

"My boy Hector telegraphed that he had found a couple of bearers for Kilwhillie and myself and was sending them to meet us in Bombay."

At this moment a neat little Dogra approached Ben Nevis.

"You are please MacDonald Sahib?" he asked with a salaam. "I am Balu Ram, to come from Tallulaghabad for your bearer," and with an unobtrusive grace he relieved his new master of the only thing he was carrying, which was a topee pressed upon him at the last moment by his hatter in London, who should have known better.

From behind Balu Ram a very tall and fierce-looking Pathan, with a moustache that stretched far beyond both his ears, stepped forward.

"Sher Khan," he announced with a salute. "I am bearer for Cameron Sahib."

When Kilwhillie looked at his new servant he seemed like an elderly Aladdin eyeing the genie of the lamp.

"I don't know why Hector sent such an enormous fellow for you, and such a little fellow for me, Hugh," Ben Nevis said, with a touch of envy in his voice.

The explanation was that the two cards which Hector had written out for the bearers had got mixed up during the journey from Tallulaghabad.

"We'd better see that you have all your baggage," said Charles Henderson. "And then your bearers can bring it up to Government House in the luggage-van. By the way, have you brought bedding-rolls?"

"Bedding-rolls?" Ben Nevis exclaimed.

"You'll want them for your journey to-morrow. I think the best thing we can do is to call in at Moffat's on our way and take them with us in the car. I'll telephone from Government House for reservations."

"Yes, but these bedding-rolls. What are they exactly?" Ben Nevis asked earnestly.

Charles Henderson explained.

"Oh, something to sleep on in the train? I thought it was some kind of eatable for the journey," Ben Nevis guffawed in genial appreciation of his own ignorance.

An hour later the two visitors were shown into the delightful little bungalow on the cliff's edge above the pale blue sea that was allotted to guests at Government House.

"Lunch is at one, sir," said Charles Henderson. "I'll come along and fetch you about ten to. Your bearers will soon be along with the baggage."

"Very nice lad that," Ben Nevis observed, when the young A.D.C. had left them. "Very good manners."

"He wouldn't be an A.D.C. long if he didn't have manners," Kilwhillie commented.

"Well, here we are in India, Hugh," the Chieftain said. "It's warm, but it's nothing like as hot as I expected it to be. By the way, I haven't had an opportunity to tell you yet, but I found out last night from Winstanley that his wife may be a cousin of yours."

"A cousin of mine?" Kilwhillie snapped. "Rubbish!"

"Yes, it appears that Mrs Winstanley's mother was a Cameron who married this chap Peppercorn."

"No cousins of mine ever married anybody called Peppercorn," Kilwhillie snapped again. "Where did she come from?"

"Oh, she came from Calcutta, but her father—that's Angela's — that's Mrs Winstanley's — grandfather came from Dundee, and his name was Cameron."

"Why on earth should you suppose that a Dundee Cameron was a cousin of mine? You'll be telling Lochiel when we get back that you met a cousin of his called Peppercorn."

Ben Nevis was still laughing heartily at the effect of such an announcement upon Lochiel when the two bearers arrived.

Ben Nevis again eyed with envy the huge Pathan who had been allotted to his friend.

"I can't think why Hector picked this enormous fellow for you, Hugh," he grumbled.

"Will Master change clothes for tiffin?" Balu, his own bearer asked.

When the new arrivals in the East met in the bungalow sitting-room they looked at one another's clothes with interest.

"As far as I can make out we're properly dressed for this climate, though I feel rather like a seaside tripper in this light grey suit," Ben Nevis said. "Oh, by the way, Hugh, Balu tells me nobody wears topees in India nowadays. Would you care to have mine?"

"Thank you, but I can exist without it," Kilwhillie replied.

"Yes, I see now why Hector got Balu for me. He takes charge of me rather in the way Toker does. I asked him if he'd ever thought of coming west. I believe he'd fit in capitally at Glenbogle."

"For goodness' sake, Donald, don't go engaging Indian servants before you've been in India a couple of hours."

"Oh, I haven't engaged him yet. But I've taken quite a fancy to the little fellow. What's your chap like?"

"He seems all right. The only thing that rather annoyed me was his asking me if I wanted him to curl my moustache."

"I doubt if he'd ever be able to get that moustache of yours to grow the other way up like his," said Ben Nevis, shaking his head.

"He's certainly not going to be allowed to try. I've no desire to walk about looking like a bicycle," Kilwhillie declared. "Ah, here's Henderson."

The A.D.C. came into the bungalow.

"I hope you've found everything comfortable. Shall we go along now? H.E. likes a gimlet before tiffin."

Sir Henry Harbottle was a florid round-faced man who

looked as if he liked several gimlets before tiffin and a good many more before dinner, and the rasp in his voice came as a surprise because one expected it to be well oiled. Lady Harbottle, who was interested in astrology, had decided that in consequence she was much better able to understand the Indian point of view than the wives of other Governors. She affected what she believed was an air of mysticism which merely suggested, however, absent-mindedness.

"Now, we must get this right. I call you 'Ben Nevis', eh? And so do you, my dear," His Excellency added. "And what do we call you, Mr Cameron?"

"That will do admirably, Sir Henry," said Kilwhillie.

"Nonsense, Hugh," Ben Nevis interposed. "You are Cameron of Kilwhillie, and I'm sure Sir Harry Henbottle— ha-ha—that's an old trick of mine—I mean Sir Henry Harbottle would prefer to call you what you're called from one end of the Highlands to the other, and that is Kilwhillie."

"I always think the Highlands are so romantic," Lady Harbottle gushed. "Charles," she murmured to the A.D.C., "there's just a little too much gin in my gimlet. Will you add a little lime-juice? Yes, so romantic," she continued, turning back to her guests. "H.E. and I once motored—where was it we motored to, Henry, in Scotland?"

"I don't remember where we went in particular," His Excellency rasped. "It was all very jolly."

"Oh, it was incredibly romantic," Lady Harbottle sighed.

"You probably went to the Trossachs," said Kilwhillie coldly. His sarcasm was ineffective.

"Yes, that's just where we did go," his hostess gushed. "It was quite lovely."

Kilwhillie was spared a rhapsody about the Trossachs by the entrance of Captain Harcourt, another A.D.C.

"Sorry, sir, I'm afraid I'm a minute or two late," said the new arrival.

"You're two and a half minutes late, Harcourt," His Excellency rasped severely, with a glance at his watch.

Ben Nevis intercepted a glance between the two A.D.C.'s and made up his mind to thaw the frigidity.

"Ah, you mustn't pay too much attention to time, Sir Henry. In the Highlands we treat time with the contempt it deserves."

"You make a great fuss, Donald, if people are late for dinner," Kilwhillie reminded him.

"Ah, dinner. Well, of course, that's different. I do like dinner to be absolutely on the dot."

At this moment the doors of the dining-room were opened by stately servants and the company moved in to lunch.

"Stuffy. Very stuffy, Hugh, if you know what I mean," Ben Nevis said to Hugh Cameron when they were back in the guest bungalow. "I'm glad we're not making a long visit here."

The other A.D.C., Captain Harcourt, knocked before Kilwhillie could reply.

"May I come in? I was wondering, sir," he asked, "if you'd like me to run you round Bombay in one of our cars. Unless you and Mr Cameron want to have a siesta."

"We'd like a drive very much, wouldn't we, Hugh?"

"You came to my rescue very kindly over that little spot of trouble before tiffin," said Captain Harcourt. "H.E. is a terror for punctuality."

"Well, I suppose these Governor wallahs have to be, poor devils," Ben Nevis barked genially.

Captain Harcourt looked a little astonished at Ben Nevis's way of referring to the Governor of Bombay, and took refuge in the tactful quack of military agreement.

"Quite, quite."

When at the end of that long first day in India Ben Nevis and Kilwhillie were sitting in the guest-bungalow sipping a last burra peg before retiring, the Chieftain observed:

"I don't believe I should like to be a Governor, Hugh."

"Well, you're never likely to be one. So I don't think you need bother about it."

"I don't believe Trixie would like being a Governor's wife, either. Did Lady Harbottle strike you as being a little bit—er—well—er?" The Chieftain tapped his head.

"I didn't have much opportunity of forming an opinion. I wasn't next her at dinner."

"No, she had that Indian parson on her left."

"Parsee, Donald, not parson. Parsees are fire-worshippers."

"Good lord, that must make them dreadfully hot in India. But why I asked you that about Lady Harbottle was because of the extraordinary things she was saying to me at dinner. She's got some kind of an instrument she calls a holoscope."

"I suppose you mean horoscope. It isn't an instrument."

"Well, what is it?"

"I'm not sure what it is exactly, but I know it isn't an instrument," Kilwhillie insisted.

"Well, never mind what this holoscope is. Suddenly she said to me 'I'm afraid I'm very extravagant. You see, the moon is in my seventh house.' We were eating curry at the time and I was so taken aback that I put a whole spoonful in my mouth and felt as if I'd put my tongue into a bee-hive. However, I cooled myself off as soon as I could with a gulp of wine and I said, 'Ah, is it?' I believe it's always the right line to take with a lunatic. You should always agree with them."

"Donald, you really oughtn't to say things like that," Kilwhillie protested.

"Yes, but did you ever hear a more idiotic remark? The moon is in my seventh house. I mean to say, it's absolute nonsense. And then a minute or two later she said, goggling those dark eyes of hers at me like a spae-wife, 'But what worries me is that Herschel and Satan are both square with Jupiter in my'—I think it was third house. I suppose I must have goggled back at her, because she suddenly waggled her finger at me and said . . . and, Hugh, she did actually say this, she said, 'Ah, I expect you call Herschel Urinus.'

I was staggered. I don't know who this fellow Herschel is, but if he heard I was calling him Urinus he might feel more than a little annoyed, and indeed I shouldn't blame him. They tell me Harbottle has another two years to go as Governor, and in my opinion his wife will be stark mad before he goes back home." The Chieftain raised his glass. "Well, slahnjervaw, Hugh. I hope they won't settle in the North when they retire. You know how ready Trixie is to think that I've made a mistake, and if Lady Harbottle told her I'd been calling people Urinus, she'd probably think I had."

Chapter 6

ANGELA WINSTANLEY

THE last impression any witnesses of the meeting between Donald MacDonald of Ben Nevis and Hector MacDonald, Younger, of Ben Nevis, when the former alighted from the train at Tallulaghabad was that an anxious father had arrived to admonish an erring son. They barked away at one another so exuberantly that even the gaggle of emaciated coolies arguing and squabbling about the disposal of the luggage under the lordly direction of Balu Ram and Sher Khan seemed the merest twittering.

"I told the Colonel," said Hector, "that as the train might be three hours late it would be better if Duncan and I met you and took you along to his bungalow. Oh, you haven't met Duncan yet. This is Duncan Robertson of Ours, who shares a bungalow with me. This is my father, Duncan."

Duncan Robertson was a tall good-looking young soldier, of whom both Ben Nevis and Kilwhillie approved immediately.

"How have the two bearers I picked for you turned out?" Hector enquired.

"My fellow's a capital chap," his father replied. "Toker couldn't have looked after me better. And Hugh likes this whopping chap with a turban you found for him. The only thing that worries Hugh at all is that he will keep trying to curl his moustache up over his ears."

"Oh, you've taken the Pathan, have you, sir?" Duncan Robertson said to Kilwhillie.

"But I meant Sher Khan for you, sir," Hector told his father.

"Well, I was a bit surprised myself," Ben Nevis admitted. Then he took his son aside. "But don't say anything more about it. I'm quite pleased with my chap and Hugh Cameron's quite pleased with his except for this moustache business. Mind you, I see what Sher Khan means, but of course he'll never get Hugh to agree. He's so used to hanging on to his moustache as it is. He'd miss it if it got behind his ears."

In the Rose-Ross bungalow the Colonel and his wife were waiting for their guests to arrive.

"I confess I shan't be sorry when all this business is over, Myra," he said. "I'm beginning to wonder whether I was wise to interfere. People are saying now that Mrs Winstanley is much more interested in John Tucker than she is in Hector MacDonald."

"She and that Lambert young woman went up to Pippla with him a week ago and apparently stayed two nights at Parker's," said Mrs Rose-Ross in disapproval.

"Yes, I know. All I hope is that the paternal opposition won't make Hector obstinate. Perhaps I ought to have let things work themselves out. However, it's too late to do anything about it. Well, well, they can't be long now. This train is disgracefully late. Ah, there they are."

In contrast with the fuss of arrival at the Rose-Ross bungalow, a meditative peace brooded over Angela Winstanley's bungalow, where she was playing to herself the Beethoven sonata called *Les Adieux*, while Maisie Lambert sat sewing.

"Only another month," she said, closing the volume of music and leaving the piano.

"Another month to what?" Maisie Lambert asked.

"To complete freedom. That's when my divorce will be made absolute."

Angela Winstanley came across to the sofa, sat down in the corner of it and lit a cigarette.

"And then what do you think you'll do?" her friend asked.

"That's just what I wish I knew. Hector's father arrives to-day," she murmured, half to herself.

"Was Hector very annoyed about our staying up at Pippla with John Tucker?"

"Well, of course he was furious. You know, Maisie, I think young men are really very boring."

"That's what you said about Herbert."

"Oh, but Herbert must have been born old. He never seemed ripe. He merely seemed withered. John Tucker was young once and he's kept the attractive part of youth but got rid of the boring part."

"It's a pity he isn't better looking," Maisie commented with a sigh.

"Good looks didn't take you far, my dear."

"They took me further than I ought to have gone," Maisie said.

"Where is this Gerald Ripwood now?" her friend asked.

"Bulger's have gone to the Frontier."

"Of course, Hector is handsome in a sort of obvious way," Angela went on. "But I believe his voice would get on my nerves. A voice is so important. John Tucker certainly isn't good-looking, but he enjoys enjoying himself. Those two evenings at Parker's were great fun. And you know he dances really well. Hector dances disastrously. I think we may have some fun with Papa. And don't forget there's an eligible bachelor with Papa."

"In what way eligible?"

"Well, apparently he owns lots of land and lives in a historic sort of house. According to Hector he has been angled for by every spinster in the Highlands. And his name is Cameron. Perhaps we're distant relations. Hector says we're to call his father 'Ben Nevis'. I said, 'Why not "Kanchenjunga" while I'm about it?' I think I shall suggest their dining with us on Wednesday. That will annoy Mrs Rose-Ross. Papa has obviously been brought out here to fetch Hector to heel and so she won't be able to stop his coming to dinner here. At the same time it'll make her look small, which will please me muchly. Hello, there's Duncan Robertson. You know, I rather like that boy."

The good-looking young subaltern was in the drawing-room a moment or two later.

"Have they arrived, Duncan?" Angela Winstanley asked.

"Have they not! Marvellous old boy, Hector's father. That's what I've come round about. Hector wants to bring him along to tea."

"No can do, Duncan. Maisie and I are going round to Scarborough Towers to have drinks with John Tucker."

Maisie was on the point of ejaculating 'Are we, Angela?' but just managed to suppress the question in time.

"That'll be rather a blow for Hector. Well, I'll toddle along. Shall I tell him 'to-morrow'?"

"I'm not sure. I think I may have to go out."

Duncan Robertson chuckled to himself as he strolled away from the bungalow. He was thinking that the Colonel need not have worried so much whether Hector was going to be hooked by Angela Winstanley. Angela Winstanley seemed to be fishing in other waters. Duncan chuckled again. He had been told about his friend's unsuccessful wooing of the American heiress when he was home in the summer, and it looked as if he should soon be hearing of another matrimonial set-back. Duncan Robertson laughed aloud. Poor old Hector, he was a comic figure in love.

And that was what Angela Winstanley seemed to be finding him as she laughed to her friend Maisie Lambert about Hector's disappointment when Duncan Robertson took back the news that she would not be at home this afternoon and might not be at home to-morrow.

"Angela, I think you're being rather unkind. After all, he is a very nice boy and he has always behaved as a gentleman should. And you did like him awfully at first."

"I'm still very fond of him, but you don't suppose I'm going to give the Rose-Ross woman the pleasure of thinking that she and her stuffy husband have upset my plans? Oh, no, Maisie. Not little Angela." She sat down at her desk to write a note. "Call Abdullah and tell him I want him to take a letter to The Towers."

Tallulaghabad was an example of the British desire to create a home from home in exile. The cantonments tried to look as much like a bit of Aldershot as possible, and Victoria Avenue, the chief residential thoroughfare, tried to look as much as possible like Camberley. Houses in various styles of late nineteenth-century Gothic were set back from the road in large gardens. Half-way down the avenue was a small gothic church in a churchyard with the resident chaplain's house next door, indistinguishable from any suburban vicarage near London. From Victoria Avenue one or two smaller avenues branched off, in one of which was the furnished bungalow rented by Mrs Winstanley, known as The Laurels; the original owner probably thought such a name would counterbalance the unfamiliar vegetation by which he felt oppressed. In every garden, whether of the smaller avenues or of grand Victoria Avenue, malis strove to grow for their British employers the flowers that reminded the exiles of home. Pansies, violets, sweet peas, delphiniums and the rest of them passed a wilted existence in spite of assiduous watering, and here and there lawns fought a losing battle with the climate. When these exiles did return home in spite of having all the pansies, violets, delphiniums and grass they wanted they would spend the rest of their lives regretting the absence of any domestic servant problems in India and wishing they were back in dear old Tallulaghabad. A bed of lanky zinnias would be their only floral link with those wonderful gardens in India of which they would brag to their friends at home.

Scarborough Towers, the residence of Mr John Tucker, was the largest and ugliest of the several large and ugly houses in Victoria Avenue, but in spite of its ugliness it was extremely comfortable and it was redolent of money.

"He must be very rich, you know," said Angela to Maisie as John Tucker's large Daimler which he had sent to fetch them from The Laurels stopped in front of the gothic entrance of the Towers and about half a dozen servants salaamed them in to the gothic entrance-hall, which was full of tiger-skins, armour, weapons and various horned heads. At the foot of the wide polished stairs that led to the first floor were the figures of two Samurai warriors in full armour whose painted faces glared ferociously.

John Tucker was coming down the stairs, his round face in contrast to the Japanese warriors beaming a cordial welcome.

"Jolly nice of you two girls to suggest coming along for cocktails. And of course you'll stay on to dinner," he said.

It was after an excellent dinner that Angela Winstanley put into words the plan she had been thinking over.

"We had such a wonderful time with you up at Pippla, John, that Maisie and I thought we'd like to go and stay there for Christmas. Could you get away?"

"I don't see why not," the little brewer replied. "I'll write and book rooms at Parker's."

"No, I don't want you to do that. I want to be on our own, and I may want to get away from Tallulaghabad almost at once."

"I can't get away myself for a couple of weeks. We're always very busy at the brewery about now, but I'll send you up with Ali in the Austin and I'll come along later. I won't be able to leave the Austin with you because I must have a second car handy down here. And anyway, you won't have much use for a car at Pippla, once it has taken you up there. When do you want to go?"

"I thought I'd write and book rooms to-night, and go in three or four days as soon as my dirzee has finished the frocks he's making for me."

"Well, you've only got to let me know when you want the Austin."

"It's awfully sweet of you, John," said Angela, resting her white ringless fingers for a moment on his plump hand.

"We fat men like to be of service to the ladies. Ha-ha, that's what we're for."

Angela would have preferred less of this genial and slightly impersonal benevolence, and a little more anxiety to do something for her that he would not do for what he called 'the ladies'. It was a little too significant that John Tucker had succeeded in remaining a bachelor until he was fifty. Still, that would make it all the more amusing to unsettle his bachelor's security.

"Do you think John Tucker is beginning to be just a little bit in love with me, Maisie?" she asked her friend when they were back in the rose-shaded sitting-room of The Laurels.

"Honestly, Angela, I don't know. I think he likes you very much."

"Yes, yes, yes," said Angela impatiently. "But do you think he's at all in love with me?"

"Honestly, dear, I simply haven't a clue," Maisie replied. "I think one only *knows*, when somebody is attracted by oneself. But if *you* think Mr Tucker is in love with you he probably is."

An unsatisfactory silence followed which was broken at last by Maisie's asking why Angela had suddenly made up her mind to go to Pippla.

"Are you trying to find out if Mr Tucker *is* in love with you? I mean, did you expect that he would go up with us?"

"Don't be so silly, Maisie. Certainly not. I'm going to Pippla in order to make it difficult for those interfering busybodies. Don't you understand that the Rose-Ross woman won't have a glimmering notion of what is happening if Hector's father and this Mr Cameron have to come up to Pippla. Hector won't be able to come, or if he comes he won't get leave for more than a day or two, and I think we might have quite a lot of fun with Hector's father. I'm going to ask them all to drinks to-morrow evening."

"Colonel and Mrs Rose-Ross too?" Maisie exclaimed.

Angela did not answer this question. She merely sighed compassionately for Maisie's stupidity. "I'll write a note to Hector right away."

Hector, who had been in a state of gloom since Duncan Robertson brought him word from Angela Winstanley that she would not be in that afternoon and probably not in to-morrow either, was much cheered up to get this invitation to drinks. His father and Kilwhillie had been invited to dine in the Clanranald Mess, and as this was a kilted occasion it would mean that his father would be at his best in his own garb when he met Angela for the first time.

Sher Khan was so delighted by his master's doublet of faded plum-coloured velvet that he made another attempt to persuade him to let his moustache be trained upward toward his ears in the style of Sher Khan's own. Indeed, he went so far as to put his hands over Kilwhillie's shoulders when he was standing in front of the glass to see that his jabot was perfectly tied and suddenly hoick up the two ends of his long drooping moustaches to demonstrate the effectiveness of the martial style.

"What the devil are you doing?" Kilwhillie spluttered.

"Sahib will be much better. I am putting on piece of wire to hold moustache behind ears."

"Drop my moustache at once, you rascal," said Kilwhillie. "Drop it, I tell you."

So might he have chastened a retriever that was clinging to a golden plover and mouthing it.

The next slight disagreement between Sher Khan and his master was over the buttons of Kilwhillie's doublet which represented Luath the famous sable hound courant of the Camerons of Kilwhillie. These buttons were of jet with a garnet for the hound's eye and a silver collar.

"Why you have dirty animal dog for buttons, Sahib?" the Pathan asked distastefully. "I get you very nice buttons in bazaar."

"I don't want any buttons from the bazaar."

"I think I get turkishes," Sher Khan persisted.

"You'll do nothing of the kind."

The Pathan sighed.

"Dog very dirty animal," he reiterated obstinately. "No good for Sahib's coat."

"You'll allow me to be the best judge of that. Your job is to polish these buttons."

At about a quarter to six Hector and his friend Duncan Robertson arrived at the Colonel's bungalow in the ancient Morris car they owned between them. Colonel Rose-Ross in his heart regretted he was not going to accompany his guests, but his wife's ascendancy had been too long established for him to defy it now. As it was, he had to face her criticism when the Morris drove off to The Laurels.

"I should have thought the proper course for Ben Nevis to take was to ignore that woman," Mrs Rose-Ross said. "He must know you wouldn't have brought him all the way to India on a wild-goose chase. All he has to do is to notify Hector that if he persists in this entanglement his allowance will be cut off."

"He could have done that without coming out to India at all," the Colonel ventured to observe. "What I'm hoping is that Ben Nevis will be able to persuade Mrs Winstanley to see things in a proper light."

Mrs Rose-Ross sniffed.

"Proper is the last word I should use for anything to do with Mrs Winstanley," she commented. "Well, it's nothing to do with me how your subalterns behave," she went on, "but I wonder what Major Cartwright will think when you go down to the Mess to-night."

"What *has* it got to do with Cartwright?" the Colonel asked with courageous asperity.

"Don't you think Paula Cartwright will be somewhat surprised when she hears that your guests were drinking with Mrs Winstanley before dinner?"

"And what has it got to do with Mrs Cartwright either?" the Colonel snapped.

Mrs Rose-Ross turned her faded forget-me-not blue eyes toward the ceiling with an expression of pained astonishment.

"It's extraordinary how easily one woman can upset a whole station. Quite extraordinary," she declared. "Well, of one thing I'm sure, which is that when Mrs Coppendale

comes out after Christmas she will do all she can to persuade
the Brigadier to get rid of Mrs Winstanley."

"I'm afraid the Brigadier won't find that so easy, whatever his wife may say."

Kilwhillie had impressed on Ben Nevis the importance of
not letting either Hector or Mrs Winstanley know that he
had met her husband. As they were driving to The Laurels
he murmured to Ben Nevis who was sitting with him at the
back of the car not to forget what he had said.

"Forget what?" Ben Nevis asked at the top of his voice.

"About meeting a certain person," Kilwhillie muttered.

"Oh, about meeting Winstanley," Ben Nevis exclaimed
at the top of his voice. "No, of course I shan't." Hector
turned round.

"Did you meet Mrs Winstanley's husband, sir?" he asked
in amazement.

"I didn't meet him exactly," his father replied.

"He was on board the *Taj Mahal*," Kilwhillie quickly
put in.

"Angela will be jolly interested to hear you saw her ex-
husband," Hector went on. "He's a pretty poor type, isn't
he?"

"Oh, he seemed a perfectly ordinary fellow—the sort of
fellow you might see in a railway-carriage," said Hector's
father.

Kilwhillie in his agitation had been tugging so hard at
his moustaches that when he got out of the car he looked
more like a mandarin than ever.

"Why *did* you talk so loudly about Winstanley?" he said
reproachfully to Ben Nevis when they were following Hector
and Duncan Robertson to the door of The Laurels along the
garden path.

"Well, you were speaking so quietly, Hugh. I wanted to
be sure I'd heard what you were talking about."

There was no time to say more before they were being
greeted by their hostess, and she was genuinely taken aback

by the appearance of Hector's father, who was wearing with the kilt his tartan doublet buttoned with silver eagles' heads. She looked from Ben Nevis to his eldest son as if she were trying to make up her mind whether he had in him enough of his father to look like this himself one day. Had she been wrong to let go of Hector so easily? As for Maisie Lambert, she was so much awed by Ben Nevis that she asked him whether he would have a gimlet or a whisky and soda in the tone of voice used in church to ask what number the hymn was.

"Thank you, I'll have whisky, please. And I suppose I must have this dreadful stuff soda with it, being in India, even if it does make it taste like pins and needles. You're very cosy here, Mrs Winstanley," the Chieftain went on, turning to his hostess.

"Oh, it's just a furnished bungalow I was lucky enough to get for six months. But I brought my piano with me from Jumbulpore."

"So I see," said the Chieftain, cocking a paternal eye at this extremely attractive young woman. "Perhaps you'll give us a tune presently?"

"Well, I don't know whether you'd call it a tune, Ben Nevis, but I'll play for you with pleasure."

"By Jove, Hugh," Mac 'ic Eachainn gobbled, for a moment suggesting slightly the sanguine vanity of a turkey-cock, "did you hear that? Pity she can't go to Bombay and give Lady Harbottle a lesson. Every time that woman called me Ben Nevis she tittered, which I found rather objectionable."

Hugh Cameron was worried. He recognised at once that Donald was already prepossessed by Mrs Winstanley, and to himself he had to admit that she was, indeed, extremely prepossessing. He began to compose in his head a cable that would make it imperative for Beatrice to come out to India at once.

"My father met Mr Winstanley on board the *Taj Mahal*," Hector was saying.

"So you met poor Herbert," Mrs Winstanley exclaimed.

"Well, I didn't exactly meet him, but we found ourselves drinking cocoa together," said Ben Nevis.

"Cocoa? Do you like cocoa too?" Mrs Winstanley laughed.

"I can't say I like the stuff. It happened to be there, if you know what I mean," Ben Nevis tried to explain to his hostess.

"Herbert had a passion for cocoa," she murmured, her dark eyes brimming with recollections of the many cups she had made for her late husband after a busy day at the bank. "I wish you'd tell me what he said about me. Not now," she added quickly. "Oh, dear, and I'm going up to Pippla in a day or two."

"You're going up to Pippla?" Hector barked.

"Yes, John Tucker's lending us one of his cars. I hate that railway journey. Maisie and I thought we'd go and spend Christmas at Parker's Hotel. Oh, dear, and I *should* so much like to hear what Herbert told you about me," Mrs Winstanley said to Ben Nevis.

"In his cocoa cups, eh?" the Chieftain guffawed.

"I wonder if you'd be able to come to tea with me to-morrow?" Mrs Winstanley asked.

"I'd be delighted."

Hugh Cameron almost groaned aloud. He might just as well have stayed at home. It was clear that Donald was going to take the bit between his teeth, and he would be left with the painful task of trying to defend to Beatrice his own failure to restrain him.

Chapter 7

THE TÊTE-À-TÊTE

"WOULD you like me to come with you to Mrs Winstanley's, Donald?" Kilwhillie asked on the following afternoon.

"No, I don't think you'd better, Hugh. I don't want the little lady to be embarrassed. I think if we have what they call a tête-à-tête . . . though why they call it that I've never been able to understand, but if we have this tête-à-tête I've a feeling we shall get to understand one another and be able to look at the situation from everybody's point of view. Mind you, I don't mind telling you I was favourably impressed, very favourably impressed, by her yesterday evening. And don't forget, Winstanley hadn't a word to say against her. I liked that fellow, Hugh. I wish he'd come and run my bank in Inverness. Not that I've anything against Macnair, but he knuckles under too much to the Head Office in Edinburgh. I've always taken a firm line with these Edinburgh wallahs. It's essential when you're dealing with affairs in the Highlands. I mean to say, look at the Department of Agriculture. They go marching round the country in plus-fours under the impression that they know all about farming, and half of them don't know the difference between a hogget and a . . . "

"Yes, but that doesn't matter at the moment," Kilwhillie interrupted. "We're in India now. We have a definite job, which is to prevent Hector from committing himself to an unsuitable marriage. All I hope is you won't let yourself be persuaded into thinking that it is a suitable marriage."

"I don't intend to be persuaded by anybody. I have as a matter of fact a definite plan of campaign of my own."

"Of your own?" Kilwhillie repeated, with a hint of apprehension in his tone.

"Yes, I intend to try and make things up between her and Winstanley."

"But they're already divorced."

"Yes, unless; that's the key word, unless, that's what nisi means."

"I know perfectly well what nisi means," said Kilwhillie irritably.

"Unless somebody produces a just cause or impediment, as they say in church. And if Angela went back to her husband that would blow the whole divorce sky-high."

"I think you're taking a very dangerous line."

"You thought I was taking a very dangerous line when I told her I'd been drinking cocoa with her husband on board the good ship *Taj Mahal*. But what was the result? She asked me to go and have tea with her this afternoon. Ah, there's the tonga."

"The what?"

"Some people call it a tum-tum. It's a sort of dog-cart. Rose-Ross offered me his motor-car, but I said I wanted to get the feeling I was in India, and you don't get that from a motor-car."

The Chieftain surged out of the Rose-Ross bungalow and a few moments later was jogging along on the way to The Laurels.

Mrs Winstanley greeted him with a kind of grateful cordiality which Ben Nevis found extremely attractive.

"This is awfully sweet of you," she murmured. "I've sent Maisie out because I want to have a long talk with you, and I think it's much easier to talk without a third person being around."

"Oh, I agree with you."

They sat down on the sofa covered with worn chintz.

"It's rather sad you're not wearing your kilt, Ben Nevis. You looked so wonderful last night."

"Well, of course, I'm not really at home in these ghastly trousers, but I never wear the kilt south of Perth except on ceremonial occasions. Last night we were dining with the

Clanranalds and we had some capital piping. Roderick Macdonald, the pipe-major, comes from my country. His father has a sizable croft in Strathdun—old John Macdonald. You're fond of music, aren't you? You ought to get Hector to bring Roderick Macdonald along one day. Yes, we had a very jolly evening. I played a curious card-game called Bumblepuppy, and lost forty chips. Do you notice how quickly I'm falling into the lingo?"

"Yes, indeed. You might have been in India all your life. And so you met my husband on the way out. Did he talk about me?"

"He hardly talked about anything else. I think it was the cocoa. Of course, I didn't tell him you knew my boy Hector. I thought it might put ideas into his head."

"That was tactful of you."

"Yes, I thought it was rather tactful, and yet you'll hear a lot of people say I'm not tactful. My friend Hugh Cameron, for instance, thinks I haven't an ounce of tact."

"Tell me about Mr Cameron. He made me feel rather shy."

"Did he? I expect that's because he's rather shy himself, especially with women. He's afraid of getting married."

"How strange! You know, Herbert was always afraid of getting married."

"Herbert? Oh, yes, of course. You called him 'Herbert', did you? I always feel that if I was called 'Herbert' I'd prefer to be called 'Bertie'. You never called him 'Bertie'?"

"You met my husband, Ben Nevis. Would it ever occur to you to call him 'Bertie'?"

"No, I see what you mean. But you know, he spoke of you with a great deal of affection. May I ask you a rather rude question? Why exactly did you want to divorce him?"

"I suppose you'll think me heartless if I tell you that it was because I was utterly and hopelessly bored. To start with, Herbert was twenty years older than myself, and as I told you a confirmed bachelor. He couldn't adapt himself to married life. He thought I was untidy and careless about

F

money. He thought I oughtn't to play the piano and forget about arranging what we were going to have for dinner. And then he was always so difficult about knowing people. He thought the soldiers and the people in the Civil Service looked down on him and he would never let me give parties. He said he might be accused of touting for business. And then there was nothing to make it worth while having such a difficult husband. You see, I wasn't at all in love with him," she sighed.

"But you married him."

"Well, you see, my father, who was with Campbell, Campbell, Campbell and Co., died."

"I'm not surprised," the Chieftain ejaculated.

Mrs Winstanley seemed puzzled.

"I mean to say I'm sorry to hear that," he said. "And instead of going to study music in London as I had planned," Mrs Winstanley continued, "I had to stay with my mother. We lived in Calcutta, and, you know, Calcutta isn't the jolliest place in the world unless you have plenty of money. My mother's health was failing and oh, well, when Herbert was appointed to Jumbulpore he asked me to marry him and offered to have my mother to live with us and it seemed a way out and . . ." Mrs Winstanley shrugged her shoulders, "and that was that. I was only twenty at the time, and at twenty we're apt to be optimistic."

"Oh, I agree. I was a howling optimist when I was twenty."

"My mother didn't live long and I inherited the little money she had. And life dragged on at Jumbulpore until at last I asked Herbert to give me my freedom. And he did."

"And what are you going to do when this decree nisi business is over? Are you thinking of marrying again?"

Ben Nevis was immensely pleased with himself over this question. He felt as sagaciously diplomatic as an ambassador in a romantic novel about the turn of the nineteenth century. So he was a little taken aback by Mrs Winstanley's counter.

"You mean am I thinking of marrying Hector? And if I said 'yes', what would you do? Do you think I should disgrace him?"

"Oh, no, of course not, No, no, no, not a bit."

"But you came out to India with the intention of stopping Hector from making what everybody told you would be a social mistake."

"Well, I'd had rather exaggerated reports, if you know what I mean. But as soon as I got into conversation with your late husband over that cocoa—we had hot buttered toast as well—well, I realised that you wouldn't be a bit like what I'd dreaded, I mean expected."

"I'll be frank with you, Ben Nevis, as you've been frank with me. I haven't yet made up my mind."

"Yes, I see what you mean," said the Chieftain.

"You've nothing to worry about until this decree nisi is made absolute. I have no intention of taking the risk of finding myself still married to Herbert Winstanley."

Ben Nevis's plan to reconcile the Winstanleys began to seem much less practicable than when he had first thought of it.

"I like Hector very much," Mrs Winstanley continued.

"Yes, he's a good lad," said his father. "He's supposed to be very like me. Do you think he's very like me?"

"I'll tell you this, Ben Nevis. I'd almost decided not to marry Hector, but when I saw you yesterday afternoon looking so absolutely splendid I began to wonder if I wasn't making a mistake in refusing to marry Hector. I saw in you what he would be like one day. It gave me quite a shock."

"A shock?" the Chieftain repeated, looking mortified.

"A shock of pleasure," Mrs Winstanley murmured quickly.

"Oh, that's awfully nice of you. Look here, hadn't I better call you 'Angela'? Your late husband, I mean your former husband, always talked about you as 'Angela' and

I began to feel I knew you as 'Angela', if you see what I mean."

"Of course I should like you to call me 'Angela'," she said softly. "But I can't promise you that I will marry Hector."

"Oh, you can't?" And anybody listening could easily have fancied a dejected tone in the voice of the Chieftain.

"You realise, because you have imagination . . ."

"No, no," Ben Nevis interposed quickly, "I'm not in the least imaginative. I know people say I am because I've taken this firm line about the Loch Ness Monster, but actually I've never suffered at all from imagination."

"But you have sympathy," Angela insisted.

"Oh, I have any amount of sympathy."

"Well, then you can realise what I have gone through ever since my divorce was granted. You'll probably say I was foolish to come back to India. You'll tell me I ought to have stayed in Canterbury. But India has been my home all my life. Yes, we used to visit my grandparents in Canterbury occasionally, but to me it was always essentially a foreign place."

"Oh, I understand that. I feel just the same about London."

"I knew you'd sympathise. People like Mrs Rose-Ross have said the most terrible things."

"But Mrs Rose-Ross is a stupid woman. In fact, she must be a very stupid woman or she wouldn't have married Rose-Ross."

"Oh, they're all alike, these memsahibs. They think India just exists to give them an importance they would never have at home in England. So when Hector began to pay me a little attention—we went riding together once or twice and he took Maisie Lambert and me for one or two drives in that car he shares with Duncan Robertson—yes, when Hector began to pay me these little attentions I was accused of trying to entangle him in matrimony. I assure you the last thing I wanted to do was to entangle Hector."

"Oh, I see that perfectly, and I'm going to tell Mrs Rose-Ross that I consider you have been grossly misjudged."

"Do you know that Hector begged me to let him introduce me to you as his fiancée, and that I said 'No'?"

"Did you really? Look at that now."

"I said I could not give him his answer until the decree nisi was made absolute. Hector agreed that it would be purely a family affair and that nobody would know anything about our engagement. But I said if the King's Proctor heard a whisper of such an engagement he would at once see that the decree was rescinded—I think that's the right word."

"It sounds just the kind of word that would be right. I can't think why these lawyer wallahs must use this extraordinary language of their own. I suppose it's because they can charge more for it."

"And as I said to Hector, 'Where should we all be if I suddenly found myself married all over again to Herbert Winstanley?'"

"I hope Hector saw your point?"

"No, I'm afraid he didn't," she sighed. "He was extremely obstinate. And so I've decided it will be wiser for me to leave Tallulaghabad for a while and spend a little time at Pippla. Mr Tucker is lending Maisie and me one of his cars to drive us up there. The train is so uncomfortable. One is going in and out of tunnels all the way. I'm only waiting for my dirzee to finish one or two frocks, and then Maisie Lambert and I will be off."

"Your dirzee?" Ben Nevis asked in bewilderment.

"My tailor—my dressmaker."

"I must remember that word," he said resolutely. "That's a pretty easy bit of Pelmanism. I'll think of jersey and then I'll remember it's something to do with clothes. I'm collecting as many Indian words as possible in order to annoy Colonel Lindsay-Wolseley at Council meetings. Did you ever run across him in India? He was what they call a Piffer and he bought Tummie after he retired from the service. A yellowish-brown man with a small grey moustache."

"That would describe quite a lot of Colonels in the Indian Army," she laughed.

"Oh, yes, that reminds me. What does 'Ko hi' mean? Last night in the mess everybody kept shouting 'Ko hi.' Does it mean 'waiter'?"

"No, it means 'Is anybody there?' It's what you shout when you want a servant to attend on you."

"I call that rather a silly way of calling for a servant. It would be a very badly run mess if there wasn't anybody there to bring along a barrow peg."

"It's not barrow peg. It's *burra* peg. A large whisky."

"I say I rather wish you weren't going away, Angela," Ben Nevis said regretfully. "I'd ask you to give me lessons in Indian. I'm getting quite keen on the language. This word 'wallah' is much more expressive than 'fellow'. I always say it now."

"Why don't you and Mr Cameron come up to Pippla?" Angela asked suddenly. "That would stop people from gossiping about Hector and me."

"By Jove, that's a jolly good idea. Between you and me I'm getting rather bored at the Rose-Rosses and I don't think it's fair to accept a wallah's hospitality if you feel bored. Yes, after these dinner parties that have been arranged I think Hugh Cameron and I *will* come up to Pippla. Is there a good hotel there?"

"There are several, but Parker's is the best. That's where Maisie and I will be staying. If you like I'll book rooms for you. Mind you, it can be quite cold in Pippla at Christmas time."

"I shan't mind that. I'll get your . . . now, don't tell me . . . thirzee?"

"Very nearly right, dirzee."

"Yes, well I'll get your dirzee to make me a thick suit."

"I think you'd better get Hector to find you a good **dirzee** for men's clothes, Ben Nevis."

"Yes, perhaps you're right. Well, I suppose I ought to be going."

The Chieftain rose and engulfed Angela's slim ringless fingers in his two massive hands.

"I want you to realise, Angela, that I am your friend," he declared solemnly. "If you decide to marry my boy Hector I shall welcome you as a daughter-in-law. If you decide not to marry him I hope that makes no difference to our friendship. It's a most extraordinary thing . . . I suppose like so many Highlanders I have a bit of what's called second sight . . . yes, it's a most extraordinary thing, but do you know from the moment your late . . . I mean your former husband talked to me about you I had a curious instinct that we should get on together like a house on fire. Now you're going up to Pippla. What about booking rooms for me and Hugh Cameron for ten days from now? I had intended to write to an old school friend of mine, the Maharaja of Bangapatam—Banjo we used to call him—to ask if we could pay him a visit for Christmas."

"But the Maharaja of Bangapatam has a house in Pippla," Angela Winstanley said. "And when we were there we heard he was coming up for Christmas."

"That's splendid. It couldn't be better," Ben Nevis declared. "Well, I must get back to the Rose-Rosses. Goodbye, Angela. We shall meet at Pippla."

And as Ben Nevis went off in his tonga Angela Winstanley sat down at the piano to play the most rousing polonaise that Chopin wrote.

"I think we're going to have lots of fun at Pippla, Maisie," she told her friend when Maisie came back to The Laurels half an hour later. "Lots and lots of fun."

As Ben Nevis drove back in the tonga the sense of having attempted something and of having done something to earn a night's repose began to be jogged out of him by the motion of the vehicle, and by the time he reached the Rose-Rosses' bungalow he was already considering the strength of the defensive position he proposed to take up and wondering if it was as strong as he could have wished.

The Chieftain, humming to himself to suggest an impregnable equanimity and in effect making a noise like an Aeolian harp in the first uneasy gusts before a gale, was making for the shelter of his own room when the Colonel appeared in the entrance of the Rose-Ross drawing-room.

"Ah, there you are, Ben Nevis. Come along and have a drink. We're all agog to hear how you got on with Mrs Winstanley. You've had quite a session, eh?"

"Oh, it was very pleasant, very pleasant indeed," the Chieftain replied in a tone of voice which he hoped suggested the insouciance he was far from feeling.

Hugh Cameron, who knew his friend's moods, at once suspected the worst. It was not often that Donald felt he was in the wrong, but on the rare occasions when he had been doubtful over something he had said or done this slightly overemphasised indifference was a sure sign of his state of mind.

The situation was saved for Ben Nevis by the arrival of his son.

"Hullo, here's Hector," he exclaimed in relief. "I don't want to say anything in front of him. He may not know I have been to—er—interview Mrs Winstanley. And I don't want to make the boy anxious."

It appeared that Hector's mission was to ask if the pipers of the Clanranalds could play at Flagstaff House on the occasion of the dinner party that Brigadier Coppendale was giving to-morrow night."

"Certainly, certainly," said the Colonel. "Only too pleased."

"Ah, I'm glad you've turned up, Hector," said his father. "I want you to get hold of a good jirzee for me."

"A jersey?" Hector exclaimed. "I doubt if I'll be able to find a jersey for you in Tallulaghabad. I could get hold of a pullover probably. Any particular colour?"

"I don't want a pullover, my boy. I want a fairly warm

suit. I'm told that it can be quite cold up at Pippla. That's why I want a jirzee . . . no, no. I've got it wrong. Dirzee. That's the word. It apparently means what we call a tailor."

"Oh, that's easy enough, but when did you decide to go up to Pippla, sir?" Hector asked.

"Well, I think Hugh and I ought to see something of the country. Besides, we don't want to abuse the hospitality of the Colonel and Mrs Rose-Ross."

"My dear Ben Nevis, my wife and I will be only too delighted for you to stay as long as you can," the Colonel protested.

"Yes, but I want Hugh Cameron to see something of the country," said Ben Nevis. "He may not have another chance of seeing India."

While the Chieftain was dressing for dinner he was visited by Hugh Cameron, who had deliberately gone along early to his room in order to find out from his friend just what had happened this afternoon.

"You're dressed very early, Hugh," the Chieftain observed. "Or am I late?"

"No, you're not at all late, Donald. But I wanted to have a few words with you before dinner."

"Well, don't talk while I'm tying my jabot, there's a good chap. Don't forget I haven't got Toker with me here and Balu isn't tall enough to help me with it. So I *must* concentrate. By the way, there was a letter from Trixie by the post. All's well, thank goodness, at Glenbogle. Mr Fletcher has a touch of bronchitis. Trixie says he's never properly shaken off that cold he got when those ruffianly hikers shut him up in the Raven's Tower. Mary and Catriona are in great form. Iain will have arrived from Cambridge by now."

"Did Beatrice ask if you'd met Mrs Winstanley yet?" Hugh enquired.

"She may have said something about Mrs Winstanley. I really don't remember. She's leaving the whole business to me. I'm going to write and tell her that whatever happens she has no reason to feel in the least worried."

"Whatever happens?"

"Now, look here, Hugh, I'm not going to hear any criticism of Mrs Winstanley. We had a most interesting talk this afternoon. She has a complete grasp of the situation and she absolutely refuses to be engaged to Hector until this nisi business is cleared up. I must say I was most impressed by her attitude. In my opinion that little woman has been disgracefully slandered. One of the reasons why we're going up to Pippla next week is because I am not prepared to hear any more unnuendoes about her. Mind you, I don't believe she intends to marry Hector. She obviously prefers older men. I've noticed that about the young women to-day. They definitely prefer older men. And of course they're right. I'll tell you something, Hugh. Do you know that Mrs Winstanley would make absolutely the right wife for you? By Jove, I can see her sitting beside Loch Whillie. What a picture, eh? Well, you'll have a great chance to make the running up at Pippla."

"Donald," said Kilwhillie, sweeping up his moustache with a ferocity that would have impressed even Sher Khan, "there are moments when you step beyond the bounds allowed even by a friendship as intimate as ours. If you ever suggest again that I could in the objectionable phrase you use make the running with Mrs Winstanley, I shall cable to Beatrice that I will not be responsible for anything that may happen out here—anything. I shall make it clear that the winter climate is agreeable and I shall advise her to fly out either with Mary or Catriona or both. And by the way, the word is 'innuendo' not 'unnuendo'."

"Well, it was only an idea that passed through my mind, Hugh. However, if the idea upsets you there's nothing more to be said."

"And this excursion to Pippla," Hugh Cameron went on. "Am I to understand that we are going to Pippla in order to see more of Mrs Winstanley?"

"Mrs Winstanley happens to be going there to spend Christmas, but that's just a coincidence. The point is we want to enjoy ourselves. I get bored by this barrack life. You were in the Brigade for four or five years and so you're used to it. As you know, I'd planned a visit to Bangapatam, but I hear now that he's going to spend Christmas in Pippla. And they tell me that Parker's Hotel at Pippla is very comfortable."

"Who told you so? Mrs Winstanley?"

"She may have said so. I really don't remember. I can't remember what everybody says."

"From what I can make out, Donald, Mrs Winstanley twisted you round her little finger this afternoon. You've put me in a most awkward position. If harm comes of this excursion to Pippla I fear I shall be blamed for not having dissuaded you from going. If we were at home I should insist on going back to Kilwhillie until you had recovered your senses. But if I arrive back in Inverness-shire without you it would inevitably be noticed. People there think we have gone to India for pleasure, and it would look as if we had quarrelled. Have you spoken yet to Hector about the future?"

"It's very difficult for a father to speak to his son about a matter like this. After all, Hector is now twenty-five. I can't treat him like a schoolboy. And I'll tell you this, Hugh. You think I don't know how to handle this business, but you can take it from me that, if I'd started making difficulties, Hector and Angela would have gone off and got married the moment they could. If Angela wants to marry Hector she'll marry him and nothing any of us can do or say will stop her. Thanks to the way I've handled the business, Angela doesn't feel she's being jiggered out of it. In fact, the more I think of it the more astonished I am at my own extraordinary tact. Now don't talk to me, Hugh. I'm going to tie my jabot."

Chapter 8

PARKER'S HOTEL

THE hill station of Pippla was less famous in fact or fiction than its grand relation Simla, which on a smaller scale it resembled, but at the same time when Ben Nevis went East it was a typical health and pleasure resort for those temporarily exhausted by carrying the white man's burden and as such it is still remembered with affection by retired soldiers and Civilians in Cheltenham, Bournemouth, Leamington and all the other harbours of their declining years.

The immediate impression made upon somebody who saw Pippla for the first time was that a few mischievous Titans had emptied part of Golder's Green on a ridge of that mountainous tangle of country which goes rolling away to the snowy ramparts of the Himalayas, and that some of the houses had slipped down the steep slope on either side and managed to lodge themselves here and there without tumbling to the bottom. Narrow paths led down from a wide terrace on the crown of the ridge to those houses which only escaped seeming like any house in the outer suburbs of London because they were built among tall deodars and looked out upon a sublime aspect. The terrace with its bandstand, empty in winter like the bandstand on a south-coast marina, was bounded on one side by a Victorian Gothic church and on the other extended to the fashionable shopping-street of Pippla known as the Promenade, which was forbidden to wheel traffic and Indians alike, except to those Indians who drew the rickshaws that were the only conveyances able to reach the houses on the slopes.

There was a tiny mountain-railway which wound its way up the six thousand feet above which Pippla stood, but the pleasantest way was to drive up by car, and it was by car

that Ben Nevis and Kilwhillie arrived, having sent on their
bearers with the luggage by the railway.

The Chieftain was taken aback for the moment when
Balu Ram, who with Sher Khan was waiting for his master
at the end of the motor road which ran round the foot of
the ridge, indicated the rickshaw in which he was to be
conveyed up what looked like a perpendicular wooded cliff
to Parker's Hotel.

"But those chaps will never be able to pull me up that,"
he protested, eyeing the two apparently emaciated rickshaw-coolies.

"Please, Master is getting inside rickshaw," Balu insisted
firmly.

"Well, if I must I suppose I must," the Chieftain woofed.

For the first time that Ben Nevis could remember his
friend Kilwhillie laughed aloud. Inasmuch as Kilwhillie
had been almost morose during the drive up in order to
mark his disapproval of what he called 'this harum-scarum
excursion' to Pippla, the Chieftain was startled by the
sound.

"Did I hear you laugh, Hugh?" he exclaimed.

"Yes, as a matter of fact I did laugh."

"But what are you laughing at?"

"I was laughing at you."

"At me?" Ben Nevis gasped in amazement.

"Yes, you look about twice as big as that queer sort of
perambulator you're sitting in."

And Kilwhillie laughed again.

"Well, I suppose it is very funny," said the Chieftain
doubtfully.

At that moment he leaned back in the rickshaw, where-
upon the two shafts went up into the air, carrying both the
rickshaw-coolies up in the air with them.

And Kilwhillie laughed aloud for the third time.

When Kilwhillie in his turn was seated in a rickshaw Ben
Nevis guffawed boisterously. Yet somehow it lacked the
spontaneity of his friend's merriment: indeed, it could

almost have been called a forced laugh. At that moment the coolies strained forward to pull their bulky passenger up the hill. As Ben Nevis saw the shafts again taking an acute angle in front of him, he said:

"We shan't either of us laugh, Hugh, if these extra-ordinary contraptions start going downhill backwards."

"Not to be afraid, Sahib," said Balu reassuringly. "Strong mens not let Master fall down *khud*."

"Cud?" the Chieftain repeated.

Balu stepped to the edge of the narrow path and pointed to the ravine.

"Down there is what Pippla mens call *khud*," he explained.

"Did you hear that, Hugh?" Ben Nevis called from his rickshaw to Kilwhillie following in the other. "If we fall over the edge we shall both be chewing the cud at the bottom."

This time Ben Nevis laughed in cordial appreciation of his own joke, but Kilwhillie did not even smile.

Presently Balu pointed to a large building which had apparently slid down from the Terrace and was now only prevented from sliding down further by huge buttresses of concrete.

"We come now to Parker's Hotel," he announced.

"It looks like a decayed fort," Ben Nevis observed.

"Very good hotel," Balu affirmed. "Me and Sher Khan see rooms for Master and Cameron Sahib. Very good rooms with balcony. Important peoples only can have these rooms. Master is being very much pleased."

Presently they passed a sleeping figure by the side of the path with a blanket round his head and the rest of his body covered only by a loin cloth.

"Is anything the matter with that poor wallah?" Ben Nevis asked sympathetically.

"No, he is rickshaw-coolie man who sleeps for a little rest," said Balu.

"But why is his head covered up in that blanket?"

"Blanket is for keep him warm. It is cold now in Pippla."

"Keep him warm?" Ben Nevis exclaimed. "But he's got practically nothing on except over his head."

"If his head being warm he is warm all over himself," Balu explained. "If his head being cold he is cold all over himself."

Parker's Hotel had begun as a small boarding-house some time in the early 'seventies of the last century, and had been steadily enlarged as time went on until it grew into the huge amorphous pile it was at the time that Ben Nevis and Kilwhillie arrived there some sixty years later. To describe it in terms of architecture is impossible, with its Italian loggias, its Oriental arches, its corrugated tin roofs which seemed to cover an enormous lean-to against the *khud*, its concrete buttresses, its passages at different levels and its innumerable staircases without one main staircase in the whole building. The large dining-room was surrounded by a verandah on three sides with a sublime view over that tossing countryside of wooded hills and deep ravines. The drawing-room was a perfect period piece of the early 'nineties when it was built. The walls were covered with pink and cream lincrusta. The mirrors were painted round the edge of the glass with lakeside vegetation so as to suggest that the glass itself was a lake. Pampas grass and bulrushes gathered dust in tall vases. The pictures were mezzotints of sentimental Royal Academy costume-dramas. The furniture was Maples in its prime. If the belles of forty years earlier with their balloon sleeves and hats balanced on top of their overcurled hair and fringes had revisited that drawing-room in Pippla they would see no change in it since they flirted there with subalterns in the days when Rudyard Kipling was young.

The bedroom allotted to Ben Nevis opened out of a sitting-room and on the other side of the landing was Kilwhillie's bedroom. A loggia ran the length of the three rooms from which it could be entered by french-windows.

"This is very jolly, Hugh," said the Chieftain, who had stepped out into the loggia to enjoy the view. "By Jove, it's almost as good as parts of the Highlands."

"It certainly is a fine view," Kilwhillie agreed. "But I still think we were unwise to come up here."

"I don't know why they have all this wire-netting everywhere. There can't be many mosquitos buzzing about at this time of year. And anyway it wouldn't keep out a bumble-bee, let alone a mosquito."

"These people must be the despair of our fellows who are trying to help run this country," Kilwhillie remarked. "Fancy thinking you can keep out mosquitos with a mesh that size."

"We may as well open them," said Ben Nevis. "They rather spoil the view, which really *is* almost as good as parts of the Highlands."

The Chieftain opened the wire doors along the parapet of the loggia and declared what an improvement it was.

"Really, you know, Hugh, now this wire is out of the way, I think this view *is* as good as parts of Perthshire or Argyll. Not the west of Inverness-shire, of course," he added hastily. "Well, I think we ought to be getting downstairs. Tiffin will be ready. And look here, Hugh, when we meet Mrs Winstanley and her friend Miss Lambert I do hope you'll be pleasant to them."

"I shall be polite, of course. But I don't intend to turn this deplorable excursion into a family party."

Balu Ram and Sher Khan were waiting for orders on the landing outside the sitting-room when their masters came out.

"I think we'll wear the kilt for dinner, to-night, don't you?" Ben Nevis suggested.

"Mightn't it seem rather ostentatious," the younger laird suggested.

"Dash it, Hugh, we're six thousand feet up where we are, which is more than a thousand feet higher than dear old Ben Nevis itself, and the air here has quite a bite in it.

That view from our balcony made me feel quite homesick. I shall wear the kilt to-night without hesitation, and if you take my advice you won't go about looking like a dumb waiter in black." He turned to the bearers. "The Sahib and myself will wear the kilt to-night. Put everything ready."

Balu jerked his head to show he understood what was required and with that jerk somehow expressed at the same time affirmative approbation.

Down in the dining-room, which looked cheerful in the December sunshine, Angela Winstanley and Maisie Lambert were already seated at a table in the window.

"Let's have coffee together afterwards, shall we?" the Chieftain suggested breezily, after he had greeted the two young women. "We had a splendid drive from Tallulaghabad, but I thought Kilwhillie and I were going to chew the cud when they dragged us up here in those gimcrack rickshaws. The two wallahs pulling me went right up in the air once or twice at the end of the shafts when I leaned back."

When Ben Nevis and Kilwhillie were seated, the Chieftain said, "I was going to suggest joining the girls at their table, but you would keep scowling, Hugh, and so I didn't."

"I think it's more dignified to lunch at our own table," his companion said.

"Well, I must say I like this place," Ben Nevis declared, gazing round the dining-room. "I was getting awfully tired of Rose-Ross's pettifogging conversation."

"For goodness' sake, Donald, not so loud," his companion begged. "Everybody in the place is staring at us."

"I wasn't talking louder than usual, Hugh. It's because we're six thousand feet up and the air is so much clearer that you think I'm talking loudly. What are we having to eat? Ah, curry. I'm getting very fond of this curry. I must get hold of some recipes to take back with me. I believe Mrs Ablewhite would make jolly good curry if I could give her a few tips. By Jove, I'll have the Lindsay-Wolseleys to lunch at Glenbogle and I'll have such a hot curry that Wolseley

G

will think he's back in the Khyber Pass slashing away at Afghans and whatnot. Yes, I'll show him what curry is. He'll think he's swallowed a mustard plaster. I'll tell Toker to put some extra chillis in his plate, though why they call them chillis I've never been able to understand. You might as well call ice-creams hot-dogs."

In the excitement of preparing a ferocious curry for his neighbour Colonel Lindsay-Wolseley when he returned to Scotland the Chieftain was incautious about the curry in front of him, and for a minute he was compelled to keep silence until his own tongue had cooled.

After lunch the two new arrivals at Parker's adjourned to the drawing-room, where they found Angela Winstanley and Maisie Lambert waiting for them.

"Poor old Hector was very cast down when we started off this morning," said his sympathetic father.

"Yes, I expect he'll miss you," Mrs Winstanley agreed.

"Oh, it's not me he's missing," the Chieftain guffawed genially. "Ha-ha-ha!"

It would be an exaggeration to assert that Kilwhillie's rather tired eyes were those of a basilisk at this moment, but they certainly did come nearer to gleaming his disapproval of that last remark than they had ever come to gleaming.

"Perhaps he'll be able to manage a spot of leave," Miss Lambert suggested compassionately.

"I doubt it," said the Chieftain. "They were talking about some regimental—now, wait a minute, what's the word—not tomato?"

"Tumasha?" Mrs Winstanley suggested.

"That's it—tamasho. I was pretty near it, wasn't I? Yes, some regimental tamasho which will keep him down in Tallulaghabad. Poor old boy. Of course, if we get this war which everybody seems to think we shall within the next year or two it will be different, but I'm bound to say I think a soldier's life in peacetime is an appalling waste of time. The other night dining with the Brigadier at Flagstaff House I thought the top of my head would explode once or twice I was so bored with the conversation. However, luckily we had some good piping. Pipe-major Macdonald played *MacDonald is Here*—that's one of our great Glenbogle tunes—as well as I've ever heard it played. My own piper Angus MacQuat couldn't have played it better. Even the Brigadier seemed to grasp that it was a jolly good tune, and of course he's as English as cricket. And that reminds me, didn't you say that the Maharaja of Bangapatam is coming here for Christmas?"

"Yes, he has a lovely house here. And he and the Maharaja of Tussore, whose state is only a few miles from Pippla, always have wonderful parties at Christmas time."

"Have you ever met him?" Ben Nevis asked.

Mrs Winstanley smiled a little sadly.

"No, I'm afraid I didn't move in such circles," she murmured.

"Well, by Jove, you shall meet him, Angela. I'll jolly well see you do."

Hugh Cameron gave his moustache an agonised tug. Donald was exceeding even his gloomiest forebodings. Where was all this going to end? He had a vision of Beatrice MacDonald eyeing him with stern reproach.

"I think we ought to take a little exercise, Donald," he said. "I suggest we walk up to what they call the Terrace."

In making this suggestion, he had not supposed that Ben Nevis would say:

"Jolly good idea. You two girls go and put your things on, and we'll wait for you downstairs."

When the girls had departed to get ready, Hugh Cameron looked at his friend in censorious amazement.

"This mountain air seems to have gone to your head, Donald. Do you realise what you've just done?"

"Of course I realise what I've done. There's nothing to realise," the Chieftain replied.

"You come out to India, dragging me with you in order to prevent Hector from plunging into a deplorable entangle-

ment. Within a fortnight of your arrival you allow yourself
to be seen escorting Mrs Winstanley all over Pippla. What
are people going to think?"

"I don't care what these sahib wallahs think," said Ben
Nevis. "I consider that Angela—by the way you'd better
call her 'Angela' and I'll tell her to call you 'Hugh'."

"You are not to tell her to call me 'Hugh'. If Mrs Winstanley dares to call me 'Hugh' I shall cable immediately to
Beatrice to fly out here and I shall go down to Bombay to
meet her. And when she arrives I shall tell her that I no
longer feel capable of handling the situation."

"I wish you could understand what I'm trying to do,
Hugh," Ben Nevis expostulated.

"What *are* you trying to do?"

"I'm trying to win Angela's confidence. When she feels
sure I am her best friend I shall be able to advise her."

"Rubbish," Kilwhillie ejaculated. "All she will feel sure
about is that she can twist you round her finger."

Ben Nevis shook his head.

"I don't know where you've been getting those ideas
about women, Hugh. Have you been reading some of those
French novels?"

Kilwhillie felt powerless to argue further with his friend.
He moved toward the door of the drawing-room.

"If we have to take this deplorable walk," he said, "we'd
better get it over as soon as possible. The Terrace will
probably be packed with people wandering about with
nothing better to do than gossip."

The Terrace was not so thronged as it would have been
in summer, but there were plenty of people walking to and
fro in the brilliant wintry sunshine, and there was nobody
who did not take an obvious interest in the quartet from
Parker's Hotel. Ben Nevis in the tweed suit made for him
by the dirzee found for him by his son did not present the
striking figure of the monarch of Glenbogle on his native
heath, but even in trousers he was much the most striking
figure on the Terrace of Pippla, and beside him Angela

Winstanley in an astrakhan coat walked in beauty like Byron's night of cloudless climes and starry skies. Kilwhillie, with whom poor Maisie Lambert was finding conversation difficult, attracted much less attention.

"And those are the Himalayas, are they?" Ben Nevis observed when they were standing on the north side of the Terrace to gaze across the miles of tossing country in between to that noble line of snow along the horizon. "By Jove, I'd like to catch a glimpse of one of these Abominable Snowmen we hear about. I suppose there's no chance of seeing them as far down as this."

"I've never heard of one being seen in Pippla," said Angela Winstanley.

"It would be a wonderful thing to be able to say that one had seen the Loch Ness Monster as I have, and even one of these Abominable Snowmen. There was one of those scientific wallahs who came up to Inverness who said he'd seen the footprints of an Abominable Snowman but he never got a glimpse of our dear old Monster."

"That house, down there among the trees, is Rosemount, the Maharaja of Bangapatam's house," said Angela Winstanley bringing the prospect nearer to prosaic reality.

"It looks rather a jolly place. I must write to old Banjo when we get back to the hotel, Hugh. Don't let me forget," Ben Nevis told him.

"I don't think he's arrived yet," Maisie Lambert said. "He usually comes about a week before Christmas for a short visit, but of course he stays much longer in the summer."

"Well, I'll send a letter to wait for him. Good old Banjo. What a century that was he made at Lord's. The Eton wallahs were absolutely paralysed. It's a stupid game, cricket, but when old Banjo was batting one could see there was something in it."

It was nearly four o'clock when the quartet got back to the hotel and, after Ben Nevis in spite of Kilwhillie's frowns had arranged to meet before dinner in the cocktail bar, he and Kilwhillie went up to their sitting-room. Presently the latter walked across the landing to see if Sher Khan had laid out his evening attire correctly.

As Ben Nevis went into his bedroom for the same purpose a shape bounded along the balcony past the window.

"Hugh!" he shouted. "Hugh! There's an Abominable Snowman. Hugh!"

But even as he bellowed for him, Hugh Cameron himself appeared in the doorway.

"My god, Donald," he said in a tremulous voice, "a large monkey has just gone off with my sporran."

"Well, I suppose it *might* have been a monkey," Ben Nevis admitted unwillingly.

"But do you realise the brute was sitting on my bed when I got into my room?" Kilwhillie said. "And when it saw me it picked up my sporran and bounded out of the window with it."

"Good lord, your window was open, then?"

"Of course it was open," Kilwhillie answered irritably. "You don't suppose the brute jumped through the glass?"

"You shouldn't have left it open," said the Chieftain. "And you shouldn't have opened those wire-netting doors. Angela says they're meant to keep out monkeys, not mosquitos."

"It was you who opened them. But never mind about that. How am I going to get back my sporran?"

"We'd better consult the Management."

The little Indian clerk who represented the Management looked up from his desk in the office that was a little larger than a cupboard and a little smaller than a room, off the narrow entrance-hall.

"A monkey has just carried off Mr Cameron's sporran," Ben Nevis announced. "What ought he to do about it?"

"What is sporran, please? It is an English sweet?" the clerk asked courteously. "I'm afraid the langur monkey will be eating it by now."

"No, no, no," said Ben Nevis, "a sporran is an article of clothing, well, not clothing exactly, but it's worn with the kilt."

"Ah," said the little clerk solemnly, "It is a respect for the dead, what is called a mourning, I think."

"No, no, no," Ben Nevis barked. "The kilt is worn by Highland regiments."

"Ah, I understand. Like a petticoat. Oh, yes, yes, of course. It is the Scotch dress."

"The sporran," Kilwhillie explained, "is a sort of pouch which is worn in front. It is actually a purse."

The little clerk's eyes glittered.

"Ah, you have lost money?"

Then he pointed to the printed notice on the wall behind his chair, which announced:

"The Management cannot be held responsible for any valuables not placed in their charge by the guests."

"There was no money in it," Kilwhillie said. "I am not trying to hold the Management responsible. I left the window of my room open and my bearer omitted to close it before he went away. What I want to know is whether there is any method of tracing these monkeys to their—well, to where they live?"

"The monkeys are living on the roof," the clerk said.

"Good lord!" Ben Nevis exclaimed. "But the roof is made of corrugated iron. They can't live on corrugated iron."

"Yes, they can live there," the clerk insisted.

"Well, I think the best thing to do will be for Sher Khan to get a ladder and climb up on the roof to see if your sporran is there, Hugh."

Word was sent for Sher Khan to report at once to his master, and Ben Nevis and Kilwhillie went back to their sitting-room. On the way upstairs Ben Nevis suddenly let out a tremendous guffaw.

"What strikes you as particularly funny, Donald?" his friend asked coldly.

"I was thinking how funny it would be if this monkey started wearing your sporran."

"I see nothing at all funny about that," the owner snapped.

"I don't know. Monkeys are very intelligent beasts," said Ben Nevis. "Of course, this particular monkey wallah might get it the wrong way round. But that would be funny too."

"It doesn't appeal at all to my sense of humour," said Kilwhillie distastefully. "Moreover, it's the only sporran I brought with me, and that means we shall have to wear dinner-jackets to-night, for I presume you don't intend to make yourself conspicuous by being the only person in a kilt this evening?"

"Well, we *must* rescue your sporran somehow, Hugh."

A minute or two later Hugh Cameron had the gratification of hearing Ben Nevis bellowing from his bathroom.

"Hugh! Hugh! One of these infernal monkeys is sitting in my bath."

"Has it got my sporran?" Hugh asked anxiously, hurrying through into the Chieftain's bedroom.

"No, but the brute is sitting there pulling my sponge to pieces and chattering at me," said Ben Nevis, hastily closing the door of the bathroom behind him.

"Well, you can't leave it in your bathroom," Kilwhillie said.

"I'm not going to be bitten by a monkey for the sake of a sponge," Ben Nevis declared. "Why the deuce don't our bearers come back?"

"You're not frightened of a monkey, are you?" Kilwhillie asked.

"Of course I'm not frightened of the brute. But I don't know how you handle a monkey covered with grey fur. It's as big as you are, Hugh."

The Chieftain rattled the door of his bathroom and bellowed, "Get out of there, you brute!"

There was a scamper of feet followed by the roar of the old-fashioned sanitary cistern emptying itself.

"Good lord," Ben Nevis gasped, "the brute must have climbed up by the plug to get out of the window."

And that, indeed, was what had happened. When Ben Nevis and Kilwhillie entered the bathroom they found among the wreckage of the Chieftain's toilet accessories Kilwhillie's sporran intact except for the contents of a tube of shaving-cream with which it was richly smeared.

"I think we'd better go out and close those wire contraptions," Ben Nevis growled.

"It's a great pity that you ever opened them," Kilwhillie commented, removing from his sporran as much shaving-cream as he could with the largest piece he could find of the Chieftain's sponge.

Chapter 9

THE MAHARAJA OF BANGAPATAM

"I WISH you would impress on your friend Mrs Winstanley that I do not dance, Donald," said Kilwhillie when he and Ben Nevis were back in the sitting-room after their first evening in Parker's Hotel.

"You used to dance *Strip the Willow* jolly well, Hugh."

"There's a great difference between *Strip the Willow* and this ghastly slithering about all over the place which they call dancing to-day. Besides, I don't even dance *Strip the Willow* nowadays. And I think I ought to warn you, Donald, that I overheard one young woman say to another that she'd like to teach you the rumba."

"What's that? A card game?" the Chieftain asked. "I hate cards."

"It's a dance," said Kilwhillie severely. "A rather disagreeably wriggling dance."

"Oh, it's a dance, is it?" Ben Nevis chuckled, a gratified expression on his high-coloured countenance.

"What she actually said was, 'Oh, darling, I'd love to teach that gorgeous creature the rumba.'"

"Gorgeous creature, eh?" Ben Nevis repeated, putting up his hands to test the neatness of his jabot.

Kilwhillie looked at his friend in astonishment.

"Do you mean to say you don't resent being called a gorgeous creature?"

"It was apparently meant as a compliment," said the Chieftain.

"It's the kind of thing some feather-headed visitor from London would say about a shorthorn bull at the Perth Cattle Sale," Kilwhillie scoffed.

"I think you ought to watch yourself over these curries, Hugh."

"What do you mean?"

"I don't believe they agree with you. I think they're lying a bit heavily on your liver. You had two helpings of the curry at dinner to-night."

"You had three."

"Ah, but I haven't got a liver. You've had one ever since I can remember. But look here, we don't want to start arguing about your liver, Hugh. I must write this letter to old Bangapatam, and let him know we're in Pippla."

The Chieftain seated himself at the gimcrack desk which is a permanent feature of all hotel sitting-rooms east or west of Suez.

Writing even the briefest note was a painful business for the Chieftain and the difficulty of it was expressed by putting out his tongue and holding it firmly between his teeth. At last he managed to finish his letter and turned to his friend.

"How's this, Hugh? *My dear Banjo . . .,*"

"How long is it since you saw the Maharaja of Bangapatam?"

"It must be about forty years. But why do you ask? Trixie met him at the Finchamptons a year or two ago when she was lunching with them in that horrid place London."

"Well," Kilwhillie began, becoming very Wykehamist, "I feel that if you haven't seen an Indian prince since he was at school with you . . ."

"Oh, we met several times when we were at the 'Varsity, but he was at Oxford," Ben Nevis put in.

"Anyway, I don't think you ought to call him by his school nickname," Kilwhillie insisted.

"You think not?"

"I feel positive about it."

"Well, I can't write 'My dear Bangapatam'."

"Why not write 'My dear Maharaja'?" Kilwhillie suggested.

"You don't think that's too formal?"

"Not at all."

Ben Nevis scratched out '*My dear Banjo*' and began again,

'*My dear Maharaja,*

I have heard with a great deal of pleasure that you will soon be visiting your house in Pippla where I am now staying with my friend Hugh Cameron of Kilwhillie at Parker's Hotel. I hope you have not forgotten Nosy MacDonald . . .

"You never told me you used to be called 'Nosy' at Harrow," Kilwhillie interrupted sharply. "I was called 'Button' at Winchester."

"Because you had a head like a button, eh?" Ben Nevis guffawed.

"Not at all," Kilwhillie replied. "It happened once when I had a bad cold that I asked for some more button."

"I never knew buttons were good for a cold. Do you heat them or something?"

"Who on earth would want to eat buttons?"

"I said 'heat' not 'eat'. You're getting awfully deaf, Hugh. I believe Sher Khan is right. I believe if you turned your moustache up behind your ears you'd find it a help for your deafness."

"I'm certainly not going to, and in any case I'm not deaf."

"I don't know. If you thought I said 'eat' when I said 'heat' for these buttons you say are good for colds . . ."

"I did not say buttons are good for colds," Kilwhillie interrupted. "I said once when I had a bad cold I asked for some more button."

Ben Nevis shook his head.

"Well, what did you do with these buttons?"

"Buttons don't come into it. I was trying to say mutton."

"Well, you don't want to use Pelmanism to remember mutton. Anybody can remember mutton."

"But mutton sounded like button when I had this bad cold."

"Did it?" Ben Nevis asked doubtfully. "Well, of course

there's no knowing what anything will sound like to you Winchester wallahs . . ."

"Go on with this letter of yours," said Kilwhillie wearily. "You'd got as far as Nosy MacDonald."

Ben Nevis continued his reading:

"You met my wife a year or two ago at the Finchamptons, but unluckily I did not get an opportunity to have a talk with you about old times forty years on,"

Ben Nevis broke off to explain that this was an allusion to the Harrow school song.

"You've never missed an opportunity to tell me that, Donald. And once at Glenbogle you tried to sing it to me. It made me feel glad that I wasn't at Harrow." The Wykehamist shuddered. "Go on with your letter," he said.

"We are both older than we were when you made that grand century at Lord's."

"Isn't that rather too obvious a remark?" Kilwhillie put in. "Of course you're both older than you were over forty years ago."

"But although we are older," Ben Nevis continued ignoring the interruption, *"we still enjoy life as much as ever."*

"How do you know he does? He may be suffering from an incurable disease," Kilwhillie interrupted again.

"How can he be suffering from an incurable disease when he comes all the way up here from the middle of India to spend Christmas? I wish you wouldn't keep interrupting, Hugh. Where was I? Oh, yes,

"we still enjoy life as much as ever and I hope that I may have the pleasure of a jolly good talk about the dear old school on the Hill when I was Nosy and you were Banjo.

"I want him to know that I haven't forgotten his nickname," Ben Nevis broke off to say.

"You will be interested to hear that I have seen the Loch Ness Monster . . ."

"No," said Kilwhillie sternly. "Cut out everything about the Loch Ness Monster."

"But I was going on to say something about the Abominable Snowmen," Ben Nevis protested.

"Cut that out too. You don't want to give the man the idea that you're a crank."

"A crank?" Ben Nevis expostulated.

"A crank," said his companion firmly, so firmly that Ben Nevis did not argue with him but stroked out the sentence.

"Hugh Cameron and myself will be staying on at Parker's Hotel over Christmas and I very much hope that we may have the pleasure of calling on you."

Ben Nevis put down the letter.

"I don't know what the etiquette of this calling business is in India, but I don't think I ought to suggest his calling on us. . . . Oh, and then I sign myself

> *Yours ever,*
> *Donald MacDonald of Ben Nevis."*

"I think 'yours ever' is too free and easy," Kilwhillie ruled. "I should say 'yours sincerely' or perhaps 'with kind regards, yours sincerely'."

"Isn't that rather too formal. I want to make Banjo feel the auld lang syne spirit. I hope he'll get his friend the Maharaja of Tussore to give us a panther beat or whatever they call it."

"That can come later when you've met," Kilwhillie commented.

"Oh, I ought to say something about Hector. I'll put in a PS. '*My oldest boy Hector is with the Clanranalds at Tallulaghabad and if he is lucky enough to get a spot of leave I hope you'll let me bring him along to Rosemount some time*—Of course. That's the way to sign the letter. *Salaams*. It's extraordinary, isn't it, how quickly I've picked up Indian? Yes, of course, that's it. *Salaams Yours sincerely*. I'll send Balu along with it to-morrow morning. I'm longing to see how my Express behaves. I had a jolly good mind to put it together and have a shot at that monkey this afternoon . . ."

"I don't think you're allowed to shoot monkeys. I believe they're sacred here."

"I never heard such peprosterous rubbish in my life. Well, I have as a matter of fact, because I believe it's against the law to shoot a fellow at home who breaks into your house unless you're already half dead yourself because he shot you first. I don't know what the world's coming to. I really don't."

Two or three days later after the despatch of that letter to Rosemount Ben Nevis surged into Kilwhillie's bedroom one morning, triumphantly bearing the answer.

"Listen to this, Hugh.

"My dear Nosy,

I was delighted to find your welcome note when I arrived at Rose-mount and even more delighted that I am to have the opportunity of renewing an old friendship. I did not realise at the time when I met Mrs MacDonald at the Finchamptons in Belgrave Square that she was the wife of Nosy MacDonald, and you had gone back to Scot-land before I found out.

Now, I can't possibly let you stay at Parker's while I'm at Rose-mount where I shall be about three weeks. So will you and your friend Mr Cameron come along in time for tiffin?

Two of my cars will be waiting at the usual place near the station and your bearers will know how to arrange about the luggage. Looking forward with great keenness to renewing an old friendship and with many kind remembrances.

Yours very sincerely,

Banjo

"And then he's written about six Indian names after that, but I can't read one of them."

Hugh Cameron applauded the idea of staying with the Maharaja, at any rate it would give Donald less opportunity to develop this menacing friendship with Mrs Winstanley.

Balu Ram and Sher Khan were both much gratified to hear that their masters were to be guests of the Maharaja, and the prospect of repacking and arranging for the transport of the baggage down to the motor road did not in the least dismay them. The sense of their own importance as the bearers of two such burra sahibs already acute was now twice as acute.

"It's terribly sad that you're leaving us so soon," Angela Winstanley said when the Chieftain gave her the news of their visit. "But you'll have a wonderful time at Rosemount," she added, with the faintest hint of a sigh.

Ben Nevis looked over his shoulder to see if Kilwhillie was within earshot, but seeing that he was not he said in the voice of a conspirator:

"And you're going to have a wonderful time at Rosemount too. I'm going to make it my particular business to see that you do. Did you ever hear a song called 'Say Au Revoir but not Good-bye'?"

"I don't believe I ever did, Ben Nevis."

"No, I don't suppose you would have. But I was very fond of it when I was a young man. Yes! Say Au Revoir but not Good-bye. I can't remember any of the rest of it, but it doesn't matter, because that's the whole point of the song, if you see what I mean."

"I do see, dear friend, if I may call you that," said Angela.

"I hope you will, by Jove. Well, I must be getting along. We're going to walk down the cud to where the cars are waiting. All right, I'm coming, Hugh," the Chieftain shouted, and he hurried away to rejoin Kilwhillie.

Rosemount was situated at the bottom of the slope on the other side of the ridge and a car could go right up to the main entrance at the end of a long drive. Externally it looked like a very large house built in the Tudor style at Sunningdale, and it might have served as a model for the ideal home of the successful business-man able to escape occasionally from the strain of making money to enjoy the simplicity of country life with the maximum of comfort. There was a cricket ground where his Highness sat in judgment on the play of the younger generation. There were lawns and hard tennis-courts. There was a squash-racquet-court, and a floodlit hard tennis-court with a pavilion along one side of it. There were lily pools, woodland walks and crazy paving, rockeries and rhododendrons galore.

Internally Rosemount was more definitely oriental in its decoration, but it was nowhere oriental at the expense of comfort. There was a ballroom and a very large drawing-room, a gymnasium, a swimming-bath, a billiards-room and a table-tennis room. The guests of his Highness were accommodated in an annexe built in the Scottish baronial style but considerably more luxurious than any of its proto-types. Between the guest-house and the rest of Rosemount was a picture-gallery the walls of which were covered with pictures from the exhibitions of the Royal Academy during the last decade of the nineteenth century.

When the car with his two guests was approaching the house along the drive the princely host was waiting to welcome them on his threshold, and the driver turned round to tell them that the figure standing there was Maharaja Sahib himself.

"Good lord!" Ben Nevis gasped in the nearest he could get to a low voice. "He's the size of an elephant. He was almost as slim as my little finger at Harrow. Extra-ordinary!"

"Not at all extraordinary," Kilwhillie contradicted. "You're a good deal bulkier yourself than you were forty years ago."

The car reached the steps leading up to the door of Rose-mount before Ben Nevis had time to argue with Kilwhillie about his physical development. At the head of them stood His Highness the Maharaja of Bangapatam, wearing a black silk jacket with jewelled buttons, beaming a welcome. In spite of his size, His highness seemed younger than his sixty years and carried his weight with a dignified grace and no little agility.

"My dear friend Nosy, I am really so glad to see you again," he exclaimed, shaking the Chieftain's hand warmly. "My house is yours."

"My dear Maharaja, I'm jolly glad to see you. The last time we met was at Jimmy's on the last night of the 'Varsity match. You made a lot of runs against us for Oxford and if we hadn't had Ranji we should have been for it. This is my friend Hugh Cameron of Kilwhillie, who hadn't the good luck to be at Harrow. He's a Wykehamist wallah."

"He is already speaking our language very fluently, isn't he?" said his Highness, with a twinkle in his dark eyes.

Ben Nevis chuckled with a touch of complacency.

"Well, I'm picking up a bit here and there, you know. But, by Jove, what a job I had to remember your name. I had to use Pelmanism at last. I could only remember 'Bang' and 'Banjo'."

"Well, 'Banjo' is pretty easy," said his Highness. "I think we will go back to 'Banjo'. I shall feel quite young again when you call me that."

By this time they had passed through the hall into the smoking-room where half a dozen nymphs and goddesses in marble assisted mutely at the smoking-room conversation carried on from deep armchairs covered in crimson morocco leather.

"What will you have before tiffin? A gimlet? Or would you prefer some of your own Scotch?"

The guests both declared for whisky.

"You'll forgive me, please, if I do not join you," said his Highness. "But my doctor is trying to keep me down to twenty-two stone. Poor chap, he does not find it at all easy."

"I've never thought of giving up whisky," said Ben Nevis. "And I'm only just under seventeen stone myself."

"Tell me now, you were never called Ben Nevis at Harrow. When Lord Finchampton told me that Mrs Mac-

Donald was the wife of Ben Nevis it never occurred to me that it was my old friend Nosy MacDonald."

"Ah, my elder brother Hector was still alive then. I wasn't Younger of Ben Nevis in those days."

"You have given me quite an idea, Nosy," said his Highness. "If you are Ben Nevis, which is quite a small mountain I think . . ."

"Oh, it's not so small as all that," its namesake protested.

"Yes, if you are Ben Nevis I think I shall ask my friend the Maharaja of Nepal to let me call myself after one of his Himalayas."

"Jolly good," Ben Nevis guffawed. "And I say, Banjo, this is a wonderful whisky. What's the brand?"

"It is Stag's Breath."

"Ah, that *is* a wonderful whisky. We can't get it in Scotland of course. It's all for export. However, I'm glad you've got hold of some of it. I thought it was all being drunk by these American wallahs."

After lunch his Highness asked his guests to excuse him until tea-time as he had to drive over to see his friend the Maharaja of Tussore.

"Tussore will be dining with us on Thursday night and I shall tell him he must arrange a good panther shoot for you. Did you bring a rifle?"

"Yes, I brought my Express, but Hugh Cameron didn't bring a rifle."

"That's easy. I have plenty here."

"Did you ever meet a Piffer called Lindsay-Wolseley?" Ben Nevis asked.

"Oh, I know him well. A very nice chap. He was in the Frontier Force Rifles."

"Well, he's come to live in Inverness-shire. So Hugh and I are rather anxious to make his mouth water with our—now wait a minute, what's the word . . . it's chicory in Pelmanism . . . shikari! Yes, we want to come back as a couple of shikaris and make Lindsay-Wolseley's mouth water."

"Speak for yourself, Donald," Kilwhillie put in. "I've no desire whatever to make Wolseley's mouth water."

"You'll like Tussore," said their host. "He always has a great Christmas party at the Palace. You'll like that too. By the way, do you play table-tennis, Nosy?"

"I never heard of it," said Ben Nevis.

"Of course you have, Donald. They were playing it on the *Taj Mahal*," Kilwhillie reminded him.

"Oh, ping-pong?" the Chieftain exclaimed. "No, I've never played that."

"It's the only game I can play nowadays," said his Highness. "I have a Czech professional here, and if you'd like to play Klopczok will be only too glad to coach you."

When the Maharaja had gone off to pay his visit to the ruler of Tussore, Ben Nevis and Kilwhillie, after taking a stroll in the garden, retired to the guest-house.

"You know, I can't do this sort of thing at Glenbogle, Hugh," said the Chieftain looking round the sitting-room provided for them. "Three boxes of Havana cigars— Partaga, Punch and Upmann. Turkish, Virginian and Egyptian cigarettes. Champagne, whisky, brandy, gin, vermouth, and what's this? Pernod? I never heard of it."

"That's absinthe," Kilwhillie told him.

"I've a good mind to taste it. Isn't that what they drink in France? Have you ever tried it, Hugh?"

"Never, and I don't intend to."

"I'm going to try it. Now wait a minute. I know how to do this. Ko hi!" he bellowed.

Simultaneously from different doors appeared Balu, Sher Khan and a couple of the Maharaja's attendants.

Ben Nevis explained that he wanted to try the bottle of Pernod. Balu translated his wants to the house-servants, one of whom uncorked the bottle, while the other produced glasses from the sideboard.

"How does one drink this stuff?" Ben Nevis asked.

Kilwhillie shook his head.

"I don't know at all."

Ben Nevis took the bottle and smelt the top.

"It smells like cough-mixture. Do you think it tastes like cough-mixture?"

He poured some into a tumbler and added water.

"Good lord," he exclaimed. "Something's gone wrong with the stuff. Or else it's a mouth-wash. It's turned cloudy, and I had a mouth-wash that did that."

Ben Nevis poured a five-finger dram from the bottle into another glass. Then he picked it up and tossed it off like a dram of whisky.

For a moment he had that look of surprise which a boxer has just before his eyes glaze and he goes down for the count.

"I never tasted anything so absolutely foul in my life," he spluttered. Then he seized a bottle of whisky and poured himself out a hefty dram in the hope of obliterating the taste of the absinthe.

"That's better," he declared. "But I think I'd better have another."

Two powerful whiskies would normally not have affected the Chieftain more than two dewdrops, but when those two powerful whiskies were mixed with about twice as much neat absinthe as a Frenchman sips well diluted for about an hour, the fumes mounted rapidly to his head.

"I must do something about this, Hugh," he said with the deliberation of a man who expects to trip over each word. "I repeat I must do something about this, I tell you."

"I think you'd better go and lie down."

The servants had left the room, but with the instinct of the perfect bearer for his master's well-being Balu came back into the room at that moment.

"Master like sleep a little," he suggested.

"Balu's right. You'd better lie down," Kilwhillie agreed.

"Sleep?" the Chieftain exclaimed. "Did you say sleep, Hugh? I never heard a more peprosterous suggestion in my life. I have no desire whatever to sleep. None. And if I did I wouldn't, if you see what I mean. No, no. I'm going to get a jogsaw, a jigsaw I should say, and ride up to the post-office in it. Yes. And when I get to the post-office I'm going to send a wire to Rose-Ross in Tal—in Tal—well, you know where I mean. And I'm going to ask him to let Hector come up for a spot of leave. Mind you, I don't say that Angela will accept him. No, I'm far from saying that. But what I do say is I think he ought to be given a chance for her to say 'No'."

"And suppose she says 'Yes'?" Kilwhillie asked in tones of icy disgust.

"If she says 'Yes' I shall welcome her to Glenbogle as a lauter-in-daw."

"If by that you mean daughter-in-law," Kilwhillie said in grave rebuke, "I can only suppose that your mind has been affected by the Indian climate."

"What is more . . . what is more, Hugh," the Chieftain went on without paying the faintest attention to his friend's condemnatory frowns, "What is more, I shall tell Angus MacQuat to compose a pibroch called Mac 'ic . . . Mac 'ic . . ." he strained at the name like a machine-gunner whose weapon has jammed. . . . 'Mac 'ic Eachainn's Nutbrown Bride'."

"I am not going to argue with you in your present state," Kilwhillie began, but the Chieftain broke in,

"My present state is A1 at Lloyd's," he affirmed.

"Your present state is disgraceful," said Kilwhillie. "In fact, you are not responsible either for your actions or for your words. I dislike having to say such a thing to a man older than myself, but I should be no friend of yours, Donald, if I allowed myself to shirk my duty. Instead of making a public exhibition of yourself in a rickshaw you should go and lie down on your bed, which Balu has prepared for you."

"I refuse to lie down. I must have some exercise," Ben Nevis insisted.

"You won't get any exercise in a rickshaw. If you want exercise I noticed a stationary bicycle in the gymnasium. Sit on that and pedal as hard as you can for half an hour."

"But if I'm in the state you think I'm in, Hugh, I shouldn't be able to steer a bicycle properly."

"You don't have to steer a stationary bicycle. It doesn't move."

"But if it doesn't move, how should I get the exercise I feel I must have? I want to get into good trim for this panther shoot. And look here, Hugh, you've got to take part in this shoot."

"I will take part in this shoot on one condition," said Kilwhillie. "If you will go and lie down until you know the difference between a jigsaw and a rickshaw, I will agree to take part in this shoot."

"Ko hi!" Ben Nevis bellowed.

And Balu Ram, who had been listening at the door to the argument, slipped quickly into the room and said:

"Master's bed ready for lie down if Master come."

Those who have drunk a very strong neat absinthe followed immediately by two powerful whiskies will know whether a kind of stupor succeeds the desire for violent action it induces at first. At any rate, Ben Nevis followed Balu into his bedroom and a few minutes later his deep regular snores told Kilwhillie that the crisis had been successfully weathered.

Chapter 10

DINNER AT ROSEMOUNT

A SECOND crisis was not long in developing. Indeed, it
developed the very evening after dinner when the
Maharaja was sitting in the smoking-room with his two
guests. Perhaps it was the mute reproach of those marble
nymphs and goddesses that made his Highness suddenly
aware of the lack of feminine society at Rosemount.

"My Christmas guests won't be arriving till next week,"
he said. "I'm afraid it's very dull here for you both with
only an old man like myself for company," he went on
apologetically.

The Maharaja was feeling his age because Klopczok, the
Czech professional, had beaten him in every set of table-
tennis before dinner.

"Not at all," said Kilwhillie quickly. "I'm a bachelor,
and I find women rather exhausting about the house."

Any effect this quiet tribute to celibacy might have had
was destroyed at once by Ben Nevis.

"I wonder if you ever met a Mrs Winstanley, Banjo?
She's the wife, or at least she *was* the wife of the British and
Oriental Bank—I mean the Manager of the Jumbulpore
branch. I believe there was some domestic something or
other, and they're now divorced."

"No, I don't remember ever meeting a Mrs Winstanley,"
said his Highness.

"Well, I met her in Tallulaghabad and when we came
up to Pippla I found she was staying with a friend at
Parker's Hotel."

The Maharaja immediately assumed that his guest was
interested in Mrs Winstanley, and his natural hospitality
prompted him to oblige Ben Nevis by giving him an opportunity to cultivate that interest.

"I shall ask her to dinner when Tussore comes here to dine on Thursday."

"Oh, that's very good of you. It would be a kindness. I thought she and her friend Miss . . . Miss . . . dash it, I've forgotten what her friend's name is. Do you remember the name of Angela Winstanley's friend, Hugh?"

"I believe it was Lambert," Kilwhillie replied as frigidly as he could because he was afraid that the Maharaja would jump to the conclusion that he was interested in Miss Lambert.

"Mrs Winstanley and Miss Lambert," his Highness repeated to himself as he noted their names with a gold pencil. "I shall send an invitation to them to-morrow morning."

"I'll take it along to Parker's," the Chieftain volunteered. "They might feel timid about the etiquette of the whole business. They're very simple folks."

"But Mrs Winstanley managed to get divorced," his Highness said, twinkling.

"Oh, there wasn't any kind of scandal," Ben Nevis assured him. "It was a case of what they call incom . . . incom . . ."

"Income Tax?" his Highness laughed.

"No, no, no. Incom . . . incom. . . . What is it, Hugh, when two people can't agree? It's a long word."

"I suppose you mean 'incompatibility'," Hugh Cameron suggested wearily.

"And Mrs Winstanley went off with somebody more compatible?" his Highness asked with a smile.

"No, no. She divorced her husband. And she's just waiting quietly now for what they call the decree nisi. She comes from Canterbury. In fact, she's what they call . . . ha-ha-ha . . . a Canterbury Belle."

Ben Nevis laughed so much at his own verbal felicity that his sporran came unbuckled. Kilwhillie did not know whether to feel more pained by the undignified behaviour of a Chieftain's sporran or by what he considered the vulgarity of the Chieftain's joke.

"Now we ought to have two more ladies to make the party right," said his Highness. "Let me see, I'll ask old Lady Pinfield. She's the widow of a judge who has a charming little house not far from Parker's. And then . . . Oh, yes, of course, Maud Nutting."

"Who's she?" Ben Nevis asked.

"Maud Nutting, the literary light of Pippla. You must have read some of her novels about life in India."

Ben Nevis shook his head. Nor did Kilwhillie seem any wiser.

"I shall certainly give you each one of Miss Nutting's novels to read before you meet her," his Highness promised.

"I've heard these novelist wallahs have a habit of putting people into their books," Ben Nevis said. "I hope your friend Miss Nutting won't put me into a book. I don't know what I'd do if I found myself in a book. Not that I read a great deal, of course."

Later that evening when Kilwhillie and he were sitting in the guest-house over a last whisky the Chieftain opened *Tooth and Claw* by Maud Nutting.

"Good lord, Hugh!" he exclaimed.

"What's the matter now?"

"Listen to this! 'Sher Khan glided behind the pillar, knife in hand, as Hugh Cameron seated himself at his desk, but the revengeful Pathan had forgotten Rover. With a low growl the retriever sprang at the throat of Hugh's faithless bearer and received the deadly blow intended for his master's heart.' Good lord! She's put you into a book already, Hugh," the Chieftain gasped.

"How can she have put me into a book when she's never met me, Donald?"

"But she has. Hugh Cameron, Sher Khan. The only thing she's got wrong is Bonzo's name. She calls him Rover. I'm going to be jolly careful what I say in front of Miss

Maud Nutting. I shan't open my mouth all through dinner."

"It's a pity you didn't make that resolution before you persuaded the Maharaja to invite Mrs Winstanley to dinner on Thursday. Do you realise that you've introduced her to Pippla society?"

"That's exactly what I want to do," Ben Nevis replied. "I thought she seemed very lonely yesterday, poor little woman, when we went off and left her."

"Do you realise, Donald, that the Maharaja was evidently under the impression that you were personally interested in Mrs Winstanley?"

"So I am."

"I mean in an unpleasant way."

"Unpleasant?"

"I believe he supposes that you are having a love affair with her. I dislike criticising a man whose hospitality I am enjoying, but, after all, we have to remember that his point of view is oriental, however well he may have played cricket for Harrow and Oxford. He imagines that you have the same point of view about women as himself."

"I don't believe old Banjo thinks anything of the kind," the suspected amorist declared. "And if he does he'll soon see that my interest in Angela is the interest a father takes in his daughter, if you know what I mean. In fact, I shall take him into my confidence and tell him about Hector."

"That would be most unfair on Hector. However, I'm getting tired of giving you good advice to which you pay not the slightest attention. I tell you frankly, Donald, that if the sea is rough on the way back I shall bitterly regret having upset my whole winter by coming out here with you."

"I think you're making a molehill out of a mountain, Hugh."

"You'll probably confide in Miss Maud Nutting next," Kilwhillie went on. "And if you do, she *will* put you into a book. But don't complain to me if you find yourself sitting in a kilt surrounded by a bevy of houris."

"I have heard it pronounced that way by a Minister," said Ben Nevis in astonishment. "But I think it's rather an affected way for *you* to pronounce it, Hugh."

"I'm going to bed," Kilwhillie announced curtly.

"I hope Sher Khan won't stick a knife into you because Bonzo isn't here to protect you," the Chieftain guffawed. "And I'm going to bed myself."

The next day Ben Nevis, leaving Kilwhillie to write letters at Rosemount, was driven to the end of the motor road in one of the Maharaja's cars but declined the pressing offers of the rickshaw-coolies to convey him up to Parker's. By the time he reached the Hotel, after taking several wrong turnings among the maze of narrow paths winding up the *khud*, the Chieftain was feeling he had had a longer walk than he intended.

"It's these vile trousers," he muttered to himself. "If I'd worn trousers all my life I should be an old man by now."

Angela Winstanley's welcome made him forget all about the discomfort of a steep uphill walk in trousers.

"Ben Nevis! Why, how sweet of you to call on two lonely females so soon. Maisie dear, isn't it sweet of him?"

"I've come on behalf of his Highness, Angela," the Chieftain announced. "He wants you and Miss Lambert . . ."

"Oh, please, call me Maisie, Mr . . . I mean, ought I really to call you Ben Nevis?" Maisie Lambert asked.

"That's absolutely right, Maisie," the Chieftain assured her. "Yes, the Maharaja wants you and Maisie to dine at Rosemount on Thursday. He'll send the car for you and I suppose you'll find some rickshaw wallahs to take you down the cud. The Maharaja of Tussore will be there, and Lady Pinfield, and an extraordinary novelist called Maud Nutting, who's apparently put Hugh Cameron into a book without knowing it."

"Ben Nevis," Angela breathed in an ecstasy, "you're the most wonderful man that ever lived."

"I remember Lady Pinfield when I was at school in

Pippla," said Maisie Lambert. "She came one year to give away the prizes. We girls were awfully frightened of her because her husband was a judge."

"We had a judge once shooting with us," Ben Nevis put in. "He couldn't hit a bird. I can't understand why they ever made him a judge. I said to him, 'Look out, Judge, or you'll be trying yourself for manslaughter.' But he had no sense of humour, poor chap."

"And fancy meeting Maud Nutting," Maisie went on. "I think her books are so very interesting. Some people are shocked by them."

"I'm not surprised," Angela commented sarcastically.

"The only one I've looked at is called *Tooth and Claw*," said the Chieftain. "That's the one with Hugh Cameron in it. And Sher Khan, his bearer."

"I don't think I've read that one," said Maisie.

"As far as I can make out it's about an Indian army officer called Hugh Cameron who falls in love with the daughter of an Indian raja in the first chapter, and then I went to sleep."

"Mr Cameron fascinates me," said Maisie Lambert.

"Does he? I must tell him that. It will be rather a new experience for old Hugh."

"Please, please, Ben Nevis," Maisie Lambert begged, "please don't tell Mr Cameron what I said. I should sink into the ground next time I saw him. What I mean is he has such a mysterious far-away look in his eyes as if when he's talking to you he was in another world."

"Yes, I know what you mean," said the Chieftain. "I think it's liver. He's always had a weak liver. He's over ten years younger than me, but he is really my most intimate friend. He can say things to me I wouldn't allow other people to think, let alone say."

"I hope you didn't ask the Maharaja to invite us to Rosemount," said Angela suddenly.

"Not at all. It was entirely his idea. I think his friend the Maharaja of Tussore likes feminine society."

"So I've always heard," Angela observed pensively. "I saw a picture of him once in the *Illustrated News of India*. He's very handsome."

"That's more than I can say for my old friend Bangapatam," said Ben Nevis. "And he was quite good-looking as a young man. Now he's about the size of St Pancras. Well, you'll see for yourselves on Thursday."

"I can't say how much I'm looking forward to Thursday," Angela murmured half to herself. "And it's all thanks to you. Dear, dear Ben Nevis," she exclaimed suddenly, her dark eyes in a glow.

The Chieftain, smiling what can only be called a sugar-daddy's gratified smile, made some amiable rumbling noises in his throat.

"Have you heard from Hector?" Angela asked.

"No, but the Maharaja says he's going to write a personal letter to Hector's Colonel to ask if he can have two or three days' leave up here at Christmas. Apparently the Maharaja of Tussore gives a terrific party every year, and no doubt we shall all be asked to it."

"I hope it will be all right for Hector to come. We mustn't do anything to interfere with his military duties, must we?" Angela pointed out with an almost maternal solicitude which, however much it might impress Donald MacDonald of Ben Nevis, would have been by no means agreeable to Hector MacDonald, Younger, of Ben Nevis.

"Well, I must be getting along back to Rosemount," said the Chieftain. "And his Highness's car will be waiting for you on Thursday at a quarter to eight."

"I feel like somebody in one of the stories in the *Arabian Nights*," said Angela Winstanley on that Thursday, when she and Maisie Lambert were seated in the Maharaja's car bound for Rosemount. "I feel this might lead to anything."

"You will be careful, Angela, won't you? That's just what I felt when Gerry Ripwood gave me those two brandy-

Macs. And it led nowhere. Nowhere at all," Maisie Lambert repeated with a sigh.

Angela shivered luxuriously under the fur rug.

"To anything," she repeated without paying the least attention to her companion's plea for prudence. "There was a moment when the lawyers were being so tiresome that I began to wish I'd never divorced Herbert. Poor old Herbert. I expect he's working late at the bank to-night. He always worked late on Thursdays."

This time she shuddered luxuriously. "But, thank goodness, I did divorce him. We should never have been going out to dinner with two Maharajas if I hadn't. I know one thing I'm going to do if Hector gets that leave. I'm going to tell Mr Cameron that I have made up my mind not to marry Hector."

"But have you absolutely made up your mind?" Maisie asked.

"I shall have by the time he arrives in Pippla," Angela replied.

"But why are you so anxious to tell Mr Cameron, Angela?"

"Because it will set his mind at rest and he won't try to keep Ben Nevis and me apart."

Maisie turned round to her friend in perplexity.

"Angela! You're not going to flirt with Ben Nevis?" she asked incredulously.

"It depends on what you call flirting. We've been having a sort of spiritual flirtation already."

"Angela, I sometimes simply don't understand what you mean."

"I'm not going to try and tempt Ben Nevis to make love to me if that's what you're afraid of."

"I must admit you did rather frighten me for a moment."

"And then of course there's John Tucker," Angela went on. "He'll be here in a few days, and I think John Tucker is going to have a surprise. He'll find that I'm not quite so stranded as he supposes. At the moment he thinks he can have all the fun he wants without the slightest threat to his unmarried security. John Tucker will find the competition rather more than he bargained for."

"It's funny that we're going to meet Maud Nutting to-night," Maisie reflected.

"Why?"

"Because you're talking exactly like one of her characters in *The Golden Horizon*."

"I never read it."

"It's about the daughter of an officer who gave some wrong order and caused a lot of trouble and had to leave the Army and she was planning how to escape from the depressing life she was leading, looking after her father."

"And did she escape?"

"No, she didn't. She got into a frightful lot of complications and in the end she jumped out of a houseboat in Kashmir and drowned herself. She made the most wonderful plans and everything went wrong. I enjoyed the book because there was another character in it who was awfully like Gerry Ripwood. Hugo Champneys was his name and he was in the Guides."

"Perhaps you'll find yourself in Maud Nutting's next book," said Angela. "Perhaps we all shall."

Miss Maud Nutting was already in the drawing-room when her prospective victims arrived. She was a plump rosy woman of about fifty with untidy faded fair hair and an amber necklace that seemed as weighty as a mayor's chain. Nobody could have been less like the authoress of the passionate tales of life in India which she had been writing with such successful fertility for more than twenty years. The Maharaja of Tussore was talking to her when Angela and Maisie were announced, and he turned quickly to look at Angela in the way that a good judge of a horse will sum up its points in one quick glance.

Ben Nevis came forward with exuberant geniality.

"Ah, here you are, and here's your host, His Highness the Maharaja of Bangapatam."

"It was very kind of you to give me the pleasure of dining with me at such short notice, Mrs Winstanley."

"It was much kinder of your Highness to give us the pleasure of dining with you. This is my friend Miss Lambert."

"How do you do, Miss Lambert," said the Maharaja. "Are you any relation of Mr William Lambert of the P.W.D.?"

"He's my father, Maharaja Sahib."

"Is he, indeed? Well, give him my kind regards. He did some great work for us in Bangapatam about five years ago. And now I want to present you to His Highness the Maharaja of Tussore."

The Maharaja of Tussore was a tall and handsome man of about forty who, unlike so many of the Indian princes, was still almost as slim as he had been when he had served during the Great War in an Indian cavalry regiment. In his own small but rich State he maintained the ceremony and dispensed the lavish hospitality of a princely ruler, but outside its confines he liked to dress and behave like any British officer in mufti. He had been twice married, but both of his Maharanis were dead, and as each had left him possible successors he had not taken another wife.

"Where have you been hiding yourself all this time, Mrs Winstanley?" he asked, and managed to convey the suggestion that he had been looking for her.

"Oh, Calcutta and Jumbulpore and Tallulaghabad and —er—Canterbury," she replied with a smile that managed to convey the suggestion that only now had she realised what absurd places they all were.

"Canterbury, eh?" said the host. "What fun we used to have there in the cricket week." And then he turned aside to welcome Lady Pinfield, whose arrival made the party complete.

In private the Maharaja of Bangapatam was wont to allude to Lady Pinfield as the Grenadier. With the determined tread of her not small feet; with her high pompadour the colour of which had changed in some twenty-five years from light-brown to grey while the coiffure remained exactly as it was when King Edward VII ascended the throne; and with her big aquiline nose and those large teeth dear to French caricaturists of Englishwomen Lady Pinfield justified the nickname. When Sir Lawrence died, his widow stayed on in Pippla, where his vacations had been spent for so many years, and none of the other British women would have ventured to contest her primacy.

"How are you, Maharaja Sahib? It's a fine clear night, but there's a nip in the air," she said in that gruff jerky voice which had decided the social fate of so many. "I'm glad to meet you, Mrs Winstanley. Are you going to reside in Pippla?"

"Oh, no," Angela replied. "This is just a quick visit. I shall be going back to England in the spring."

"Oh, yes?" said Lady Pinfield. "To what part of England?"

"To Canterbury."

"Indeed, to Canterbury? Have you met the Archbishop?"

"Not the new Archbishop," said Angela, by which Lady Pinfield was at liberty to suppose that she had met his predecessor.

"And this is Ben Nevis," the host announced, obviously taking a good deal of pleasure in making the Grenadier get out of step for a moment.

"I didn't quite catch the name."

"Ben Nevis," his Highness repeated.

"How d'ye do, Mr Nevis?" said the Grenadier.

"No, no, Lady Pinfield, he's not Mr Benjamin Nevis. He is Ben Nevis, a great Highland chief,—MacDonald of Ben Nevis," His Highness explained.

"How d'ye do, Lady Pinfield? How d'ye do, how d'ye do?" Ben Nevis woofed.

The Chieftain in his own garb was a sufficiently impressive figure to make Lady Pinfield realise that she had been less successful in asserting her primacy in Pippla society than she had come to accept as axiomatic.

"Of course, I don't really know Scotland at all," she said rather lamely.

"And this is Kilwhillie," his Highness went on.

"Another Highland chief?" Lady Pinfield enquired with a kind of arch condescension.

"Oh, this is quite a gathering of the clans," the host said. "MacDonald of Ben Nevis and Cameron of Kilwhillie."

"And wasn't it dreadful, Lady Pinfield," exclaimed Maud Nutting. "I used Mr Cameron's name in a book."

"Which book was that, Maud?"

"*Tooth and Claw.*"

"Ah, I didn't read that, as you know," said Lady Pinfield. Fond as she was of Maud Nutting, the Grenadier always refused to read those of her books which she heard were advanced: literary taste in Pippla still considered Rudyard Kipling's story of the Gadsbys rather daring.

"I've started to read it," Ben Nevis announced. "But I'm rather a slow reader because I never can remember where I've got to in a book and so I expect I read a lot of pages over twice, and even three times."

Two khitmatgars opened the doors of the drawing-room to show that dinner was served.

"Now, I want you to take the other end of the table, Nosy," said the host. Lady Pinfield looked a little puzzled for a moment, but recovered complete equanimity when his Highness asked her to sit on his right. "Mrs Winstanley, will you sit on my left? Tussore, I'm putting you next to Mrs Winstanley, and Miss Nutting, will you sit next his Highness? Miss Lambert, will you sit on the left of the Chief? Kilwhillie, you're between Lady Pinfield and Miss Lambert."

"And how are you enjoying your visit to India, Ben Nevis?" asked Miss Nutting.

Before he could reply the sound of the pipes was heard and into the dining-room came two ex-pipers from one of the Dogra regiments playing *Wi' a Hundred Pipers an' a'*, which they followed up with *The Road to the Isles* as they marched round and round the table.

"Oh, jolly good, Banjo," Ben Nevis bellowed in a voice that rang out above the skirling of the pipes. "Jolly good!"

Lady Pinfield fancied nervously that her pompadour might at any moment be blown from her head by this blast of sound, but feeling that the reputation of the British Raj was at stake she courageously tried to tap a not small foot in time with the music. The other guests in the formidable noise seemed to be cowering like a picnic-party under a tree in a thunderstorm. Even Kilwhillie was blinking.

"Jolly good! Jolly good!" Ben Nevis bellowed enthusiastically. "I must have a dram with the pipers."

His Highness called for whisky.

"Slahnjervaw," said Ben Nevis, raising a glass of Stag's Breath.

"Salaam, Sahib," said the pipers, before they drained their glasses like veterans.

"Wonderful," Ben Nevis boomed solemnly in the hush that succeeded. "Don't know when I've been so much moved. Wonderful," he repeated, and a large tear from one of his choleric blue eyes fell into his soup.

"Do you play the bagpipes, Ben Nevis?" Angela Winstanley asked.

"No, I'm not really musical at all," he replied. "But Hector plays rather well."

"Oh, he does?" Angela murmured. She had by now definitely made up her mind to refuse Hector's hand. And the prudence of this resolve was confirmed by hearing that Hector played the bagpipes.

"You are not fond of music, Mrs Winstanley?" the Maharaja of Tussore asked.

"I love music," Angela exclaimed indignantly. "At one time I was going to study the piano with the idea of becoming a professional pianist."

The Maharaja was obviously surprised and pleased.

"Indeed? I am passionately fond of music," he told her. "I wonder if I can persuade you and your friend, Miss Lambert, to pay me a visit at Tussore? I have a Steinway, but perhaps you prefer a Bechstein? I have a Bechstein too."

Angela turned round and looked directly into his dark eyes.

"Who is your favourite composer?" she asked.

"For the piano?"

She nodded.

"That depends on the time and the place and the player. But always I can surrender to Chopin."

"If I come to Tussore I will play Chopin to you," Angela promised.

"But of course you will come to Tussore. You know that we are much further down than Pippla."

"It will be warmer," said Angela.

"Very much warmer," the Maharaja agreed.

From the other side of the table Lady Pinfield was studying the newcomer to Pippla. She must find out from her host after dinner just exactly who she was. Apparently she had not met Tussore before this evening, or she would have suspected that Bangapatam had invited her to please him. Indians, however well bred, were capable of doing that kind of thing. Yet, unless an elaborate game of 'let's pretend' was being played, Mrs Winstanley and the Maharaja of Tussore had never met before this evening.

"And are *you* enjoying your visit to India?" Lady Pinfield turned to ask Kilwhillie, her right hand neighbour.

"I'm not disliking it so much as I expected," he replied.

"You expected to dislike India?" Lady Pinfield exclaimed. "I never heard of anybody who expected to dislike India nowadays. We've done so much for them. Mind you, it's not easy to know India. I've lived here for over thirty years, and I don't consider that I really know India."

"Don't you, Lady Pinfield?" her host put in, twinkling.

"No, and my late husband who as a judge had a very

wide experience was always being surprised by unexpected behaviour which did not seem to surprise Indians at all."

"Have you been surprised by Indian behaviour yet?" his Highness asked Kilwhillie.

"Not nearly so much as I have been by the behaviour of British people out here," Kilwhillie replied, looking steadily at Ben Nevis, who at this moment was urging Maud Nutting to visit Inverness-shire and write a book about it.

"I was just telling Miss Nutting she ought to come and write a book about Inverness-shire, Hugh. You'd like her to visit you at Kilwhillie, wouldn't you?"

"I'm afraid my bachelor establishment wouldn't give Miss Nutting much to write about," said Kilwhillie. "A little fishing and a little shooting are all we have."

"Ah, that reminds me," said the host to the Maharaja of Tussore. "Ben Nevis is very anxious to shoot a panther. Couldn't you arrange a beat?"

"With the greatest pleasure," the Maharaja of Tussore replied. "That can be arranged for Saturday. Your Christmas guests won't be arriving till next week, will they, Bangapatam?"

"That's agreed," said the latter. "We'll start from here about half-past ten and reach Tussore in time for an early lunch."

"That will be excellent." The Maharaja of Tussore turned to Angela Winstanley. "Have you ever seen a panther shoot?" he asked her.

"Never."

"Would you like to?"

"I'd love to."

"You'll bring Mrs Winstanley and Miss Lambert, please," said the Maharaja of Tussore to their host. "And you, Lady Pinfield?" he went on, diplomacy putting the brake on desire. "And of course Miss Nutting?"

"It's most kind of you, Maharaja Sahib, but though I used to accompany my late husband on shikari . . ."

"I know what that means," Ben Nevis burst in.

Kilwhillie looked at his friend as the owner of a large dog might look at it for jumping up suddenly and upsetting a tea-table.

"I've never done so since he died," Lady Pinfield concluded.

"I'd love to come," said Miss Nutting. "I've never seen a panther shoot."

"You wrote a very elaborate account of a panther shoot in one of your books, Maud," she was reminded by Lady Pinfield, with a touch of acerbity.

"Yes, I know. It's in *Freckles*. Freckles was a subaltern in Bulger's Horse," his creator told the company. "Guy Harford was his name."

Maisie Lambert was on the verge of saying something, but she caught Angela Winstanley's eye and refrained.

"Several kind friends corrected the details," Miss Nutting went on. "And one or two reviewers picked out the panther shoot as one of the best things in the book."

"Then you shall see on Saturday how well your imagination worked," the Maharaja of Tussore told the novelist.

When they were drinking their nightcaps in the guest-house, Ben Nevis asked Hugh Cameron if he had noticed how much interested Tussore had seemed in Angela Winstanley.

"I never notice that kind of thing," his friend replied distastefully.

"Well, when she was playing the piano after dinner I started to say something," the Chieftain said. "Somebody playing the piano always makes me want to say something. And Tussore looked at me and said 'Hush'. You could have knocked me down like a feather. I know these Maharaja wallahs are quite important people in their own country. But even so it's extraordinary for somebody to say 'hush' to somebody in somebody else's house when somebody is playing the piano. It never happened to me before. I was absolutely staggered. However, as he's arranging this shoot for us I didn't like to do anything about it. So I said nothing."

"Which is what he wanted you to say," Kilwhillie commented.

"Still, it was a very jolly evening," the Chieftain admitted. "Old Lady Pinfield was a bit stupid, I thought. Fancy having to explain to a judge's wife that I wasn't Benjamin Nevis. But I liked the novelist woman; I shan't mind a bit if she puts me into a book. Trixie might be a bit annoyed, but I shan't mind. And if she gets the description of my dress wrong you could help her to get it right. I mean, I wouldn't like to appear in a book wearing my skeen doo on the wrong leg or being described in kilts. I think if she does want to put me in a book I must get her to come to Glenbogle. And, by Jove, if she can write a good account of a panther shoot without ever having seen one, think what a wonderful account she could give of the Monster. Well, I think we ought to go to bed, Hugh. You mustn't keep me up talking. I'm going to ask old Banjo to find me a place where I can have some practice with this Express rifle of mine. So you mustn't keep me up talking, Hugh."

Chapter 11

A LITTLE PRACTICE

THE next day Kilwhillie was roused by Balu's bringing him his morning tea.

"Where's Sher Khan?" he asked.

"Master take Sher Khan for shoot and tell me bring Cameron Sahib his chota hazri."

"Shoot?" Kilwhillie repeated. "Shoot what?"

Balu Ram gave a propitiatory shrug to indicate his ignorance of the quarry.

"What clothes I put for Sahib?" he asked.

Kilwhillie found the ministrations of the little Dogra soothing and efficient; apart from a faint anxiety about what Ben Nevis was up to, he did not in the least mind having his own bearer taken away from him without warning.

"Where's Nosy?" the Maharaja asked when he and Kilwhillie met at breakfast.

"Apparently he's gone out shooting and taken my bearer with him."

The Maharaja chuckled.

"I bet he's determined to carry off the honours to-morrow. I wonder what he's shooting at. Not your bearer, I hope?"

For a moment Kilwhillie thought his host was serious, but realised that he was not in time to be able to smile faintly.

"You're going to take part in the shoot to-morrow, of course?" the Maharaja went on.

"I'm afraid I didn't bring my rifle with me."

"I can lend you a Gibb's Metford, which is excellent for panther. I'm using a Holland and Holland myself."

"But I've never done any panther-shooting," Kilwhillie demurred.

"Nor has Nosy," the Maharaja reminded him. "But we must give Miss Nutting a chance to see more than one gun in action."

"What is the exact procedure?"

"We shall leave here about half-past ten and get to Tussore in time for an early lunch. Then we shall drive to wherever Tussore has arranged for the beaters to ring the panthers. One usually takes up a position on a platform to get a fair shot as the beasts break cover and cross the open ground. By the way, you'll want to remember that they are moving much faster than they seem to be moving."

The Maharaja went on for a while with reminiscences of bygone sport and then said suddenly:

"Tell me, do you think Nosy was upset by the attention Mrs Winstanley was receiving from Tussore last night?"

Kilwhillie looked at his host in bewilderment, the piece of kidney he was about to put into his mouth remaining upon his fork in suspension. "Why should he be upset?"

"Ah, well, I suppose he's learned philosophy by now and can face calmly the disillusionment of age," said the Maharaja. "We all have to come to it. Klopczok beats me every other time now at table-tennis. That's what it means to grow old. Mind you, she's a very very attractive little woman, and I can well understand what Nosy feels about her. Yes, yes, we can be as philosophical as we like, but all the same it hurts."

"I'm afraid I must seem very dull," said Kilwhillie, "but I really don't understand where philosophy comes into it."

"You think he's deluding himself, eh?" the Maharaja went on. "Yes, that happens to us all too often when we get past sixty. I haven't seen Nosy for many years, but he has changed very little in essentials from what he was in his early twenties, very little indeed. Indeed, he's no different from what he was when he was at school."

"I suppose he was pretty noisy, eh?" Kilwhillie asked.

"Noisy? I never heard anybody make so much noise. I remember once when somebody pushed him into the swimming-pool he made as much noise as ever, bubbling and blowing under the water. It was an extraordinary effect. Well, I hope he won't let himself be upset too much over Mrs Winstanley."

"Oh, I think he feels less worried than he did," said Kilwhillie who supposed from the last remark that Ben Nevis must have been confiding in the Maharaja about Hector.

"I'm glad of that. I thought he must have learned philosophy by now. After all, my dear fellow, nobody can escape growing old. And once we start trying to think we can cheat age by indulging in the follies of youth we're bound to suffer for it."

By now Kilwhillie had decided that the Indian approach to a domestic problem was from an angle so remote from the British approach that Ben Nevis had made another of his impulsive mistakes in confiding to the Maharaja his anxiety over Hector. At the same time the Maharaja himself was supposing that Kilwhillie with the notorious inability of the British to face facts was refusing to face the fact of his friend's infatuation with Mrs Winstanley.

At this moment the subject of this discussion at cross-purposes came into the breakfast-room, looking curiously subdued.

"Good-morning, Banjo. Good-morning, Hugh," he said. "I'm afraid I'm rather late for breakfast."

"Oh, breakfast is a movable feast at Rosemount," his host assured him. "I hope Kilwhillie and I have left you enough after your shooting exercise."

Ben Nevis looked round from the side table where he was helping himself from the hot-plate.

"You didn't hear what happened?" he asked keenly.

"We've heard nothing at all," the Maharaja replied. "Not even a shot," he added with a chuckle.

Ben Nevis took his seat at table and started upon the kidneys and bacon.

"This is very good bacon, Banjo," he said presently. "Do they go in much for bacon here?"

"Not the Muslims."

"I was thinking more about the British residents."

"They most of them eat plenty of it," the Maharaja told him.

"Yes, I realise that," the Chieftain said. "What I really meant was 'Do any of them go in for keeping pigs?'"

"I don't think I ever heard of them keeping pigs in Pippla, but for all I know some of them may keep pigs. Why do you ask?"

"Oh, no reason in particular. Just curiosity," the Chieftain replied with a rather too much accentuated unconcern to seem quite natural. "By the way, I owe you an apology, Hugh, for borrowing Sher Khan this morning, but I thought he'd be more up to what I wanted to do than my own bearer. I hope Balu looked after you properly."

"What *did* you want to do, Nosy?" his host asked.

"I wanted to try this Express rifle I bought in Inverness before we left. It's a new kind of shooting for me."

"And what did you practise on?" the Maharaja asked.

"What did I practise on?" Ben Nevis repeated in a tone which to Kilwhillie's astonishment sounded embarrassed; in all the years he had known him he had very rarely seen him embarrassed or heard him sound embarrassed. "Well— er—" Ben Nevis went on, "Sher Khan pulled along a plank which he got hold of somewhere by a longish rope. I asked him last night if he thought he could do this for me. And it worked very well. We got down by that rocky slope at the bottom of your garden, Banjo, because Sher Khan told me that panthers like to lie up among rocks."

"I know where you mean," said the Maharaja. "Just above old Major Crumbleholme's place."

"Crumplehorn? What an extraordinary name!"

"Not Crumplehorn. Crumbleholme."

"Well, that's an extraordinary name too. Who is he?" Ben Nevis asked.

"He used to be in Campbell's Sikhs, but he retired before the war. He must be over seventy now. He's been living in

Pippla for years. And how silly of me! You asked just now if any of the British residents kept pigs. Why, Major Crumbleholme keeps pigs."

"Oh, he does?" Ben Nevis muttered gloomily. "Of course, he *would*, being a Campbell."

"He's not a Campbell, Donald," Kilwhillie put in. "The Maharaja said he was in Campbell's Sikhs. It's a regiment."

At this moment one of the servants came in and said something to the Maharaja.

"Well, here's a coincidence," the latter exclaimed. "We are talking about Major Crumbleholme and he has come to call on me on a matter of business. I wonder what the old boy wants?"

Ben Nevis cleared his throat. "Well, I think before you see this wallah, Banjo, you'd better hear exactly what did happen about an hour ago. The whole business was an unfortunate accident, but this is how it happened. As I told you, Sher Khan was dragging this plank along the rocks just beyond your grounds. I had a couple of shots with my Express, both of which hit the plank plumb in the middle. I was rather pleased about this because, though the plank wasn't moving at the pace of a panther, a plank is a good deal smaller than a panther. Well, then Sher Khan carried on with the plank and I had another shot, and when I went down to see where I'd hit it, Sher Khan was looking at a dead pig, which apparently I'd shot. You see, just as I fired at the plank this confounded pig must have been lying asleep in front of it. Sher Khan apparently doesn't like pigs. All he said was something about its being a dirty animal, and in fact he seemed delighted I'd killed it. I'm bound to admit that it did look very like a domestic pig, but it wasn't until I was eating that excellent bacon of yours, Banjo, that it occurred to me it might really be a pig belonging to somebody. That's why I asked if anybody kept pigs in Pippla. And now I can't help feeling this—this Major Crumple . . ."

"Crumbleholme," said the Maharaja.

"This Major Crumbleholme—I never heard a more peprosterous name in my life—yes, I can't help feeling this Major wallah may be the owner of it. What's the best thing for me to do? It's most awkward, isn't it? What would you do, Hugh?"

"There's only one thing you can possibly do," Kilwhillie told his friend. "You'll have to apologise to Major Crumbleholme for shooting his pig and offer to make good any damage you've done."

"Naturally, I'm quite prepared to do that," Ben Nevis said with as much dignity as a man who has shot a neighbour's pig can muster. "All the same, if people leave pigs sleeping about among rocks they oughtn't to be surprised if something happens to them. I've always said that about chickens. If you let your chickens go dashing about in the middle of the road you oughtn't to be surprised if one of them gets run over by a motor-car. What sort of wallah is this Major wallah?"

"I don't know him at all well," said the Maharaja. "He's been in here once or twice. He collects butterflies."

"Collects butterflies?" the Chieftain echoed in amazement. "But I thought you said he'd retired from the Army before the war. He must be a man of seventy, at least. And he collects butterflies? Good lord! Look here, Hugh, I wish you'd go and see him and explain that shooting this pig of his was an accident and say I shall be delighted to pay any price he cares to put on the animal."

"No," said Kilwhillie firmly. "You shot the pig and you must explain to the owner of it what happened."

Ben Nevis turned to the Maharaja, but his Highness was by now shaking like an enormous jelly with laughter.

"You'll have to go yourself, Nosy," he managed to gasp, and then went on shaking.

"Well, if I must I suppose I must," the Chieftain said. "I must get his name right, though."

"Crumbleholme," Kilwhillie repeated slowly.

"I'll think of sweetbread," the Chieftain announced.

"Oh, Nosy, Nosy," his Highness wheezed in a paroxysm of mirth, "why on earth are you going to think of sweet-bread?"

"It's Pelmanism. You think of crumbs and bread, and then you think of home, sweet home. Then you think of sweetbread and remember that this wallah's name is Campbellholme."

"But it isn't," Kilwhillie pointed out. "It's Crumble-holme."

"Yes, that's what I meant, but he was in a regiment called Campbell's Sikhs. You know, these Campbells are absolutely impossible people. Not content with getting everybody out of Argyll except themselves and then trying to put the Kinlochleven Aluminium Works on the Argyll rates, which fortunately for us in Inverness-shire was stopped by Lochiel . . . what was I saying? It makes my blood boil when I think of that attempt to bag Kinlochleven for the Argyll rates . . . yes, and now here they are in India collaring everything too. Jute and Sikhs and . . ."

"And a place called Campbellpore," the Maharaja added.

"You don't mean to say they collared a whole town in India? Good lord! It's staggering. It really is."

And the misdeeds of the Campbells so preyed upon the mind of Ben Nevis when he was on his way to interview Major Crumbleholme that when he saw a wizened little man in a suit of Lovat tweed standing in the Maharaja's drawing-room he said:

"Major Campbell, I believe?"

"No, sir," the little man rapped out sharply. "My name is Crumbleholme."

"That's what I mean," Ben Nevis barked. "I believe you've come about a pig."

"A pig? What pig?" the Major snapped. "I've come to ask his Highness for a subscription to the Pippla branch of the Society for the Prevention of Cruelty to Animals."

"But I thought you kept pigs," Ben Nevis said.

"So I do, sir. Have you any objection to my keeping pigs?" Major Crumbleholme snapped.

"Have you missed one of your pigs lately?"

"Why should I miss one of my pigs?" the Major asked. "I don't keep my pigs as pets, sir. I keep them in order to have decent bacon. I'm very fond of bacon, but I like good bacon. And by keeping my own pigs I get good bacon."

"Well, I'm afraid I shot one of your pigs this morning."

"You shot one of my pigs, sir?" the little Major exclaimed. "How dare you shoot one of my pigs?"

"Yes, I was trying out an Express rifle before we go on a panther shoot with the Maharaja of Tussore to-morrow, and I happened to shoot one of your pigs."

"It's very difficult to mistake a pig for a panther, sir."

"I didn't think your pig was a panther. I thought it was a plank."

"My pigs bear no resemblance whatever to planks, sir," the Major said angrily. "My pigs are well fed and well looked after."

"This pig wasn't well looked after," Ben Nevis declared. "It was lying about in the rocks beyond the Maharaja's grounds."

"That is my land, sir, and my pigs are entitled to use it. They like sunning themselves, and it does them good to sun themselves in winter time. And let me add, sir, that you were no more entitled to shoot planks on my land than pigs. I don't know who you are, sir, but unless you're a socialist you ought to know that a man's property is his own."

"My name is MacDonald—Donald MacDonald of Ben Nevis."

"Where's that?"

"Ben Nevis is the highest ben in Great Britain," said the Chieftain grandly.

"A mere pimple!" the Major scoffed.

"A mere what? Did you say a pimple?" the Chieftain gasped.

"To those of us who like myself are familiar with the Himalayas," the Major added.

In happier circumstances Ben Nevis might have asked Major Crumbleholme if he had ever seen any Abominable Snowmen, but his Highland pride had been too deeply wounded for him to surrender either to curiosity or to credulity.

"I don't think there's any reason to prolong this interview," he said with dignity. "If you will let me know how many—er—chips I owe you for this pig I shall be glad to pay at once."

"The value of a pig at the present moment is 150 rupees and I shall be glad if you will take steps to have the carcass removed. I do not want to have my night's rest ruined by jackals," said the Major.

Ben Nevis thrust his hand into his pocket and with stately precision counted out the sum in notes.

"Good-morning to you, sir," said Major Crumbleholme. "I shall not trouble the Maharaja of Bangapatam for a subscription. It would be ironical, sir, to ask His Highness to subscribe to the Society for the Prevention of Cruelty to Animals when he is apparently unable to prevent his guests from killing harmless pigs upon his neighbour's land."

Major Crumbleholme swung round and marched out of the room.

"And this wretched little frizzled-up butterfly-collector the size of a peanut had the insolence, Hugh, the infernal insolence to say that Ben Nevis was a pimple. I've not been in such a rage with anybody since the secretary of the Hikers' Union came mincing up to me on Drumcockie last Twelfth. Crumb is what he ought to be called, for that's what he looked like. Well, the Campbells can have him! Ko hi!"

Balu Ram hurried in to the sitting-room.

"Bring me a burra burra burra peg," Ben Nevis told his bearer. "A moth-eaten bug-hunter calling Ben Nevis a pimple," he growled.

K

Chapter 12

PANTHERS

'LAUGH and grow fat,' says the adage, but the Maharaja of Bangapatam was so fat already that laughter probably had a slimming effect. At any rate he had not been so active at table-tennis for a long time as he was that evening before dinner after laughing at intervals about Ben Nevis and Major Crumbleholme's pig throughout the day. Klopczok, his Czech professional, who had been winning every other set recently, was beaten in four sets, and what is more was so obviously piqued by his employer's victories that nobody could have supposed that he was letting him win for diplomatic reasons.

His Highness came into the smoking-room before dinner in a mood of rich benevolence; he was so full of good-humour that he allowed himself one or two pre-prandial gimlets and at dinner drank three or four glasses of champagne. Kilwhillie, under the influence of Major Crumbleholme's pig, was almost debonair, and amused his host by telling him the story of the hikers who had been imprisoned by Ben Nevis in the dungeon at Glenbogle Castle.

"Do you remember Lord Buntingdon at Harrow, Maharaja? He's the President of the National Union of Hikers and he really was an extremely comical figure in shorts."

"I knew him well," the Maharaja replied. "He was Ouse in those days and was always known as Oozy. He collects tortoises. You ought to have gone to Ouse Hall, Nosy, and shot one of his tortoises."

But the Chieftain did not respond. The comparison of Ben Nevis to a pimple seemed in retrospect more outrageous than when it fell from the thin lips of Major Crumbleholme. He had been brooding over it ever since.

"Shall I invite the Major to come with us to-morrow?"

the Maharaja suggested. "You might have a chance to shoot him, Nosy."

"Ha-ha-ha," his guest laughed with the melancholy sound of the Atlantic in the depth of a cave at the base of a cliff in the farthest Hebrides.

"Never mind, my dear Nosy," his Highness consoled him. "I shall arrange a pleasant surprise for you to-morrow."

This pleasant surprise proved to be the despatch of Ben Nevis in one car with Mrs Winstanley while he and Kilwhillie escorted Miss Nutting and Miss Lambert in the other.

"But won't that make rather too many in your car, Maharaja? Hadn't I better go with Donald and Mrs Winstanley?" Kilwhillie suggested.

"Now, don't be a spoil-sport, my dear Kilwhillie," said his Highness. "You are quite as bad as the Major."

"What has the Major been doing?" Miss Nutting asked. "You know, we poor novelists are always looking for copy."

"Then you shall sit by me, and we'll put Kilwhillie and Miss Lambert in front of us."

The Maharaja had been right in thinking that the arrangement would please Ben Nevis. Seated beside Angela Winstanley on the way to Tussore, the spirits of the Chieftain returned.

"Do you know a wallah called Major Crumbleholme?" he asked.

"No, I've never heard of him," she replied. "What does he do?"

"He breeds pigs and collects butterflies. A most unpleasant type. He was in Campbell's Sikhs, if you've ever heard of such a regiment."

"Indeed I have," said Angela. "It's rather a crack regiment."

"I wouldn't pay much attention to that. The Campbells always make out they're better than anybody else. I mean to say, you'll hear some boobies claim the Argylls are as good as the Clanranalds, which of course is utter nonsense.

By the way, his Highness is writing to ask Hector's Colonel if the boy can spend Christmas up here at Rosemount."

"You told me; that will be very jolly," Angela said.

"Yes, I thought you'd be pleased."

Yet an observer who had noticed the way that the bow of Angela's mouth had grown suddenly taut might have wondered if she was really as pleased as she declared she was.

"Yes, I've been thinking over things since I came up to Pippla," the Chieftain went on. "The air here is much clearer than it was in Tallulaghabad and I've been wondering whether a father has any right to try and interfere in the private affairs of his son."

"That rather depends on the son," Angela said.

"Oh, yes, quite so. I agree with you absolutely. But Hector is very like me in many ways and when I found how very much I took to you at once I said to myself, 'Supposing you were the same age as Hector, wouldn't you feel you were entitled to marry the girl you wanted to marry?' Look here, Angela, I'm going to be quite frank with you. I came out to India under the impression that Hector had got himself tangled up with a designing woman, if you know what I mean."

"I do indeed," Angela murmured.

"Instead of which I find you'd been grossly . . . what's the word? . . . grossly . . . er . . . maligned. Yes, that's it. Maligned. I don't mind telling you that I began to suspect as much when I was drinking cocoa with your late husband on board the *Taj Mahal*. In fact, I said to my friend, Hugh Cameron . . ."

"Who doesn't approve of me at all," Angela interposed.

"Oh, well, dear old Hugh. He doesn't approve of anything. He was at Winchester, you know, and they have what they call notions, and one of these notions is that if you're not a Wykehamist you don't know anything about anything at all. Curious people, very. But you mustn't be put off by this stiff sort of manner he has. He's a splendid chap. Loyal as a trivet. I mean to say, we have trouble sometimes with the Campbells. And with the Macintoshes. And we should have trouble with the Mackenzies. Only fortunately they're all on the Ross-shire County Council. Except old General Mackenzie of Mam, and he's only interested in his rock-garden. My wife's very fond of him, but I get tired of these Latin names. Yes, as I was saying, Hugh Cameron is always back to back with me. That's why he came out to India of course. He had a wrong impression of you too."

"And still has," Angela said.

"Yes, but you must remember Hugh hasn't got my quick mind. He can't change his mind in a flash as I can. He's got into the habit of hanging on to that moustache of his and stroking it, and if he isn't stroking his moustache he's stroking Bonzo."

"Bonzo?"

"That's his dog. Now, I never stroke anything, and so I know my own mind. But I'll tell you this, Angela. If you married Hector, in another two years or so you'd find that Hugh Cameron would be absolutely devoted to you. I'm sure of that."

Angela Winstanley looked out of the car at the landscape swiftly passing. They had just turned off the corkscrew road down to the plains and were driving through a country of low wooded ridges intersected by stony glens.

"We must be getting near to Tussore," she said. Then she turned to Ben Nevis. "You needn't worry about Hector and me. He's too young for me."

"You're not much older than he is."

"Oh, in actual years only one, but in reality I'm a very great deal older than Hector. Even older than you, dear Ben Nevis. India is not a country to keep people young. You didn't realise, did you, why the Maharaja put you and me together in this car? I do. He thought he would give you an opportunity to make love to me, because he is quite sure that you wouldn't have suggested his inviting me to Rosemount unless you were interested in me."

"Well, I am interested in you."

"Ah, yes, but not in the way the Maharaja supposes." She put her slim ringless hand for a moment on the back of his. "You dear big innocent," she murmured.

"But it would never enter my head to try and make love to you," the Chieftain protested.

"Of course not. But it would never enter the Maharaja's head that you wouldn't."

"Extraordinary!" the Chieftain ejaculated.

"But I'm very grateful to him for that mistake. If he hadn't made it I shouldn't have been invited to Rosemount and I shouldn't have had a chance of being invited to the Maharaja of Tussore's Christmas party. I should just have been one of the people staying at Parker's until I went back to Tallulaghabad to wonder about the future. Oh, and that reminds me. John Tucker is coming up to Parker's for Christmas and it would be kind if you'd get him an invitation to Rosemount. He has been very kind to me and he's most hospitable."

"I know. I went round to his place, and he gave me some jolly good whisky. Young Duncan Robertson took me round there one evening. Hector wouldn't come. I liked him very much."

"He's another of the lovers that the mem-sahibs of Tallulaghabad have allotted to me."

"Good lord!" Ben Nevis ejaculated.

"And now I'm going to tell you something seriously," Angela went on, "which I told you before half jokingly. Just before you arrived in Tallulaghabad I'd practically made up my mind to refuse absolutely to marry Hector. I said to myself that he would be sure to become boring as he grew older, and that he would also become stuffy and ugly. And then when you came to call on me that first evening you looked so marvellous in your kilt—yes, Hector has taught me not to say kilts—and so handsome in a fierce kind of way that I began to wonder if after all I shouldn't like to marry Hector and go back to that house he talks about— lodge he called it."

"I wonder which one he was thinking of. We have rather a nice lodge by Loch Hoch."

"That's the one."

"I think you'd be very comfortable there, Angela," said the Chieftain.

"Dear Ben Nevis. Dear, dear Ben Nevis," she said. "You know as well as I do that it wouldn't work. I was never meant to be the wife of a Highland chief, any more," she quickly added, "than I was meant to be the wife of a bank manager or of a clergyman. Look," she said suddenly, "that must be Tussore we can see."

Angela was right, and a few minutes later the car drove under the great portico of the Maharaja's palace, where two sentries in uniforms of brilliant blue presented arms as Ben Nevis and Mrs Winstanley walked up the marble steps to be received by the salaams of what seemed an army of attendants.

"Welcome to Tussore," said His Highness the Maharaja, who was waiting to receive his guests in the colonnaded marble hall of the Palace. Hardly had he shaken hands with Angela Winstanley and Ben Nevis than a fanfare of trumpets announced the arrival of His Highness the Maharaja of Bangapatam. The Princes greeted one another with a ceremoniousness that seemed to call for robes of satin and bejewelled turbans rather than check suits of plus-fours.

On the way to the comfortable and cosy room where drinks were being served before an early tiffin the Maharaja pointed out one or two of the treasures in his famous Palace.

"And this is my music-room, Mrs Winstanley," he said, opening a door and leading the way in. She saw a Steinway concert grand and a smaller Bechstein grand, a cluster of music stands, the huge horn of an E.M. Ginn Gramophone, cabinets packed with gramophone records, a large Persian carpet on the inlaid floor, and on the white walls many silk Persian rugs.

"Will you play the Bechstein?" he asked.

"I don't think your other guests will want to listen

to music before tiffin, Maharaja Sahib," she said.

"But I want to hear you play," his Highness insisted.

"Your Highness means you want to hear *how* I play in the cold light of morning," Angela said with a smile. "I shall try not to disappoint you some other time."

A quick frown passed between the Maharaja's dark eyes; he was not used to refusal. However, it was but a momentary displeasure and he bowed his acceptance of it.

After lunch, when the guests were preparing to get into the three waiting cars, the host met with a serene refusal when Angela instead of getting into his car said she thought the ladies should keep together. So the host had Ben Nevis as his companion and the Maharaja of Bangapatam had Kilwhillie.

"Mrs Winstanley seems very anxious for feminine company," said the Maharaja of Tussore to the Chieftain. "I hope you didn't frighten her, Ben Nevis, on the way down from Pippla."

"No, no, no, we were discussing her future plans," said Ben Nevis. "You know, of course, that she's waiting for her divorce to be over and done with?"

"Yes, I had heard that. She is a very attractive woman," said the Maharaja.

"Oh, most attractive. And so natural. That's what I like about her. I should welcome her as a daughter-in-law."

"As a daughter-in-law?" the Maharaja repeated in amazement.

"I mean to say, if she decided to marry my boy Hector. He's in the Clanranalds down in Tallulaghabad. But it looks to me as if she were going to refuse him. But you never know."

The Maharaja of Tussore was silent for a minute or two. So this was the explanation of his guest's interest in Mrs Winstanley. Bangapatam had been wrong.

"My own opinion, for what it is worth, is that Mrs Winstanley intends to marry this wallah Tucker," Ben Nevis announced.

"Who's he?" the Maharaja asked quickly.

"He has a brewery in Tallulaghabad. I believe he's coming up to Pippla in a few days.

"He is, is he?" the Maharaja muttered.

Ben Nevis, who had realised that the Maharaja was attracted by Angela Winstanley, was determined not to let him think that she was going to be his for the asking.

"And mind you," he went on, "I wouldn't be at all sure that she and her former husband won't come together again."

"What?" the Maharaja exclaimed.

"As a matter of fact I met him on the *Taj Mahal*. Quite a good chap and very fond of cocoa. Mind you, I don't think he was the right husband for Angela, but she might feel that it would save a lot of bother if she went back to him. He's a quiet sort of wallah, and if he didn't drink too much of this cocoa I believe they might settle down together again quite happily."

Ben Nevis said no more about Angela Winstanley's prospects of matrimony: he felt that he had got his own back for that 'hush' with which the Maharaja had rebuked him for conversation while Angela was playing the piano at Rosemount.

After a drive of about twenty miles the cars stopped beside a low hill and all walked down to take up positions on a low platform at the head of a glade between stretches of scrubby woodland.

"Not a sound above a whisper," the Maharaja of Bangapatam warned all the novices at the panther beat.

"I can't whisper properly," Ben Nevis croaked. "So I shan't say a word. My head stalker always insists on that at home."

"Miss Nutting, please," the Maharaja of Tussore whispered, "I'm afraid you must take off your hat. It is too bright and might make the panther turn off when he comes this way."

"Oh, dear," Miss Nutting whispered in a flutter of

agitation. I ought to have left it in the car. Why didn't you warn me?"

Everybody said "Hush", and Miss Nutting became so agitated that she might have stepped backward off the platform if Kilwhillie had not grasped her arm. She smiled at him so gratefully that he very nearly let go of her arm. However, the offending hat was successfully removed and sent back to the car by a bearer.

Then the noise of the two hundred beaters who had ringed a couple of panthers started.

"Good lord!" Ben Nevis ejaculated. "I don't know why we're all whispering. I can hardly hear myself speak at the top of my voice above that yelling. We don't yell like that when we're beating for grouse."

"Hush!" everybody hissed.

After a quarter of an hour of yelling the female panther came lolloping along toward the platform.

"It's your shot, Nosy," cried Bangapatam.

Ben Nevis fired without making the panther change her course. Then the Maharaja fired, and to the manifest delight of Ben Nevis also missed.

"Here comes the male," cried Tussore, firing as he spoke. The panther went bounding on.

"I can't help feeling glad that the panthers got away," said Angela. "They *are* so like large cats, and I love cats."

"Oh, do you, Mrs Winstanley?" Miss Nutting asked her reproachfully. "I like dogs so much better than cats. I had a darling scottie once and he was carried off by a panther. So I have no pity on panthers. Poor Mac! He was an absolute angel. I just had to say 'Cats' and he was after them in a flash."

"Until a big cat gobbled him up," Angela observed.

"We shan't see the female again," the host said. "But we'll go on a bit to the tower and we may get another shot at the male."

Miss Nutting asked why the female would not be seen again.

"The beaters don't want to lose her," the Maharaja replied. "They like to have panthers about because it keeps woodcutters from poaching their wood."

"I wish we had a few panthers in Glenbogle," said Ben Nevis. "I doubt if we should see a single hiker, even in August."

The top of the tower, which was some twenty feet high, was reached by wooden steps round the outside. It stood in a space of open ground about a hundred yards square which the panther had to cross when it broke cover. The yelling of the beaters began again. After about twenty minutes the male panther appeared in the open, moving at speed but seeming almost to amble along toward the cover beyond.

Ben Nevis fired and missed.

"Nosy, Nosy," Banjo murmured, but he too missed.

And it was Kilwhillie who to everybody's surprise and above all to his own hit the quarry. Moreover, his bullet killed the panther stone dead.

The congratulations were warm, the applause was loud. The marksman stroked his moustache in embarrassment.

"You must have it stuffed, Hugh," the Chieftain declared, "and take it back with you to Kilwhillie."

"I'm not going to cart a stuffed panther about with me," said the hero of the afternoon. "It would mean an endless argument with the Customs. But I'll take the skin back with me and hang it up in the gunroom."

Kilwhillie's panther was measured, and when it was pronounced to be seven feet eleven inches over all the victor received fresh congratulations on having killed an animal of unusual size.

"I shall tell Macfarlane when I get back that I'm very disappointed with this Express he sold me," Ben Nevis announced.

"I don't think that's fair, Nosy. What about the pig you shot yesterday morning?"

And at the recollection the Maharaja of Bangapatam began to shake once more with inextinguishable laughter.

"A wounded pig can be a pretty tough customer," the Maharaja of Tussore observed.

"But it wasn't a wild pig," the other Maharaja managed to wheeze. "It was one of Major Crumbleholme's pigs."

"Oh, you didn't shoot one of the Major's precious pigs?" cried Miss Nutting. "Oh, how too utterly marvellous!"

The Maharaja of Tussore decided that enough had been said about the pig. He did not want his guest to suppose that he was enjoying the story in retaliation for what he might suppose he himself had been told about Mrs Winstanley during the drive to the beat.

"I shall see that your panther will be ready for you when you leave India," he told Kilwhillie. "Will you drive with me now to the Palace?"

The ladies drove back together again. Ben Nevis was with the Maharaja of Bangapatam.

"Look here, Banjo," he remonstrated. "I think we've heard enough about this confounded pig. I don't want the story going round all over Inverness-shire."

"You wouldn't like me to have it stuffed so that you can show it to Lindsay-Wolseley?" the Maharaja chuckled.

"I certainly don't want Wolseley to hear about it," Ben Nevis said. "He's always pestering the Departure of Agriculture wallahs to persuade our people to keep pigs."

"But he's bound to hear about it, Nosy. Somebody is sure to write and tell him. Besides, Maud Nutting will put it in a book."

"You don't mean that?" Ben Nevis asked in consternation.

"I do indeed."

"Do you mean to say that these book-writers can go about putting anything they like into a book?"

"Of course they can," the Maharaja affirmed.

"And they'll be able to read at home about my having shot a pig by mistake in India?" Ben Nevis gasped.

"Oh, she won't put you in by name, Nosy. She'll probably call you Campbell."

"That I will not be called," Ben Nevis vowed.

"Ah, well, you'll have to make yourself very agreeable to her when we get back to the Palace and then perhaps she won't put you into a book."

"I'm not going salaaming all over Miss Nutting, if that's what you mean, Banjo."

The friend of his schooldays patted Ben Nevis affectionately.

"Don't worry, my dear Nosy, I don't really think Maud Nutting has any intention of putting you and the Major's pig into a book. But you mustn't be angry with me for laughing about it because it really was a damn funny business. And now I'll tell *you* something to laugh at. I woke in the night and I began to laugh about you and the Major's pig and I laughed so much that I turned over and fell out of bed. My goodness, what a whopper I came! And when I rolled over to get up I rolled right under the bed. I couldn't make out what had happened. I thought the ceiling had fallen down on me."

The Maharaja began to shake again with unquenchable laughter, and this time Ben Nevis laughed with him.

"I don't think you and I had better go and listen to Mrs Winstanley playing," said the Maharaja, "because if we begin to laugh in the middle of the music Tussore will be absolutely furious. He has no sense of humour at all when he is interested in a woman. And I think he is very interested in Mrs Winstanley. I hope you're not annoyed about that."

"My dear Banjo, it's nothing to do with me. It's my boy Hector who's in love with Angela."

"Oh, that's it, is it? Ah, now I understand. Oh, we must certainly get him up here for Christmas. Well, that's most amusing. I thought it was you who were interested in little Mrs Winstanley. And I wouldn't blame you. All the same, when we get to our age, Nosy, it's wiser not to surrender to these infatuations."

When after tea the Maharaja of Tussore asked Angela to play to him for a little before they drove back to Pippla the ladies accompanied him to the music-room where for nearly half an hour Angela played nocturnes, études, and impromptus of Chopin to her host.

"Yes, you play Chopin much better than any woman I ever heard," the Maharaja told Angela. "I hope you and Miss Lambert will come and spend Christmas with me here. We shall have a big party on Christmas night."

"Your Highness is more than kind, but a friend of mine, Mr John Tucker, is coming up to spend Christmas at Parker's Hotel and we can't leave him to amuse himself all alone in Parker's."

The Maharaja frowned for a moment.

"But you will come to dinner and stay to dance afterwards?" he asked.

"If we may bring Mr Tucker we shall be delighted. He will have his car."

"I shall send an invitation to Mr Tucker," the Maharaja said. "He runs the Golden Lion Brewery in Tallulaghabad, doesn't he? A plump little man?"

"Plumpish," Angela admitted.

"Perhaps you and Miss Lambert would give me the pleasure of lunching with me on Tuesday and of giving me a long afternoon of music? My new Military Adviser will be arriving in Pippla on Tuesday morning and a car can bring you and him to Tussore."

"That would be lovely, Maharaja Sahib," said Angela. "What is the name of your military adviser?"

"Captain Gerald Ripwood of Bulger's Horse," the Maharaja replied.

The breathless squeak emitted by Maisie Lambert was muffled by the gurgle of joy from Maud Nutting.

"Oh, how too topping," she cried. "Freckles, my favourite character of all, was in Bulger's Horse. Good-bye, Maharaja Sahib, and thank you again for an absolutely marvellous day. I can't say how much I'm looking forward to your Christmas party."

Chapter 13

FEMININE PROBLEMS

MAISIE LAMBERT thought the drive back from Tussore was the longest she had ever taken, for she was palpitating to talk about what to her seemed the world-shaking news so quietly announced by the Maharaja. The nervous tension was not relaxed by having to listen to Miss Nutting talk all the way to Pippla about the astonishing coincidence of hearing on the very same day as she had seen a panther shoot that an officer of Bulger's Horse was going to arrive almost immediately in Tussore.

"You see when I was writing about Freckles I really fell in love with Guy Harford myself. You haven't read *Freckles*, have you, Miss Lambert? I shall send a copy round to Parker's this evening. You'll see how very like a real panther shoot is to the one I described in my book, except of course that Guy Harford himself shot three panthers and he could have shot a fourth but he wanted his friend Dick Carstairs to show Kitty Kenderdyne what a good shot he is. Kitty is the daughter of the Governor and Dick is madly in love with her, but I musn't spoil the story by telling you beforehand what happens."

"No, you mustn't do that, Miss Nutting," Angela agreed earnestly. Listening to the outlines of a tale was not her idea of entertainment.

An hour later Maisie Lambert was at last able to ask the question which she was longing to ask.

"Oh, Angela, what *am* I to do?"

"I don't know why you're letting yourself get into such a state, my dear Maisie. I'm quite sure Gerry Ripwood will be asking what *he* is to do when he presents himself here next Tuesday and finds who it is he has to escort to Tussore. But we'll talk about it after dinner. I want to have a bath. And you'll be in a better condition to discuss the future after a bath."

So it was not until after dinner that Maisie was able to say once more to her friend, "But, Angela, what *am* I to do?"

They were sitting in a corner of that drawing-room haunted by the ghosts of young women in balloon sleeves who must often have asked that question in the days when Rudyard Kipling was young. Two rubbers of contract were being played in the middle of the room and round the log fire several mem-sahibs were knitting and gently gossiping. The men were mostly reading *The Statesman* or *The Civil and Military Gazette*.

"I don't think we can discuss such a delicate subject here," Angela replied.

"Well, can't we go up to your bedroom?" Maisie begged in despair. "I feel I shall have a nervous breakdown if I can't ask your advice."

"We'll have a sitting-room to ourselves next week when John Tucker comes," Angela said.

"My dear, I can't wait till then to talk about Gerry. He'll be here before John Tucker arrives. Oh, do let's go up to your room or mine."

At last Angela relented and they went upstairs to her room at the top of the hotel, where the fire had been lit. As they sat down on either side of it there was a noise like stage thunder above their heads.

"What's that?" Maisie exclaimed in affright.

"It's the monkeys chasing one another on the roof," she was told with a laugh from her friend. "They're probably quarrelling about love. Monkeys have their complications too."

"I don't know what I shall do when Gerry arrives on Tuesday," said Maisie. "I haven't seen him for three years. Who would have dreamed that he would have come to Pippla like this?"

"My dear girl, he is going to be much more embarrassed than you. That's a sure thing. It's much worse for a man who has walked out on a girl to meet her after three years than it is for the girl who's been walked out on, if you see what I mean, as my dear Ben Nevis says."

"Yes, but suppose he feels that he treated me badly and wants to marry me now?"

"Wishful thinking, Maisie, my dear. Just wishful thinking."

Maisie shook her head sadly.

"You're awfully cynical, aren't you, Angela?"

"No, not cynical, Maisie. Merely practical. There's a time in the morning when we wake from our dreams."

"Yes, but I gave him so much," Maisie said tremulously.

"I know. And the little more of brandy-Macs and how much it is—or at any rate how much it leads to."

"You know, sometimes I think you're absolutely heartless, Angela."

Angela flicked the ash from her cigarette into the fire.

"Yes, Maisie," she assented with a sigh. "Sometimes I think the same."

"I wonder if he's changed much," Maisie speculated.

"One of the tragedies—no, not tragedies, that's too pompous a word—one of the ironies of life is that men change externally less than women and more inwardly, whereas with women it is just the reverse."

"You mean he'll think I look older?" Maisie asked anxiously.

"Of course he will. You can't be jilted in India and spend three years fretting about it without looking older."

"And so I suppose he'll say to himself how right he was to break off our engagement," Maisie sighed disconsolately.

"It may not be quite as simple as that. It may depend on what happens at Tussore," Angela told her.

"But what could happen there that would have anything to do with Gerry?"

"Quite a lot."

"As for instance?"

L

"As for instance if the Maharaja asked me to marry him," Angela said slowly.

"Angela! You're not talking seriously?"

"Quite seriously. You heard me refuse to stay at Tussore?"

"Yes, but that was because of John Tucker."

"That was the excuse I made, but Tussore himself knew perfectly well what the real reason was," Angela said.

"What was the real reason?"

"That I wasn't prepared to be his mistress. So now he has to think again and decide how much he wants me. He may, of course, decide that he doesn't want me enough to ask me to marry him. We shall see."

Maisie stared at her friend in awe.

"If anybody else but you had said that to me I should have laughed," she declared. "But somehow when you say it, it sounds as if it really might happen."

Angela bent over and stirred the logs with a poker until the flames began to dance in the grate.

"Let us suppose that Tussore does ask me to marry him. What do I say? He is not much over forty. He is still slim and certainly very handsome. He is genuinely devoted to music. I think music is what people call a ruling passion. He has had two Maharanis. Both are dead, but each presented him with a possible heir. So he hasn't got to worry about that. I don't want to live in England. I love India. Even the dull life I've spent so far in India hasn't destroyed a particle of that love. I can imagine nothing better than life in India with all the money you want. Yes, I think *if* Tussore asks me to marry him I shall say 'Yes'; but John Tucker might ask me to marry him, and I might have to make up my mind which of the two I would accept. John Tucker could also give me all I wanted."

"And Hector MacDonald? You've quite decided about him?" Maisie asked.

"Oh, I never seriously contemplated marrying poor Hector. It was amusing to find that I was upsetting the mem-sahibs of Tallulaghabad and to know that Hector's father was being summoned out to India to rescue his son from a designing female. And it was rather a sweet revenge to know that Papa would be quite pleased now if I did agree to marry his son. But once I knew that, I realised that nothing would induce me to do so. Nevertheless, I'll admit, Maisie, that when I first saw Ben Nevis I did wonder if perhaps I might not marry Hector. However, I very soon faced the acid fact that Hector would not be like his father for another forty years and I couldn't see myself putting up with Hector even for the next ten years."

Maisie, who had listened patiently, as indeed she always did, to Angela talking about herself, thought she might venture to bring the conversation back to Gerry Ripwood.

"You haven't advised me yet what I am to do," she reminded her friend.

"Do you want to marry Gerald Ripwood?" Angela asked.

"I think I'm still in love with him," Maisie replied. "That's why it was such a shock when the Maharaja said he was coming to Tussore."

"Then if you want to marry him," Angela said, "you must hope that Tussore will ask me to marry him and that I shall say 'Yes'."

"But what has that to do with Gerry?" Maisie asked in bewilderment.

"Why, if I know anything about Gerry Ripwood . . . and I know of nothing except to his disadvantage . . . I fancy you will begin to look very like the knife that helps him to spread the butter on the right side of his bread. In other words, if he thinks he can establish himself comfortably at Tussore he will keep in with me."

"But, Angela, I wouldn't like to think that Gerry was marrying me for that reason. I mean to say, after the way he treated me I should want to feel that he felt he had made a mistake and that he wanted me because he loved me."
Angela was going to say something, but Maisie went on quickly, "You mustn't blame Gerry for what happened. I

was weak, and if a girl is weak she must not put all the blame on the man. Gerry may have thought that if I was weak with him I might be weak with other men after we were married."

"Maisie, Maisie, please don't talk such blithering nonsense. Ripwood behaved like a cad and there was no excuse for the way he let you down. However, if you think you'll be happier married to him I'm quite willing to help you find out if you're right. But you'd better make up your mind that the only reason why Gerald Ripwood will marry you is if he thinks it will help his future career. Hector told me he's not one of the most popular characters in the Indian Army and I should imagine that he has taken this job at Tussore in the hope of its leading on to a permanent job with one of the Princes. And now as I've answered your question . . ."

"But you haven't answered it, Angela," Maisie protested. "What *am* I to do when Gerry comes here on Tuesday?"

"Be calm and cool and collected."

"But I don't think I can. You've no idea how my heart was beating all the way from Tussore, and when the Maharaja first said that about Gerry Ripwood coming to be his military adviser I nearly screamed."

"Well, go to bed now and start preparing yourself to be apparently quite indifferent. Remember you have the advantage because you know that you're going to meet Ripwood and he doesn't know that he's going to meet you. You've had your shock. He hasn't had his yet. So go to bed. I want to go to bed because I have a lot of hard thinking to do."

"About what, Angela?"

"About my future. Early next month I shall be absolutely free, and I have to decide what I want to do with my freedom."

"I wish I could be as calm as you are," Maisie said wistfully. "I do so admire your poise. I think you're wonderful."

"Go to bed," Angela told her friend.

"I shan't sleep a wink. Do you think I ought to tell my father that I'll be meeting Gerry again?"

"Oh, for heaven's sake, Maisie, what's it got to do with your father? Captain Ripwood isn't a job for the Public Works Department. He's a job for you, and you alone. With a little help from Angela perhaps, and I shall find it amusing to handle Captain Gerald Ripwood. And for the last time, go to bed, Maisie."

The monkeys were running about again over the corrugated iron roof of Parker's Hotel as Maisie went out of Angela's bedroom.

Chapter 14

ROSEMOUNT GUESTS

"I THINK old Banjo has collected rather a lot of stick-in-the-muds for Christmas," Ben Nevis said to Kilwhillie when they were sitting over their burra nightcaps in the guest-house two days later.

"Not so loud, Donald. There are others sleeping here now."

"I know. All those stick-in-the-muds are here," Ben Nevis agreed. "It was very lucky for Banjo that I wrote to let him know we were in Pippla. By Jove, it was."

The stick-in-the-muds who had come to stay at Rosemount with the Maharaja of Bangapatam for Christmas were Sir John Fussell, a Bombay nabob with financial interests in Bangapatam, and his wife; Mr and Mrs James Pedder-Wilson, he a Member of Parliament, who on the strength of these visits to India, each taking a few weeks, had acquired a reputation in the House as an authority on Indian affairs; Jeffrey Hearne, a political journalist who, the Indian princes believed, had the Prime Minister's ear; Croker Bates, the film director, who was making an expensive tour through the East in order to gauge the possibility of a super-film about Marco Polo; an Anglo-Indian film star called Pearl Romaine; and Mrs Kibbler, an American enquirer as she called herself.

"I shouldn't have described them all as stick-in-the-muds," said Kilwhillie. "That American woman I was sitting next to never stopped asking me questions all through dinner."

"What kind of questions, Hugh?"

"Idiotic questions," Kilwhillie replied. "She asked me if I had ever managed to project my essential self outside my earthly body. Apparently she can sit back in a chair and watch her essential self climbing up the wall of a room."

"Good lord! What did you say?" the Chieftain asked.

"I said 'No'. What would you expect me to say? And then she asked me if I had tried the effect of standing on my head to meditate? She said it cleared the mind."

"Good lord!" the Chieftain ejaculated again. "She sounds as mad as that woman in Bombay—Lady Harbottle. I hope you told her you couldn't stand on your head in a kilt."

"Certainly not," said Hugh. "She'd have asked questions about that. You'd better sit next her to-morrow. She'll ask you questions about the Loch Ness Monster. And you'll like that."

"She sounds quite intelligent after all," the Chieftain decided. "I think you must have misunderstood what she was saying when she told you she could climb up wallpaper. I know it annoys you to say so, but I think you *are* getting deaf, Hugh. Well, I had a frightful evening. I sat between the wife of that political wallah who kept telling me where she and that pie-faced husband of hers had been visiting in India. She kept telling me about what she called stratistics."

"I'm not too deaf to hear you mispronounce English words, Donald," said Hugh Cameron. "It is statistics, not stratistics."

"I know perfectly well it isn't statistics."

"But it is."

"It is what?"

"It is statistics," said Kilwhillie.

"That's what I said. There you are. That's a proof you're getting deaf if you thought I said statistics. Anyway, I began to feel that feeling I have when I'm bored and the top of my head sort of boils inside. But Lady Fussell, who was sitting on my other side, was just as boring. Have you ever heard of stuff called M and B?"

"Yes, it's what they give people for pneumonia," said Kilwhillie.

"Well, apparently some people can't eat eggs if they

have this M and B, and apparently this wallah Sir John Fussell did eat eggs and I got so bored with hearing about his symptoms that I turned round again to talk to the woman who'd been boring me with stratistics. And after dinner I tried talking to the film star. Well, I've never seen one of those films, but I'm not surprised you don't like them, Hugh, if they're as boring as this woman was. Good lord, if Hector had wanted to marry *her* then I *would* have put my foot down. I asked Banjo about her and apparently the idea is that she is to play a part in some film which that boring film wallah is making in Banjo's State. You know, if I didn't think dear old Banjo might be offended I'd suggest that we'll go down and stay at Parker's."

"No," said Kilwhillie firmly, "we cannot possibly go to Parker's Hotel. It would be an unpardonable breach of good manners. Moreover, the Maharaja has written to ask Rose-Ross if Hector can have leave for Christmas, and if Hector is coming up to Pippla it would be monstrous to fling him into the arms of Mrs Winstanley by staying at Parker's."

"That's a very strong expression, Hugh. You don't often use strong expressions like that," said Ben Nevis.

"Fortunately people don't behave in a way that calls for such strong expressions," Kilwhillie retorted severely. "And now I think we had better go to bed."

Kilwhillie had hardly had time to unbutton his doublet when the Chieftain came surging into his bedroom waving a letter.

"Read this, Hugh," he barked. "What on earth shall I say?"

Hugh Cameron took the letter and read:

> *Norfolk Cottage,*
> *Pippla*
>
> Dear Ben Nevis,
>
> *I hope I'm not committing a faux pas by writing 'Ben Nevis'. If I am, please forgive an ignorant Englishwoman and don't tear this note up.*

I have a request to make which I do hope you will consider favourably. It is the custom every year to give a children's party at the Club on Christmas Eve when we have a Christmas tree with presents for the kiddies and when Santa Claus arrives in person to hand them to the lucky recipients. We always try to persuade a visitor to play the part of Santa Claus ever since some years ago one of the children who recognised Major Crumbleholme pulled off his beard and the Ladies' Committee decided that in future we should always have somebody whom the children wouldn't recognise.

This brings me to the point. The Ladies' Committee met this afternoon and it was unanimously decided to ask you to be kind enough to be Santa Claus this year. Please please *do not refuse. We all feel that you would make an ideal Santa Claus and that if you agreed to help us our Children's party on Christmas Eve would be the most successful we have ever had.*

The red gown that Santa Claus always wears may be a little short for you but my dirzee will be able to put that right.

I wonder, should you be kind enough to accept our invitation, if you would come and have tea with me to-morrow when my dirzee could measure you for the hooded gown and when you could try on the beard.

I'm afraid that you'll think it awful cheek of me to ask you to do this, but everybody has been so much impressed by your personality and so envious of my good fortune in having met you that I could not refuse to write to you and put our request before you. Please say yes. His Highness has always very kindly consented to attend the Santa Claus ceremony and as usual he has been most generous again this year in subscribing toward the fund for presents.

I shall await your answer with trepidation and meanwhile

> *I remain*
>
> > *Yours very sincerely,*
> >
> > > *Maud Nutting*

PS. What a wonderful shot your friend Mr Cameron is—I don't know how to spell his second name. I have seldom been so thrilled in my life as I was when I saw the panther fall to his unerring eye on Saturday afternoon.

"What on earth shall I say, Hugh?" Ben Nevis asked.

"I think you ought to say 'Yes'," Kilwhillie replied. "It is a small return we can make for the hospitality we have enjoyed."

"We?" the Chieftain repeated indignantly. "But you aren't going to do anything."

"I shall subscribe to the fund for the presents," Kilwhillie announced.

"I think you're getting out of this rather easily, Hugh. I'll tell you what. I'll ask Banjo to lend me one of those heads he has of that animal with crinkly horns whose name I never can remember and one of the bearskin rugs and then you can come in with me."

"And what should I be supposed to be?" Kilwhillie asked sarcastically.

"A reindeer, of course," said Ben Nevis. "You must have seen these Santa Claus reindeer on Christmas cards."

"Even if the head of a markhor looked in the least like the head of a reindeer the suggestion would be absurd. You don't seriously think I'm prepared to walk about in a hot room among a lot of excited children covered with a bearskin rug?"

"You wouldn't have to walk about. You could lie down at my feet," Ben Nevis urged.

"That would be unsufferably stuffy. Anyway, I don't intend to dress up for this performance."

"But I've got to dress up," Ben Nevis pointed out. "I don't look any more like Santa Claus than you look like a reindeer."

"I disagree with you, Donald. You are much more like Santa Claus. Very much more like."

"Nobody has ever told me before that I'm like Santa Claus," Ben Nevis expostulated.

"I'm not saying that you are like Santa Claus, Donald. What I'm saying is that you are more like Santa Claus than I am like a reindeer. Anyway, this is a ridiculous argument to start at this time of night and I think we'd both be wise to get to bed."

Next morning Ben Nevis found himself having breakfast at the same time as Mr Croker Bates, the film director.

"Ah, you're just the man I want to see," said the Chieftain. "You'll be able to give me some advice. I suppose you must have made some of these films about Santa Claus?"

Croker Bates, a small dark man, cast a bilious eye toward Ben Nevis over a cup of tea. Like so many film directors he believed he was a creative artist and he fancied that his fellow-guest hardly appreciated this.

"I don't make films about Santa Claus," he said coldly.

"Well, of course, I don't know anything about films," said the Chieftain. "I've never seen one in my life and I don't suppose I ever shall. But I always understood you film wallahs were ready to tackle any subject."

"I'm afraid Santa Claus might be considered rather *vieux jeu*," Croker Bates said, with a contemptuous smile.

"You ought to come along to the Club on Christmas Eve and see Santa Claus giving away the presents. You'll probably get some good ideas for one of those films you make. Tell me, is Miss Romaine a good filmer?"

"I consider her one of our greatest stars," Croker Bates averred solemnly.

"Really? She didn't twinkle very brightly last night. I couldn't get a word out of her. I suppose she brightens up when she's in a film. And what exactly do you do, Mr Bates?"

"I am a director."

"Oh, I thought you had something to do with arranging the film. Bangapatam must have got it wrong."

"A director has more to do with the making of a film than anybody," Croker Bates said irritably.

"Ah, I see—what you call a working director, not a guinea pig. And now you're going to make a film about polo in Bangapatam. Well, I'm told his team is considered one of the best in India."

"I am making a film about Marco Polo."

"How does that differ from ordinary polo?" Ben Nevis asked.

"Marco Polo, the Venetian traveller who visited Khubla Khan. Circumstances are not suitable for making films in Peking at the moment. So we are setting the Oriental background in Bangapatam. Pearl Romaine is to play the bride Marco Polo brought back from Peking for the Khan of Persia. He and she fall in love with one another but Marco Polo is true to his promise, and Cocacin . . ."

"Who?"

"That is the name of the young bride. The part Pearl Romaine will play. She will be wonderful in the great scene in which she parts with Marco Polo in order to marry Ghazan. We have an unusually fine script in which no fewer than five scriptwriters have collaborated, with help from me of course. Production costs will be in the region of £500,000, Mr MacDonald. As a Scotchman you'll be interested to learn that Ronald Campbell is to play Marco Polo."

Mr Croker Bates, feeling that he had by now put Ben Nevis thoroughly in his place, took a deep draught of tea.

When the Chieftain went that afternoon to Norfolk Cottage to tell Miss Nutting of his willingness to be Santa Claus at the children's party on Christmas Eve he gave her an account of his conversation with Mr Croker Bates as if he was relating some experience he had had with the village idiot. He was therefore astonished when she expressed a lively desire to be introduced to Mr Croker Bates.

"What on earth for?" he asked.

"Because he's considered one of the best film directors in the world," she said. "And he might read one or two of my books with the idea of filming them."

Ben Nevis did not know enough about the film industry to tell Miss Nutting that film directors as a rule lacked the mental concentration to read through even one book, let alone two.

"Well, I'll introduce you to him with pleasure," he promised. "And if you like I'll lend him that book of yours called *Tooth and Claw*."

"Wouldn't *Freckles* be better? And then he could get in the panther shoot."

"I don't think you'll persuade Hugh Cameron to appear in a film. He wouldn't even come to the party with me dressed as a reindeer."

"But I shouldn't expect Mr Cameron to play a part. Didn't you say Ronald Campbell was going to be in the film about Marco Polo? He'd make a splendid Freckles— Guy Harford of Bulger's Horse."

"Of course, I don't know anything about this film wallah Campbell," Ben Nevis said dubiously. "But I suppose we must admit that the Campbells have produced some quite good soldiers, and he might be able to play this freckled wallah from Bulger's Horse."

"But the great thing is to persuade Mr Croker Bates to read my book," Miss Nutting impressed on the Chieftain. "Perhaps if his Highness were to say something to him he might pay attention."

"I'll talk to the Maharaja myself," Ben Nevis promised. "This film wallah didn't seem to think I knew much about films. I upset him apparently by asking if he had ever made a film of Santa Claus. I couldn't quite make out what he called Santa Claus. It sounded like 'verger', but I don't think it can have been that. And then he went off into this frightful rigmarole about Marco Polo."

"Well, I shall keep my fingers crossed and hope for the best," said Miss Nutting. "And now shall we try on your beard?"

"What an enormous contraption!" Ben Nevis exclaimed. "Are you sure this is a beard? It looks to me more like a hearthrug. Oh, I see. You hook it on behind your ears."

The Chieftain put on the beard and looked at himself in the mirror over the mantelpiece.

"Good lord!" he ejaculated. "I remind myself of something. What is it? I know. It's a hassock which burst in our chapel at Glenbogle Castle. It tickles my nose rather. I hope I shan't sneeze it off."

The dirzee came in at that moment with the scarlet hooded gown.

"When the hood is up it hides where your beard is hooked on," Miss Nutting pointed out. "And of course we're going to re-trim the gown with fresh cotton-wool for the party. The gown is just about six inches too short."

Miss Nutting turned to the dirzee and addressed him in fluent kitchen Urdu. He twitched his head in a sidelong nod from time to time to indicate that he understood what she was telling him to do.

"They're so wonderfully quick at grasping what one wants," Miss Nutting said proudly.

"But you speak the lingo so well," the Chieftain said. "I'm picking it up gradually. Of course, I used to talk fluent Gaelic with my old nurse long ago, and I think that's a great help with other languages. I've forgotten most of the Gaelic I knew, but after a bit of Gaelic you're prepared for anything, if you see what I mean."

"I'd love to visit the Highlands one day. Next time I'm in England I simply must go north."

"And you'll have to come and stay with us in Glenbogle," said the Chieftain. "Mind you, I can't promise to show you the Loch Ness Monster, but you're more likely to see it with me than with anybody else. I've seen it myself several times. Kilwhillie has seen it too. But he won't talk about it. He thinks it sounds boastful. He's a very retiring wallah."

"I admired him so much on that wonderful day we had at Tussore. What a magnificent shot!"

"Yes, he's a fine shot on his day."

"So cool."

"Oh, he's very cool."

"Tell me, how does one spell his name?"

Ben Nevis obliged her with the spelling of Kilwhillie.

"And he's so modest," Miss Nutting went on.

"I think he's too modest," said Ben Nevis.

"But it's such an endearing quality in a man."

"Yes, but I think it's this modesty of his which has kept him from marrying."

"Perhaps he had a disappointment when he was a young man," Miss Nutting murmured with a sigh.

"I think he did have one or two, but I never talk to him about that kind of thing. He's my most intimate friend, but I never intrude, if you know what I mean."

"I do indeed," Miss Nutting declared with emotion. "Some secrets are sacred."

"Yes, you must certainly come and stay with us at Glenbogle. Kilwhillie House is at the head of Glenbore, which is the next glen to ours. It's a romantic old house with some very interesting relics of the '45. We were both of us out in the '45—not Hugh and myself, of course, but our people. We shouldn't have had any of this Bolshie nonsense to-day if the Prince had won. However, there you are. It was not to be, as they say."

Soon after this sad reflection Ben Nevis set out back to Rosemount, and the strenuous ascent of the khud worked upon his imagination with thoughts of home.

He found Kilwhillie writing letters in the sitting-room they shared.

"I've had a very pleasant afternoon with Miss Nutting, Hugh," he announced. "I tried on my Santa Claus rig-out, and it's quite . . . now what's the Indian for all right? Something like Tokay. Never mind, I've forgotten for the moment. I say, Hugh, does your moustache tickle your chin much?"

"Certainly not. Why should it?"

"Well, this enormous beard tickled my nose like anything. If I sneeze it off at the party you must stand by to hang it over my ears again before the children see what's happened. Well, you've made a conquest anyway, Hugh."

"How do you mean?" Kilwhillie asked suspiciously.

"I mean, Miss Nutting has fallen in love with you, and by Jove, Hugh, I think she'd make you a splendid wife."

"Thank you, Donald, I prefer to judge for myself who would make me a splendid wife. Miss Nutting must be at least fifty."

"She's not much over forty," Ben Nevis urged. "In fact, she may not be forty yet. It may be the climate. She's exactly the wife you want. Of course I didn't even hint at such a thing."

"I should hope you didn't," said Kilwhillie ."But frankly, Donald, your behaviour since you landed in India has been so irresponsible . . ."

"Irresponsible?"

"Irresponsible," Kilwhillie repeated firmly. "So irresponsible . . ."

"Well, don't keep repeating that idiotic word, Hugh. I'm not a poll-parrot."

"So irresponsible that I don't know where you'll end by landing us both."

"I can't help it, Hugh, if Miss Nutting has fallen in love with you. I didn't feel called upon to say that the shot with which you hit that panther was something uncommonly like a fluke. Naturally I let her think that you were a jolly good shot. And I really don't know why it should annoy you for Miss Nutting to fall in love with you. She's an exceptionally nice woman. As you know, I've no desire at all for you to get married, but if you do get married I'd rather you married Miss Nutting than . . ."

"Donald," his friend interrupted, "I should be very much obliged if you would say no more about marriage. I have no intention of getting married, and if I had, Miss Nutting would be the last woman whom I should think of in connection with such a state."

"Well, you seem to have fascinated her, Hugh. She could

hardly talk of anything all the afternoon except you. Oh, yes, I remember now, she said you were one of the most endearing men she had ever known. But I didn't encourage her, Hugh. You mustn't think that. In fact, I told her flatly that I didn't believe you'd take part in a film which she hopes this film wallah will do about this book of hers called *Freckles*."

Kilwhillie closed his eyes wearily.

"I shall be very thankful to find myself on a boat homeward bound," he declared, "however rough it is."

M

Chapter 15

LUNCH AND MUSIC AT TUSSORE

ANGELA had been right in anticipating that Captain Gerald Ripwood of the 9th Baluchistan Rifles (Bulger's Horse) would be taken aback when he called at Parker's Hotel on that December morning two or three days before Christmas, and in order to secure him the maximum embarrassment she received him alone before Maisie came into the Hotel drawing-room. Captain Ripwood was now about thirty-five—a tall thin man with a profile, a black toothbrush moustache and a sallow complexion. The check suit he was wearing enhanced the slightly raffish effect of his personality, and his dark eyes had the calculating expression of one who is always hoping to sell somebody a horse.

"Mrs Winstanley?" he asked, showing a row of rather large white teeth in an insincere smile. "His Highness telegraphed to me that I was to call here for you and escort you to Tussore."

"Did you have a good journey?" Angela enquired.

"The train was very crowded from Pindi onwards, and my coupé was as dusty as usual, but it wasn't too bad. Are you going to stay with his Highness?"

"No, my friend and I are going to lunch at the Palace. You are going to be the military adviser, aren't you?"

"Yes, I'm to put the Tussore Lancers into fighting trim," he replied with a cautious little laugh. "I was at Kohat with Bulger's and there's nothing much doing on the Frontier just now. I was glad to get away. Indeed, I'll be frank with you, Mrs Winstanley, and admit that I shouldn't be sorry to get away for good . . . if I could find a snug little job as Personal Assistant to one of the Princes. You mentioned a friend just now. Who is she?"

And it was at this moment that Maisie Lambert entered the drawing-room.

"Maisie!" he exclaimed. Then he pulled himself together. "I haven't seen you for a long time." He turned to Angela. "You didn't tell me that your friend was an old friend of mine. Does his Highness know?" he asked quickly.

Angela cut in.

"That you and Maisie were engaged to be married? No, and there's no reason why he should know that you were anything more than old friends."

"Quite, quite," Captain Ripwood quacked gently.

"Well, I'll go and put my things on," said Angela. "You're ready, Maisie. You can entertain Captain Ripwood for a few minutes."

With this she left the drawing-room, smiling not at Captain Ripwood when he opened the door for her but over his shoulder at Maisie.

"Well, I must say I had a bit of a shock when you walked in just now, Maisie. You were the last person I expected to escort to Tussore," the Captain told her.

"I'm sure I was, Gerry. You can imagine what a shock it was for me when the Maharaja told us who was going to accompany us to Tussore."

"Listen, Maisie. I know it looked at the time as if I was treating you shabbily, but honestly it wouldn't have done for us to get married three years ago. You thought it was because I got tired of you, but you do yourself an injustice by thinking that. You do really. I realised I couldn't afford to get married. There was nothing personal in it. I had to be practical. And it's vitally important that I should make a good impression on Tussore. How well do you know him?"

"Angela and I only met him for the first time last week."

"Angela Winstanley. Where have I heard that name? Who is she?" Gerald Ripwood asked.

"She was the wife of the Manager of the British and Oriental Bank at Jumbulpore. But Angela has just divorced him."

"Yes, I remember now hearing about it," said Ripwood. "And does she know Tussore well?"

"I told you, Gerry, she and I only met him last week. But I think he's greatly attracted by her. The Maharaja is very keen on music and Angela plays the piano beautifully."

"I see," but before Gerald Ripwood could say any more a man with one of those long rectangular chins which are usually the mark of sententious egoism came into the room. This was the political journalist who was a guest of the Maharaja of Bangapatam and who was believed by the Indian Princes to have the ear of the Prime Minister.

"I'm Jeffrey Hearne," he announced. "I'm staying at Rosemount, and the Maharaja suggested that I should beg a lift in your car to Tussore. He's anxious for me to tell the Maharaja of Tussore what I told him last night about a talk I had with the Prime Minister just before I left London. You're Captain Ripwood, aren't you? I understand you're going to be military adviser at Tussore. I don't mind telling you in confidence that the P.M. is very pleased with the way the Princes are tackling the military situation. Things are beginning to look very sticky in Europe. What's the feeling in the Indian Army?"

"The feeling in the Indian Army is that the Government at home are not showing the slightest sign of tackling the military situation out here," Captain Ripwood replied.

"Ah, well, of course the P.M. has to consider the whole picture. As I said to Pedder-Wilson last night, this is not the moment to make Parliament uneasy about India. The P.M. has a terrific job on his shoulders and I don't think that's always quite appreciated. Winston has been making a lot of mischief lately, but he has a very small following in the House, and the country hasn't forgotten Gallipoli yet."

The Maharaja was by no means pleased by the arrival of Mr Jeffrey Hearne in Tussore. He had been looking forward to an afternoon of music and had no desire whatever to hear what the Prime Minister was thinking.

"I'm sorry, sir," his new military adviser said, "I didn't think you'd want Mr Hearne, but as he brought a message from Rosemount I didn't see how I could refuse to bring him along in the car."

"No, it's not your fault, Captain Ripwood," the Maharaja said. "I'll send him back to Pippla after tiffin. Mrs Winstanley and Miss Lambert can go back later."

"I used to know Miss Lambert, sir. It was quite a surprise when I arrived at Parker's."

"Had you met Mrs Winstanley before?" the Maharaja asked.

"No, I'd never met her. What an attractive woman she is, sir. Would you like me to go back with Mr Hearne? I can collect my bearer in Pippla with the rest of my baggage."

"Yes, that's a good idea."

So, soon after tiffin was over the new military adviser managed with great tact to get rid of Mr Hearne, who had been boring the Maharaja with long stories about the advice he had given to the Prime Minister on various occasions.

"I wonder you never went into Parliament yourself, Mr Hearne," the Maharaja remarked.

"That's what everybody asks," Mr Hearne said. "And I always reply, 'No, I'm more useful outside Parliament.' I have my ear to the ground and I'm in a position to know what is being said outside the lobbies. And that's what the P.M. wants. Well, you know what it is, Maharaja. There are so many Members who think about nothing but getting somewhere and they think they'll get somewhere quicker by agreeing with the P.M. I've no axe to grind. The P.M. knows that he'll get an absolutely straightforward and downright answer from me however disagreeable it may be. Besides, I get around. I've been in close touch lately with the Arabs. And, of course, India . . . well, I don't believe anybody at home is in such close touch with Indian opinion. Moreover, I've not made the mistake so many of these politicians made of supposing that Congress is the only thing that matters in India. That's where the Labour people and the Liberals always fall down. I'm a realist. 'Well, Hearne," the P.M. said to me just before I left England, 'I hear you're going out to India to have another look round. Come and see me as soon as you get back. I want to hear your impressions.' 'You can count on me, Prime Minister,' I said. 'I haven't let you down yet.' 'No,' he said, 'you never have, Hearne.' Now, I doubt if there's another political journalist to whom the P.M. would say that, and though I mention it myself, it's true, Maharaja. And it's lucky I came out to India just now because Pedder-Wilson, who by the way is also staying at Rosemount, will go back to England without a notion of what the situation really is. That fellow has a genius for getting hold of the wrong end of the stick. Fortunately I shall get back about the same time as he does, and if I think he's misleading the House I shan't hesitate to say so. I shall write an article in the *Sunday Trump* and Pedder-Wilson will have to look out."

"Have you talked at all about India to Ben Nevis?" the Maharaja asked.

"To that comic Highlander staying at Rosemount? No, I haven't much use for these effete aristocrats who come out here to sponge a free holiday at the expense of one ruling Prince or another on the strength of having been at school or at Oxford with him."

"I don't think you could call Ben Nevis effete, Mr Hearne," Angela interposed.

"Well, he seemed to have a high opinion of himself which I found rather exaggerated. He asked me if I'd ever seen an Abominable Snowman. Well, I mean to say, that's not the sort of thing you ask a political journalist in my position." Mr Jeffrey Hearne shook his head in compassion for such ignorance.

The military adviser came into the drawing-room where they were sitting after lunch and listening to Mr Hearne's tireless and fluent self-recommendation.

"The car is ready, Mr Hearne, when you are," he announced.

"Won't you have another brandy?" the Maharaja suggested.

"No, thanks very much. I make it a rule never to drink much in the middle of the day. People often ask me how I manage to get through all I do, and I tell them, 'By rationing myself very strictly all day.' When I was in Malaya last year . . ."

Angela looked round quickly at the Maharaja. She fancied that he had uttered a low groan.

"I was saying, Mrs Winstanley," the political journalist went on, with a hint of rebuke in his tone for her lack of attention, "that when I was in Malaya last year I used to be called One Drink Hearne at Raffles'. Of course, it was said in chaff, but, by George, I believe they were genuinely impressed by it all the same. Well, I must be getting back to Rosemount. I promised Bangapatam that I would tell him exactly what the P.M. said about the position of the Princes if the Government decided to intensify the process of devolution in India. The P.M. is keen to do this if it's practicable—*if* it's practicable, and I know Bangapatam is anxious to hear what the P.M.'s ideas are from somebody who has the P.M.'s ear."

"Then came they to a land where it was always afternoon," Angela Winstanley murmured.

When at last Mr Jeffrey Hearne had gone, the Maharaja exclaimed, "My god, what an appalling bore that fellow is! I hope Bangapatam will enjoy his afternoon."

"In that land where it is always P.M.," said Angela.

"Ah, I see what you meant now," the Maharaja laughed. "I wonder if Mr Hearne saw what you meant."

"I don't think so. I think he just thought I was another of these stupid women who don't understand politics."

"Has your friend Mr Tucker arrived in Pippla yet, Mrs Winstanley?"

"No, he won't be arriving till to-morrow evening," Angela replied.

"Perhaps you will kindly give him a note from my secretary inviting him to dinner on Christmas night?"

"I shall do so with pleasure, Maharaja Sahib."

"And now do you not think that we might charm away the memory of Mr Hearne with a little music? I am impatient to hear you play again."

They walked along to the music-room.

"Will you try the Steinway?" the host asked.

"I think the Bechstein is better suited to my playing," Angela told him.

She seated herself and played two ballades of Chopin.

"Have you the sonatas of Beethoven?" she asked. "If you have, I'll play you the Appassionata, but you must turn over for me."

"I shall turn over for you with very great pleasure," said the Maharaja.

And as he stood beside Angela to turn for her the pages of the Beethoven sonata, Maisie Lambert sitting back in a deep armchair was dreaming dreams of a delightful bungalow not far from the Palace at Tussore to which Gerry was coming back from a long day spent in personally assisting the Maharaja to administer his State. He would be a little tired, but his eyes would light up when he saw her and he would say, 'Nobody mixes such a good gimlet as you, Maisie darling. How I bless the day when you and I decided to get married!' And then their Goanese cook . . . or should they have a Mugg cook . . . Ethel Maxton might find her a treasure in Chittagong . . . well, anyway, he would be one of the best cooks in India and the dinner would be absolutely perfect. 'You certainly are a wonderful housekeeper, Maisie darling.' And after dinner they would sit and talk about what Gerry had been doing all day. 'I don't know what I should do without your husband, Mrs

Ripwood. He has made life twice as easy for me.' Or would the Maharaja call Gerry and her by their first names? After all, Angela would be calling her Maisie and he could hardly call Gerry Captain Ripwood. 'I don't know what I should do without Gerry, Maisie. He has made life twice as easy for me since he became my personal assistant.' What would Gerry be paid? Hardly less than 1500 a month with a house rent free and free fuel and probably nice presents from time to time. Gerry obviously hadn't disliked meeting her again suddenly like that. He had been a little embarrassed at first. But that was natural. And he *had* insisted that the reason why he had broken off their marriage was because he couldn't afford to get married. He had begged her to believe that it was not because he had got tired of her. 'Of course, it's a pity we couldn't get married three years ago, Maisie, but never mind, it's just as wonderful now. Come along, darling, let's go to bed.'

The Appassionata came to an end at that moment, and Maisie in the deep armchair blushed as if when the music stopped her thoughts were audible.

"That was marvellous," said the host. "I wonder if you will be so kind, Mrs Winstanley, as to play one of Beethoven's violin sonatas with me?"

"You play the violin, Maharaja Sahib," Angela exclaimed with evident pleasure.

"As a hopeless amateur. I won't attempt the Kreutzer."

"Nor would I," said Angela. "But I think I could read the Spring Sonata well enough at sight if you know that."

"That is the very one I was going to suggest," the Maharaja exclaimed.

And as Maisie Lambert in that deep armchair watched the duet she decided that the slim handsome Maharaja could not help asking Angela to be his Maharani, so completely in accord did the pair of them seem. But would Angela marry him if he asked her? She must do all she could to make life as a Maharani seem the most wonderful prospect in the world. And of course Angela would want to travel in Europe and meet famous musicians, which would mean that Gerry might be left in Tussore to keep an eye on everything while the Maharaja was away. Of course, she should *not* like to think that Gerry had married her because he thought it would help his position with the Maharaja. He would have to show her that he loved her for herself. Should she put him to the test? It was just like one of Maud Nutting's stories. But a novelist could always make things end happily, whatever misunderstandings and disappointments kept the reader anxious to know what was going to happen. It would be awful if she put Gerry to the test and he failed her. After all, he had failed her once because he thought he couldn't afford to get married. If he thought that he wasn't going to become a permanency in Tussore he might fail her again. Wouldn't it be better to wait and see if he really was still in love with her, and if she thought he was, wouldn't it be wiser to let him see how useful she could be to him in his career? But everything depended now on whether the Maharaja asked Angela to marry him and on whether Angela would accept him if he did. Considering how much surprised Gerry must have been this morning, he had been wonderfully self-possessed. And he was still the same fascinating Gerry he had always been. She loved the way he patted his moustache and that sidelong look in his eyes when he had assured her that the only reason he had broken off their marriage was because he couldn't afford it. And she could hardly have expected him to throw his arms round her the moment Angela went out of the room. The only man whose kisses had ever thrilled her . . . the only man. Yes, she loved him as much as that night when . . .

The Spring Sonata finished, and once again Maisie was blushing at her thoughts.

"Why, you play splendidly, Maharaja Sahib," Angela declared. "We must study . . ."

"Yes?" the Maharaja asked when she paused abruptly.

"I was going to say the Kreutzer Sonata, but when shall we have an opportunity?"

"Listen," he said in a low voice, "why don't you stay here? Miss Lambert can go back in the car and fetch all your things and at the same time bring her own. Please stay."

Angela looked into his dark eager eyes. Then she shook her head.

"No, it would be imprudent," she seemed to decide. "The decree nisi of my divorce will not be made absolute until early in the New Year."

"And then?" he pressed.

"Why, then I shall be back in Tallulaghabad and packing up to go to England."

"But you told me you loved India better than England."

"So I do, but I shouldn't love India living on alimony from my ex-husband."

"Perhaps Mr Tucker will ask you to marry him," said the Maharaja.

"Perhaps he will, Maharaja Sahib. I shouldn't be at all surprised," Angela declared, her eyes hard and bright.

"And will you accept his offer?"

"Isn't that a question I must answer when the offer is made, Maharaja Sahib? And now I think it's high time Miss Lambert and I were going back to Pippla."

"But you'll have some tea before you go?" he asked.

"Well, perhaps a very quick cup while the car is coming round."

"You're very anxious to leave Tussore," said the host, with a touch of petulance in his tone.

"On the contrary, Maharaja Sahib. It has been a completely delightful afternoon, and I will show my gratitude by playing you a polonaise on your Steinway."

"But that was magnificent," he exclaimed when the last chord had crashed and Angela came down from the dias upon which the great instrument stood. "May I say something to you, Mrs Winstanley?"

"Your Highness is in your own Palace," she murmured.

"You disturb me."

"Disturb you?"

"You disturb me very much."

"Then I must soothe you," she said and going to the Bechstein she played Chopin's Nocturne in E flat with an almost shameless *rubato*.

"You have passion," murmured the Maharaja, who had been watching her with glowing eyes as she played, her eyes fixed on his throughout.

"And now this quick cup of tea," she said lightly.

Ten minutes later Angela and Maisie were driving back to Pippla in a roseate sunset through which dark birds were flying home to roost.

"I think the Maharaja is in love with you, Angela," said her friend.

"Yes, but he hasn't yet given up hope of making me his mistress," Angela observed. "So I think it's just as well that John Tucker is coming to-morrow."

But John Tucker was already at Parker's Hotel when they arrived.

"Hullo, you two girls. I got away from the brewery a day sooner than I expected," he announced. "I've said we'll have dinner in my room. I want to hear all the Pippla gossip."

When they were sitting at the table in John Tucker's comfortable room Angela's resolve to secure her future as soon as possible was strengthened. It made such a difference to the enjoyment of life in an hotel like Parker's if you could always withdraw to the privacy of your own room. Otherwise you were merely one of what were collectively known as the residents whose only privilege was to sit afternoon and evening in that faded drawing-room there to talk quietly over their knitting or to play a rubber of contract or to crackle their way through *The Statesman* and *The Civil and Military Gazette*. And she should not be able even to do that often on the money she should have at her disposal.

"And so the Big Chief deserted you, eh, for the prodigal hospitality of Rosemount?" John Tucker chuckled.

"Yes, but we did dine with the Maharaja one evening," Maisie said.

"And I'll bet it was a good dinner. Old Bangapatam always does his guests well. He's a remarkable fellow. As wise as Solomon and absolutely loyal to the British Raj. I drink to his health."

John Tucker raised the glass of champagne.

"He and Ben Nevis were at school together and had hardly seen one another since," Angela said. "You know, John, I've come to like Ben Nevis so much."

"I haven't had a chance to get to know him. He came round to the Towers one evening and complimented me upon my whisky, but that's the extent of our acquaintance-ship. And what about young MacDonald?"

"He'll arrive on Christmas Eve. There's to be a children's party at the Club and Ben Nevis is to be Santa Claus."

"Yes, they roped me in for that one year," John Tucker grinned.

"And then on Christmas night we go to dine with Tussore," Angela went on. "You've had your invitation."

"Yes, it's the first time I've been asked. I suppose I have to thank you for that honour, Angela," John Tucker said, his grey eyes twinkling.

"Well, he obviously realised that Maisie and I wouldn't go without you," she said.

Soon after dinner was finished Maisie Lambert asked if she might be excused as she had a headache, and Angela was left alone with John Tucker.

"You don't mind if I smoke a cigar?" he asked.

"Good gracious, what superfluous politeness!" Angela laughed.

"Well, these Parker's sitting-rooms are not very large," he said.

"Not after your palatial accommodation at Scarborough Towers."

"Or at Tussore, eh?" he added. "How did you meet the Maharaja?"

"We met him at Rosemount, and then he asked us to the panther shoot he arranged for our two Highlanders."

"And then he asked you again to lunch to-day?"

"Yes, with a Mr Hearne, who is such a friend of the P.M., as he calls the Prime Minister."

"That self-important bore? Is he here again?" John Tucker exclaimed.

"He's staying at Rosemount."

"Well, old Bangapatam must think it's worth while to be bored by him. Ours is an extraordinary country. Why wandering Paul Prys like Jeffrey Hearne should be supposed capable of giving better advice about India than business-men on the spot is beyond me. However, that's the way we run our Empire, and it's the way we shall go on running it, I suppose, until there's no Empire left to run."

"I think poor Tussore found him pretty heavy going," Angela laughed. "He sent him back to Pippla as soon as he could after tiffin with his new military adviser."

"And you and Maisie stayed on?"

"He wanted me to play for him."

"Yes, I've heard he considers himself musical."

"And he is very musical," Angela said indignantly. "There's no question of considering. He plays the violin himself with a great deal of taste and genuine feeling."

"And you accompanied him?"

"We played a Beethoven sonata together."

"Quite a highbrow afternoon," said John Tucker. "And who is the new military adviser?"

"Well, that's quite a story. I told you that Maisie Lambert was once engaged to be married to Gerald Ripwood of Bulger's."

"Who once borrowed two hundred chips from me when they were stationed at Tallulaghabad. He was quite an agreeable rotter, but I think Maisie was well rid of him."

"Well, perhaps you'll get your two hundred chips back,

John, because Gerald Ripwood is now military adviser to
His Highness the Maharaja of Tussore."

"And how did Maisie take that?" he asked, his face
crinkled in a rosy smile.

"She says she is still in love with him."

"Oh dear, oh dear, you women. I can't think how I've
managed to remain a bachelor all those years. The age of
miracles isn't past in spite of what they say."

"You old fraud, you've never had the slightest difficulty
in remaining a bachelor," Angela told him. "You're just
not interested in women."

"Ah, no, Angela, I'm not going to stand for that. What
brought me up to Pippla for Christmas?"

"Your Daimler."

"You know, you ought to go and live in America on
wisecracks."

"Like a monkey, eh? We don't hear them in your room."

"Don't hear what?"

"The monkeys. In my bedroom upstairs I hear them
chasing one another over the corrugated iron roof every
time I wake in the night."

"Really? Look here, you must have a more comfortable
room. I'll see the manager to-morrow."

"Nonsense, John. I should miss my monkey revelry. They
help me to keep a sense of proportion. Besides, John, I
don't want to be just one more little woman whose
comfort you have made your concern. Perhaps I have
what is called a nasty mind, but I always suspect the
squire of dames."

"Suspect him of what?"

"I leave you to guess."

"When does this decree nisi of yours become absolute?"
he asked abruptly.

"I believe that January 12th is the exact date."

He flicked the ash of his cigar into the fire. "And then
you'll be free to marry again," he said thoughtfully.

"I know exactly what you're thinking, John," she told

him, "but if it requires such weighty consideration, don't do it."

"Don't do what?"

"What entirely against your better judgment you are thinking of doing," Angela said.

"You mean asking you to marry me?"

"Oh, John, John," she laughed, "what could have put such a ridiculous notion into your head? Thank you, I've already been married to one confirmed bachelor, and I'm still too young to repeat the experiment."

"I haven't asked you yet," John Tucker reminded her. "So you don't have to refuse me in advance."

"John, don't be a bear. You'll make me think you feel that I'm trying to lead you on. And that would spoil the jolly Christmas we're going to have."

"At Tussore."

"You seem to disapprove of Tussore."

"His reputation is not of the best, you know."

"In what way?"

"In the way of women."

"If you think there's the least likelihood of my becoming his mistress, set your mind at rest, John. I'll admit that sometimes I wonder about the future, but that kind of solution never presents itself. I am fundamentally respectable. Probably I shall go to England in the spring and settle down with my grandmother in Canterbury. Oh, I shall be the wife of a country parson yet."

"Doesn't young MacDonald want to marry you?"

"You know that. And don't tell me you haven't heard from your friend Colonel Rose-Ross that Hector's father was brought out here to save his son from a dangerous woman. What you may not have heard is that Hector's father would now be only too delighted if I would accept his son's hand."

"You might do worse, Angela."

"No doubt, but unfortunately I have a strong streak of honesty in me. And though I've flirted with Hector, and if you like to put it that way, amused myself with Hector, I wouldn't let him down by pretending that I loved him enough to marry him. Probably everybody is laughing at old Ben Nevis and thinking that he has allowed himself to be fooled by me, but in fact Ben Nevis is much cleverer than most of you are—and that goes for you, John—in that he recognised in me a fundamental decency. And I wouldn't let him down, either."

"Look here, Angela . . ." and then John Tucker stopped.

"You think the fence is too high?" she laughed with a touch of mockery in her laugh. "I'm going to bed, John. Don't look so careworn. We're going to have lots of fun over Christmas."

N

Chapter 16

SANTA CLAUS

DOWN in Tallulaghabad Duncan Robertson was saying to Hector MacDonald what a pity it was that John Tucker couldn't have waited until Christmas Eve so that they could have driven up with him and spared themselves the discomfort of their own car.

"I'm not particularly keen to be driven up to Pippla by Tucker," Hector commented with dignity.

"I only thought we shouldn't have had to start at dawn. Anyway, it's marvellous, buzzing off like this. It was awfully sporting of your father to get Bangapatam to ask the Colonel for leave for me as well as you."

"Do you know that Mrs Rose-Ross tried to persuade the Colonel to refuse us leave, Duncan?"

"No!"

"That woman is a menace," Hector declared. "When I went round this evening before dinner to say thank you to the Colonel, he hadn't come in and the khitmatgar showed me into her. 'So, you're going up to Pippla, I hear, for Christmas?' she started right off, and then she said, 'Well, I'll tell you quite frankly, Hector, that the Colonel granted leave to you and Duncan Robertson against my advice.' I was absolutely staggered for a moment."

"What did you say?" Duncan asked.

"I couldn't think of anything to say. At least I couldn't think of anything I could say, if you know what I mean. There was only one word I could think of, and I couldn't say that. And then she went on, 'I know you'll think it has nothing to do with me, Hector, but after all you must remember that I have to take the place of your mother out here, and do you think that your mother would be pleased to hear that you were going up to Pippla in the circumstances?' 'Under what circumstances, Mrs Rose-Ross?' I asked."

"That was a good come-back, Hector. What did she say to that?"

"It did stymie her for a moment, but only for a moment. 'Under the circumstances of your name being coupled with this Mrs Winstanley.' I think if she'd said 'that Mrs Winstanley' I should have let fly, but I said, 'If people choose to couple my name with Mrs Winstanley that is their business.'"

"That is not their business would have been a bit more pungent," the audience suggested.

"I wish you wouldn't interrupt, Duncan. How the deuce can I tell you what I said if you keep interrupting. Where was I? Oh, yes, 'that is their business,' I said, 'but it has nothing to do with me.'"

"I don't think that was very pungent."

"Damn it, Duncan, I'm not a walking pepperpot, I wasn't trying to be pungent. I was trying to keep cool, and it was devilish difficult because the back of my head was beginning to boil. 'Well', she went on, 'I've done my duty, but if you're determined to behave like a headstrong wilful boy your friends cannot help you.' Yes, she actually called me a headstrong wilful boy. I was staggered, Duncan. Why, an Admiral's wife wouldn't talk to a snotty like that. So I said icily . . ."

"If your head was boiling you can't have sounded very icy," Duncan put in.

"So I said icily," Hector repeated, "'I happen to be twenty-five, Mrs Rose-Ross, and I no longer consider myself a boy.' And then what do you think she did?"

"Tittered," Duncan Robertson guessed promptly.

"As a matter of fact that's exactly what she did do. But how on earth did you guess?" Hector asked in surprise. "Yes, she tittered. And then she said, 'Dear me, hark at Methuselah.' Well, I don't know what you think, Duncan. But I think for the wife of the commanding officer to call a subaltern of seven years' seniority Methuselah is a pretty bad show."

"What did you say then?" Duncan asked.

"Well, the Colonel came in at that moment, and so I couldn't do what I was going to do."

"What were you going to do?"

"I was going to laugh sarcastically."

"You could have done that whether the Colonel came in or not," Duncan pointed out.

"Don't be a clot, Duncan. What would the Colonel have thought if the moment he came into the room I'd said 'Ha-ha-ha'?"

"He'd probably have thought you were laughing at a joke made by the Mother of the Battalion. He'd have been quite gratified. I don't suppose he ever gets a chance to laugh at any of her jokes himself. However, all's well that ends well and on Christmas Eve you and I will be over the hills and far away until December 27th."

And by starting very early Hector and Duncan reached Rosemount before noon on Christmas Eve.

"I'm jolly glad you were able to get up to Pippla in time for tiffin, Hector," his father barked. "The Maharaja was worried we should be thirteen at table. So he asked the Machell girls, and if you and Duncan Robertson hadn't turned up we *should* have been thirteen at table."

"Are they the daughters of the Q.M.G.?"

"They're the daughters of Sir Oliver Machell. He's a General."

"That *is* the Q.M.G."

"Well, the General and Lady Machell have to go to Delhi and the girls are staying with Lady Pinfield," said the Chieftain. "It was rather amusing when Lady Pinfield wrote to the Maharaja, asking him to ask them to lunch because she would be busy with the blunderbust for this children's party. I read their name as Mac-Hell. I thought dear old Banjo was going to burst, he laughed so much."

"And who else is here, sir?"

"Well, I don't mind telling you between you and me that they're the dreariest collection of stick-in-the-muds I've met for years. There's a wallah with a face like an undercooked beefsteak and kidney pudding called Pedder-Wilson with a boring wife. He's an M.P. And then there's a financial wallah called Sir John Fussell with an equally boring wife. Then there's a fellow called Jeffrey Hearne who's a newspaper wallah with a chin leading up to his face like front-door steps, and a film wallah called Croker Bates, and it's a jolly good name for him. He's got a film star with him called Pearl Romaine."

"Is she here, sir?" Duncan Robertson asked, brightening. "She's rather a favourite of mine at the movies."

"She doesn't move around much here," the Chieftain said. "She just lolls about like a piece of damp blotting-paper with two blots for her eyes and a blot of red ink for her mouth. And finally there's an American called Knibbler . . . K-N-I-B—I thought her name was Kibbler at first . . ."

"It is Kibbler," Hugh Cameron put in wearily. "You'll be calling me Knilwhillie in a minute."

The Chieftain guffawed with delight.

"Jolly good name for you, Hugh. I must remember that when you start objecting to everything I do. 'Knilwhillie objecting again,' I shall say. Well, this Mrs Kibbler isn't so bad. She was tremendously interested in the Loch Ness Monster. And she's arranged for us to see the mango-trick, though of course she won't hear of its being called a trick. Then later this afternoon I'm going to be Santa Claus and give the kids their presents from the Christmas tree. And then to-morrow evening we all go to Tussore for the Maharaja's party, which is apparently rather a tremendous affair."

Hector asked his father if he was proposing to dress up as Santa Claus.

"Of course I'm going to dress up," his father replied indignantly. "That's why Miss Nutting asked me."

"Who's Miss Nutting, sir?"

"She's a novelist."

"Is that Maud Nutting, sir?" Duncan Robertson asked. "I've read one or two of her books."

"I'm reading one now as a matter of fact. It's called *Tooth and Claw*. It's very interesting, because Hugh Cameron's in it. And Sher Khan, his bearer. And she very nearly put his dog Bonzo in too."

"What an extraordinary thing for anybody to do," Duncan Robertson exclaimed. "Where did you meet her, sir?" he asked, turning to Kilwhillie.

"I never met Miss Nutting till I came to Pippla," Kilwhillie replied. "By coincidence my name was used in the book and also the name of my bearer."

"Well, you take it all as a simple coincidence, but Mrs Knibbler—Kibbler—believes there's far more in it than that. She thinks you projected yourself into Miss Nutting's . . . now, wait a moment what was it . . . oh, yes, it's Miss Nutting's astral consciousness. Astral has something to do with the stars, but I'm not quite clear what."

"Rubbish!" Kilwhillie snapped.

"You can't go about saying 'rubbish' like that, Hugh. You're as bad as one of those scientific wallahs who came trooping up to Inverness to investigate the Monster."

"I think it's time we went along to the smoking-room," said Kilwhillie. "Lunch will be ready any minute now."

When he and Duncan Robertson had gone on, Hector asked his father if he had seen anything of Angela Winstanley.

"I've seen a lot of her, my boy, but I'm afraid you're going to be disappointed. Yes, I made it quite clear to her that I should welcome her as a daughter-in-law, but she was adamant. I expect you'll want to hear from her own lips how adamantous she is and you'll get an opportunity to-morrow when you're dancing with her at Tussore. But I thought it was my duty to warn you that you hadn't a

chance, my dear boy, of changing her mind. I'm very disappointed about it myself, because I think she would have
made you a jolly good wife. But there you are. That's what
they call life, eh? You must keep a stiff upper lip and try
again, what? And I want you to get hold of some bells if
you can."

"Bells?" Hector exclaimed.

"Yes, I thought if you and Duncan drove me along to the
Club with a lot of bells it would thrill the children when they
heard those bells."

"Why?"

"Santa Claus, my dear boy, Santa Claus. I tried to get
dear old Hugh to be a reindeer, but he was in one of his
livery moods and he wouldn't do it. He was being Knilwhillie, what? I say, I'm awfully pleased with that joke.
But come along now, we mustn't keep them waiting for
tiffin."

The guests were already gathered in the smoking-room
when Ben Nevis and the Younger of Ben Nevis joined
them.

The Maharaja in his black silk jacket with the jewelled
buttons was in a shimmer of hospitality. These Christmas
days at Rosemount were dear to his heart. Enid and
Penelope Machell, the daughters of the Quartermaster-
General, were the only additions to the party. Penelope,
the younger, dark and petite, was not unlike what Angela
Winstanley must have been like at the age of nineteen, and
the cloud which his father's news had cast over Hector was
lightened by finding himself next to her at tiffin.

After coffee the party went out into the garden to see the
juggler whom Mrs Kibbler had secured to convert the
assembled guests to her own belief in the mysteries of yoga.
The preliminary snake-charming was disposed of by Jeffrey
Hearne as nothing at all because the poison-glands had
been removed and therefore anybody could do as much as
the charmer since there was no danger of being bitten.

"Well, if it's so easy as all that, Mr Hearne, why don't

you give us a demonstration yourself?" the Chieftain asked with a touch of aggressiveness in his tone.

"I don't happen to play that pipe-instrument," the Prime Minister's confidant sniffed.

"There you are," the Chieftain said. "So it's not so easy after all, is it?"

However, even the knowledgeable Mr Hearne had to admit that he was baffled by the mango-trick. As for Ben Nevis, he was almost as much excited by the growth of the mango-tree from a seed into a fruity bush in less than half an hour as he had been by his first sight of the Loch Ness Monster.

"Of course, it must be a trick," said Jeffrey Hearne. "But I'm bound to say I don't know how he managed to hide the different stages of the mango-tree's growth under that blanket and basket."

"I'm told that they do it by cutting themselves under the armpit with a razor and smearing the blood first on the seed and then on the twigs," Mrs Kibbler said. "That of course implies that they are capable of projecting from their own essential selves the necessary vegetative force."

"It's a pity we can't take this chap back with us, Donald," said Kilwhillie. "He might teach the Forestry Commission how to grow trees."

"Oh, jolly good, Hugh," the Chieftain guffawed. "I must remember that joke of yours. If I meet that brute who ringed all the birches in Glen Urquhart in order to plant his beastly asparagus and spinach instead, I'll say, 'What you want is a mango wallah from India to teach you your job? Do you have these Forestry wallahs in India, Banjo?"

"Oh, yes," the Maharaja replied, "the Department of Woods and Forests does a very big job."

"Well, I hope they do it better than our Forestry wallahs in the Highlands. If they can see a good bit of sheep-grazing within easy reach of a road they aren't happy till they've covered it with spinach and asparagus."

"Spinach and asparagus?" the Maharaja exclaimed.

"That's what these beastly spruces and whatnots look like when they're young. They won't be happy till they've made every brae look as if it was covered with green baize."

"I should like to take you up on that, Ben Nevis," said Pedder-Wilson. "Reafforestation is the policy of the Government because we must be able to rely on growing enough soft timber for pit-props."

"I'm not prepared to see the beauty of the Highlands spoilt in order to prop up a lot of pits," Ben Nevis declared heatedly.

"Oh, Mr MacDonald, you are displaying the most wonderful aura now," Mrs Kibbler exclaimed.

"Aura?"

"Yes, don't you remember what I was telling you about people's auras? I said that your aura was ultramarine. Well, I see now that it has rich purple shades in it. I had a friend in Philadelphia who was very successful in photographing auras. I would dearly like to have Mr Otis Snorker photograph your aura."

"I should have thought our friend Ben Nevis would have had a tartan aura," the Maharaja laughed.

"And what do you think of the mango-trick, Mr Bates?" the Chieftain asked.

"Please don't call it a trick," Mrs Kibbler begged. "How would you like it if I called the Loch Ness Monster a trick?"

"Yes, I see what you mean," Ben Nevis answered gravely.

"It's difficult for anybody who knows what can be done on the screen to accept what one has just seen as anything except a clever trick," said Mr Croker Bates. "I don't profess to know how it is done, but I am perfectly sure that it is merely a clever trick."

"Can you see Mr Bates's aura?" the Chieftain asked Mrs Kibbler.

"I certainly can," she replied.

"And what colour is it?"

"Well, it's a sort of muddy kind of greenish-grey," Mrs Kibbler declared.

The Maharaja felt that the atmosphere was becoming less imbued with the Christmas spirit than it ought to be, and after complimenting the juggler and the snake-charmer on the entertainment they had provided, he dismissed them with a generous tribute to their accomplishment.

"Well, I think I'll go and get ready for my Santa Claus blunderbust," Ben Nevis announced. "I wish Mr Fletcher, my chaplain at Glenbogle, were here. I should have got him to write me a short verse to say to the children when I appear from my sleigh."

"Why, I'll be delighted to write a little verse for you," Mrs Kibbler volunteered. "Just four lines, eh?"

"I say, that's jolly good of you, Mrs Kibbler," the Chieftain woofed.

An hour later Kilwhillie, who was writing letters, turned round to see who was coming into the room and gave a perceptible start at the rush of red surging through the door.

"Ha-ha, Hugh, you jumped. I saw you jump. You thought it was Mephistophanes coming for you, what?" the Chieftain barked triumphantly. "Dash this beard. Every time I open my mouth it gets full of this beard. Do you find your mouth gets full of your moustache sometimes?"

"Never," Kilwhillie replied tersely.

"All the same," Ben Nevis continued, "I rather like the effect of this beard. I remind myself of my dear old father. I may decide to grow a real beard."

"Don't start until you can shut yourself up alone somewhere for at least six weeks. It's most unpleasant for other people to watch the process."

"I might start when we go on board for the voyage home. Sailors often grow beards on board. I think salt must be a good manure for young beards."

Kilwhillie's face registered disgust. "What a revolting expression to use, Donald, even for the revolting process of growing a beard, particularly revolting to watch when one may be feeling seasick."

"Well, what I came in for, Hugh, was to ask you if you'd

hear me recite this poetry that Mrs Kibbler has kindly written for me. I said it over perfectly to myself without my beard, but I want to practise it now with my beard. Are you ready?"

"I'm sitting here waiting for you to begin. I can't be more ready than that."

"Here are the lines. Banjo's secretary kindly typed them out for me. Hector and young Duncan Robertson went along to call at Parker's and see if they could get hold of some bells. Well, are you ready?"

"I've told you I am perfectly ready," Kilwhillie answered.

"The only thing is that Mrs Kibbler made up six lines instead of four, but I hope I shall be able to remember them."

The Chieftain cleared his throat and began:

> "*I've just arrived from icy climes*
> *To welcome children large and small,*
> *And celebrate these festive times*
> *With Christmas gifts for large and small.*"

" 'One and all'," Kilwhillie corrected.

"Are you sure, Hugh?" Santa Claus asked.

Kilwhillie showed him the typescript.

"Ah, yes, I see where I went wrong. It's 'large and small' the first time. . . . As a matter of fact I suggested 'short and tall', but Mrs Kibbler thought some of the parents might be offended if they heard me calling their children short. Oh, and another thing. Mrs Kibbler wrote 'icy clime' at first so that she could say 'this festive time', but I said they might think it was 'icy climb' with a 'b' instead of an 'e' and think I was an Abominable Snowman from the Himalayas and panic. So Mrs Kibbler put 'icy climes' instead of 'icy clime'. I'd better start again."

"If you had come from the Himalayas you'd probably have had more than one climb," Kilwhillie pointed out. "So I don't see why you wanted to change 'climes'."

"Oh, for goodness sake, Hugh, don't make me change back to 'icy clime': I've had the most frightful job forgetting that and remembering 'icy climes'. Now, are you ready?"

"Yes, yes, yes," the prompter snapped.

> "*I've just arrived from icy climes*
> *To welcome children short and small . . .*"

"Large and small," the prompter corrected.

"I knew it was that," Santa Claus expostulated.

"Why didn't you say it, then?" the prompter asked.

"I can't say anything if you keep interrupting to tell me I'm saying it wrong," Santa Claus said so indignantly that he filled his mouth with hair and in trying to blow it out managed to unhook one side of his beard.

"You'll want to be careful that doesn't happen at the party," Kilwhillie warned his friend when Ben Nevis had got the hook of the beard back over his ear.

"Look here, Hugh, I came in to ask you to hear if I had this piece of poetry off by heart. I don't want you to give me a lecture about beards. Now, are you ready?"

The Chieftain cleared his throat again and declaimed:

> "*I've just arrived from icy climes*
> *To welcome children large and small,*
> *And celebrate these festive times*
> *With Christmas gifts for one and all.*"

He paused for a moment to look at Kilwhillie with triumph shining from his choleric blue eye, and then at the top of his voice he concluded:

> "*So, children, greet with loud applause*
> *Your benefactor, Santa Claus.*

"I thought 'benefactor' was rather a long word for children," said Ben Nevis, "and I suggested 'Your old friend Santa Claus', but Mrs Kibbler said 'your old friend Santa Claus' didn't scan. 'Scan what?' I asked. 'Just didn't scan,' she said. I don't know what she meant, but she seemed set on this long word 'benefactor', and as she'd gone to the trouble of writing this poetry for me I didn't like to argue with her. Phew! this beard makes me feel like a curry. Does your moustache ever make you feel like a curry, Hugh?"

"Why on earth should my moustache make me feel like a curry? It's not much larger than your own."

"No, it's not any larger in one way but it's at least six inches longer than mine at each end, and you keep dabbing at it as if you were perspiring underneath."

"I advise you to concentrate on this beard of yours instead of worrying about my moustache," Kilwhillie said testily.

"I'm not worrying about your moustache, Hugh. After all it isn't hooked on. Oh, that reminds me, have you tried smoking a hookah yet?"

"No, and I don't intend to."

"Well, you've got that hookah your grandfather brought back from India and I thought it would be jolly good some time when we're dining at Kilwhillie if we arrived and found you sitting cross-legged and smoking a hookah. Lindsay-Wolseley would think he was back with his beloved Piffers."

"This dressing up to perform as Santa Claus seems to have gone to your head, Donald. You'll be having amateur theatricals at Glenbogle if you aren't careful. You don't look unlike King Lear at this moment."

Further discussion about the future of Glenbogle entertainment was stopped by the return of Hector and Duncan, each carrying a handbell.

"These are all we could get hold of, sir," said Duncan, ringing his.

"But that doesn't sound like a sleigh-bell," the Chieftain protested. "That sounds more like the bell these muffin-wallahs go ringing about in that frightful place, London."

"They were the only bells we could find," Hector told his father.

"Did you ask Mrs Winstanley?"

"She wasn't in," Hector replied gloomily.

"I think if I ring these two bells outside the front window of the car, sir," Duncan Robertson suggested, "the effect will be quite good."

"Well, I hope they won't think I'm a fire-engine," said the Chieftain doubtfully. "I don't want to start a panic."

"If you take my advice," Kilwhillie said, "you'll give up those bells."

And in the end Kilwhillie's advice was heeded.

The Maharaja insisted that all his guests at Rosemount should attend the children's party at the Club. Pedder-Wilson, Croker Bates and Jeffrey Hearne tried to excuse themselves, but their host would not hear of it.

"No, no," he insisted, "this is a great occasion in Pippla. It's the only time that the use of the ballroom is granted by the Committee and we must show an appreciation of such public-spirited behaviour."

Miss Pearl Romaine seemed inclined to protest at being dragged off to look at a performance in which she was not the central figure, but Croker Bates, who did not want to offend his host and thereby lose the opportunity of getting the film of Marco Polo made in Bangapatam, shook his head at the recalcitrant star from behind the massive shape of the Maharaja, and Miss Romaine languidly agreed to go to the Club.

"Now, look here, Nosy," the host continued. "You should stay quietly here for half an hour because you don't want to arrive while the children are still having tea. I shall send back Miss Nutting for you at the right moment, and then she can come in and announce that Santa Claus has arrived."

"I say, Banjo, I think you ought to have been a filmer. Don't you think the Maharaja ought to have been a filmer, Mr Bates?"

The Rosemount guests went off to the Club in three of the Maharaja's cars, and Ben Nevis retired to his room to don his red gown and beard.

"Master look very good," said Balu Ram. "Sher Khan

want to make beard red and curl him, but I say no good."

"Make my beard red? What on earth was his idea in doing that?" the Chieftain barked.

Balu shrugged his shoulders.

"Muslim mens make beards red for show they are still good for womens."

"What an extraordinary idea! Why should red beards be better for women than any other colour?"

Balu smiled discreetly to show that he appreciated the feigned innocence of his master.

"Sher Khan give Cameron Sahib henna for put on moustache."

"What's henna?"

"Henna make red hairs," Balu explained.

"Good lord! What did Cameron Sahib do?"

"Cameron Sahib is being angry with Sher Khan."

"I'm not surprised. I'm glad you didn't let Sher Khan start painting my beard. It would have looked more like a hearthrug than ever. You can't read English, can you?"

Balu Ram smiled with a deprecating gesture at what he supposed was intended by his master to be a joke.

"If you had been able to read English, Balu, I should have got you to hear me recite this poetry I'm going to recite at the Club. Never mind, I'll say it over to myself once or twice."

This the anxious Santa Claus proceeded to do, while Balu Ram under the impression that his master was praying stood motionless with an expression of solemn respect.

"Yes, I think I've got it well into my head now," Santa Claus decided after the third repetition of Mrs Kibbler's poem. "Go and see if the car has come back for me, Balu."

Presently the little bearer returned with the news that Miss Sahib had arrived.

"Well, here I am, Miss Nutting," said Santa Claus. "And by Jove, do you know I'm feeling rather nervous. Is my beard shaking?"

"No, no, it's as steady as a rock," Miss Nutting assured him.

"I'm not used to this sort of thing. Of course, I make a speech every year at our Glenbogle Gathering, but that's different. I'm among my own people, if you know what I mean. However, if I get through this business this afternoon I may start a Christmas tree at Kenspeckle—that's our nearest village. Would you mind hearing me say this poetry that Mrs Kibbler wrote for me? I've got the words here somewhere if I can find them in this red contraption I'm wearing."

And once again Ben Nevis declaimed Mrs Kibbler's poem.

"Bravo, bravo," Miss Nutting cried. "Not a word wrong. What a nice woman Mrs Kibbler is! She told me some wonderful stories about her experiences with yoga. I asked her if she would let me use some of them in the book I'm writing now."

"Does it make your wrist ache much writing these books? I find if I write two or three letters my wrist always begins to ache. I asked MacGregor—that's our Doctor—if he thought it was a symptom of anything serious, but he thought it was only because I wrote so few letters."

"No, it doesn't make my wrist ache," Miss Nutting said. "But it sometimes makes my head ache."

"Ah, I'm not surprised," said the Chieftain sagely. "It gives me a headache to read a book. That's why I . . . hullo," the Chieftain broke off, "we're there! I'm shaking like a fly-rod."

"You'll be perfectly all right," Miss Nutting assured him. "I'll go in first and I shall say, 'Children, children, Santa Claus is here.'"

"I see, and then I'll come right in and start off with this poetry. I shall be all right when I've got that off my chest."

There is no need to describe the scene in the ballroom of the Club. The children replete with cake and here and there smeared with éclairs looked like children at any other

Christmas party. The large Christmas tree except that it was a deodar and not a spruce looked like any other Christmas tree. The grown-ups wore the same expression of slightly strained good-will that grown-ups always wear at Christmas parties. The only positively disagreeable-looking person present was the Club Steward, who was counting the spots on the floor.

Miss Nutting entered the ballroom clapping her hands, "Children, children," she cried, "I have great news for you. Santa Claus is here!"

The children had no chance to be prodded by their mothers and aunts and ayahs into welcoming cheers before Santa Claus himself came surging in looking like the scarlet mass at Waterloo answering Wellington's mythical order 'Up, Guards, and at 'em'! In a voice that roared louder than that of the most passionate stag in October in wild Glenbogle, Santa Claus greeted his little friends:

> *"I've just arrived from icy climes*
> *To welcome children large and small,*
> *And celebrate these festive times*
> *With Christmas gifts for one and all.*
> *So, children, greet with loud applause*
> *Your benefactor, Santa Claus."*

The children were so much awed by this tremendous voice that some of the sceptics who had been boasting that they knew who Santa Claus was were inclined to recant, wondering if after all they had been wrong and if in fact this *was* Santa Claus. Then some of the children in the front row began to cry loudly and had to be led into corners by their mothers and aunts and ayahs to be threatened or cajoled into silence.

It was Lady Pinfield who saved the situation by diverting the attention of the children from the Maharaja of Bangapatam who was leaning against the wall of the ballroom shaking with unquenchable laughter.

"Welcome, dear Santa Claus," she said, stepping forward

o

to greet him. "Will you be kind enough to hand the presents to the lucky recipients whose names I shall call out in turn?" With this Lady Pinfield opened her lorgnette and examined the list handed to her by Miss Nutting, who whispered something to her.

"Oh, yes, the girls will take their presents from the right-hand side of the tree, the boys from the left."

Fortunately for Santa Claus, who was not sure which side of the tree Lady Pinfield meant, the first little girl was old enough and self-confident enough to correct him when he was about to hand her a wooden railway-engine. He thought that he detected in her eye an eager glance in the direction of a box of chocolates, and grateful to her presence of mind over the railway-engine, he handed it to her, bellowing as he did so, 'Slahnjervaw'. Self-confident though she was, the little girl could not help recoiling in alarm, and some of the younger children burst into tears again.

"Tut-tut-tut, he shouldn't have said that," Kilwhillie muttered to Mrs Kibbler, by whom he was standing at the back of the room.

"Why not, Mr Cameron?"

"It's Gaelic. It's what you say in Gaelic when you drink somebody's health."

"Wonderful," Mrs Kibbler murmured. "That was his essential self projecting itself. And how beautifully he recited my little poem."

"I thought he said it much too loudly," Kilwhillie objected.

"No, no, I felt a cold blast go right through the room as he said 'icy climes'. I wished I'd made the poem longer."

"I'm very glad you didn't. I was agreeably surprised when he got those six lines right."

Santa Claus, unaware of Kilwhillie's disapproval, continued to roar 'Slahnjervaw' to each recipient of his gifts.

"I don't think the old man's doing too badly," Hector MacDonald said to Angela Winstanley, by whose side he had managed to find himself at last.

"He's doing wonderfully, Hector. I'm sure you didn't do as well as that, John, when *you* were Santa Claus."

"No, I didn't," John Tucker admitted. "Besides, they all knew who it was. But they *are* completely mystified by your dad, MacDonald."

This was true. Indeed, the mystification was so profound that Jack Harlowe, the ten-year-old son of the manager of Finlay's Bank and a leading sceptic about the reality of Santa Claus, found that his scepticism was causing him to lose face with his small companions.

"I bet you it isn't Santa Claus really," he challenged.

"Well, who is it?" they squeaked.

"I don't know who it is," said Jack Harlowe, "but I bet you it's a person dressed up as Santa Claus."

"I bet you won't pull his beard off, Jack Harlowe," another boy challenged.

"I won't do that," said Jack Harlowe, "because there was such a row when Claude Anstruther pulled off old Crumblebum's beard, but I'll stick a pin into him and if it really is Santa Claus he won't feel it."

"Why not?"

"How can anybody who isn't a person feel a pin, you ass?" Jack Harlowe demanded scornfully.

"Well, I bet you won't stick a pin in him," said the boy, confounded for the moment by logic.

"I bet you I will, George Hunter."

Thus it befell that when Santa Claus bent down to extract a doll from the lower branches of the deodar to present it to a wide-eyed little girl, he suddenly shot upright, bellowing, "Good lord, what was that?"

In the excitement created by that agonised bellow of Santa Claus, Jack Harlowe managed to rejoin his companions without being suspected as the assailant.

"There you are, George Hunter," he said, "I told you it was a person."

"Did you stick it in far?" asked the suitably impressed George Hunter.

"I stuck it in as far as it would go," he answered with simple pride.

Back at Rosemount, when they were talking over the success of the party, Bangapatam asked what had made Ben Nevis yell like that.

"I thought I'd been bitten by a snake," he said. "I never felt anything like it."

"It must have been a twinge of rheumatism," Kilwhillie suggested.

"A twinge of rheumatism doesn't feel as if somebody had stuck a large pin into you," Ben Nevis argued.

"Unfortunately I haven't my books with me," Mrs Kibbler said. "But I shall go into this mystery when I can get to them and I will write and let you know what it probably was."

"It is time we all had a good drink," the host decided.

"Well, I must say I think I deserve a dram," the Chieftain declared. "Lady Pinfield and Miss Nutting both told me I was the best Santa Claus they've ever had in Pippla."

Chapter 17

THE MAHARAJA'S CHRISTMAS PARTY

WHEN Maisie Lambert went into Angela Winstanley's room at Parker's Hotel on Christmas morning to greet her with seasonable wishes she found her sitting up in bed and looking at a bracelet of small rubies.

"Oh, Angela darling, what a lovely bracelet!" she exclaimed.

"John Tucker has just sent this up. I feel rather like one of the little girls who was handed a present by Ben Nevis yesterday afternoon. *A Merry Christmas from John,* she read from the accompanying card.

"He sent me this little brooch. Wasn't it sweet of him?" Maisie said, showing her friend a silver basket with a bouquet of tiny semi-precious stones. "I do think it's so pretty."

"John very very nearly asked me to marry him that night he arrived," Angela told her friend.

"What would you have said if he had?"

"I really don't know, Maisie. I'm in that state of mind when 'safety first' seems an extremely attractive proposition.

"Then why don't you accept Hector MacDonald?"

"I've already told you why not. If John had asked me you can be sure that he would have carefully considered the future from *his* point of view. John thinks first of John. He knows I would play the game with him, but what John is asking himself is whether the game is worth it."

"But I think the Maharaja . . ." Maisie began.

"We'll leave Tussore out of it," Angela interrupted curtly.

"I'm sorry, Angela. I thought . . ."

"Yes, yes," said Angela impatiently. "We're going to the

party to-night and we'll talk about it afterwards, not before-hand."

It was a quarter to eleven when after innumerable cham-pagne cocktails sixty guests sat down that Christmas night in the great dining-hall of white marble at the Palace of Tussore to dine with His Highness the Maharaja off gold plate. The host at the head of the long table of richly carved teak was wearing a black and gold brocaded jacket with yellow sapphire buttons; at the other end was the Maharaja of Bangapatam in a jacket of deep-blue watered silk with lozenge-shaped buttons of lapis lazuli. Precedence was respected so that both Princes sat between the four wives or widows of senior officials. The green facings and scarlet mess-jackets of the two Clanranald Highlanders and the vivid canary-yellow mess-jacket of Captain Ripwood of Bulger's Horse were colourfully reinforced by the tartan doublet of Ben Nevis and the plum-velvet doublet of Kilwhillie.

The Chieftain found himself next to Lady Pinfield, who was on the left of the host.

"We were so grateful to you for the truly impressive way in which you performed your arduous task yesterday," she told him. "Did you find out what was the cause of that sudden sharp spasm of pain?"

"My bearer says was it a pin."

"A pin?" she exclaimed.

"Yes, a pin, not a Pinfield, what?" Ben Nevis guffawed genially. "Yes, apparently he found this long pin in that red contraption I was wearing."

"How very careless of Maud Nutting's dirzee to leave a pin in the gown. Most careless."

"Yes, but what I can't make out is how this pin ran right into me. I didn't sit down on it. I was bending over in the opposite direction. Mrs Kibbler thinks it's something to do with this extraordinary business called yoga, but then she thinks everything has something to do with yoga. I mean to say, I was telling her about a dream I had that I was an elephant, and what do you think she said? She said 'But you were an elephant once, and in your dream you were remembering what you had done or left undone when you were an elephant.' 'The only thing I could leave undone when I was an elephant would be my trunk,' I said. I thought that was rather good, what? But Mrs Kibbler didn't seem to understand my joke. She told me she had been a seagull once."

"I don't think this sharp pain of yours has anything to do with yoga. I think it was probably an ant. Some of our Indian ants can nip one ferociously. Isn't that Mr Tucker I see over there?" Lady Pinfield went on to ask, raising her lorgnette. "Who is that rather good-looking young woman next to him?"

"That's Mrs Winstanley, whom you met at Rosemount."

"Ah, so it is. And I see that very nice and very pretty girl Penelope Machell is sitting next to your son. She and her sister are great friends of mine, and the General and his wife are a delightful couple. What a pity they've had to go to Delhi. The Commander-in-Chief is apt to be a little thoughtless when he wants something done urgently. One would have thought that it could have waited until after Christmas, whatever it was."

"This is a jolly good turkey, isn't it?" Ben Nevis said with relish. "I never tasted a better."

"Our host is very proud of his turkeys. They thrive wonderfully in Tussore. I hope you won't let yourself be prejudiced against the Maharaja," Lady Pinfield said in a low voice.

"Why should I be?"

"Well, people talk, you know. I've been putting my foot down on Pippla gossip for years, but it doesn't seem to be any use. Yes, people say that he is not to be trusted . . ." Lady Pinfield lowered her voice still more . . . "over women. Well, all I can say is that he has never conducted himself towards me other than as a perfect gentleman." She turned to her host. "I was just telling our friend, Maharaja Sahib, what wonderful turkeys you have."

"I never enjoyed a Christmas dinner more," Ben Nevis averred.

The host raised his glass of champagne.

"I drink your health."

"Slahnjervaw!" Ben Nevis barked. "That means great health in our language. You know, you'll have to come to Scotland, Maharaja. You really will. Several of my friends have jolly good lodges which they let with the shooting every year. And I must say I *should* like to return your hospitality in Glenbogle. You can always rely on keeut mealy fahltcher from me."

"I'm afraid I didn't quite follow that," said the host.

"I slip sometimes into our dear old Gaelic. That means 'A hundred thousand welcomes'."

"Very cordial indeed," observed the host with a smile.

The dinner went on as merrily as dinners do when every single guest has all the champagne to drink he can want.

Kilwhillie was almost volubly explaining to Mrs Pedder-Wilson the mistakes the Government were always making in their treatment of the Highlands. Mrs Pedder-Wilson was more than voluble in explaining to Kilwhillie why her husband had felt compelled to refuse to be Parliamentary Secretary to the Ministry of Gas and Electricity because he felt that in such a post his knowledge of Indian affairs would be wasted. Miss Pearl Romaine looked almost interested in what Duncan Robertson was saying to her and Duncan Robertson was rattling away to Miss Pearl Romaine like an auctioneer. Jeffrey Hearne was telling Miss Nutting that he had read a book of hers called *Beyond the Snows* with immense interest, and Miss Nutting, who had never written a book called *Beyond the Snows*, hoped under the encouragement of champagne that he had read another book of hers called *The Golden Horizon* and was confusing it with *Beyond the Snows*. Croker Bates was beginning to wonder whether a film about Yoga might not be an idea for a follow up of Marco Polo as he listened to Mrs Kibbler telling him of an extraordinary experience she had had in

Sikkim. Hector MacDonald was telling Miss Penelope Machell that since he had been stationed in India he had come to the conclusion the Indian Army was a better show than it was believed to be at home. Captain Gerald Ripwood was hoping that Miss Maisie Lambert realised how eagerly he was counting the minutes until the moment when he and she would be dancing their first dance together for three years.

"Our friend Tussore certainly knows how to give his guests a good dinner," John Tucker said to Angela. "Plum pudding with blue flames and holly complete!"

"I wonder if he's a good dancer," she said pensively.

"Probably. And I'm not too bad myself."

"You shall have the first waltz with me, John," she promised.

When the dessert was cleared the host rose.

"Ladies and gentlemen, will you please be upstanding and drink to the King-Emperor."

'The King-Emperor' everybody murmured with respect.

Cigars and cigarettes were lit, and the Maharaja of Bangapatam rose.

"Ladies and gentlemen, it is my privilege on these occasions to propose the health of our host His Highness the Maharaja of Tussore. I do not think there is much that I can say to add flavour to the marvellous repast with which he has regaled us, and indeed I fear to intrude upon the memory of that glorious plum pudding with my dull words. Nevertheless, I must beg your indulgence for a moment or two. Every year when I come to Tussore to join in this celebration I say to myself that this year it has been the most enjoyable we have had yet. But this year I do think that it has surpassed every other occasion.

"Perhaps I am influenced in thinking this because I have with me at Rosemount a friend of my boyhood—MacDonald of Ben Nevis, whom at Harrow we always knew as Nosy MacDonald. He has distinguished himself since he came to Pippla by one notable exploit as a shikari, and to that he has added a triumphant appearance as Santa Claus. With him to-night is his son Hector MacDonald of that famous regiment—the Duke of Clarence's Clanranald Highlanders, the Inverness-shire Greens, of so much Indian history. With him too is another Highland laird, Cameron of Kilwhillie, who outshot us all the other day and bagged one of the biggest panthers I remember. There are many other guests of his Highness whom I should like to mention to-night, but as there are sixty of us who have been dining with him this evening I think it might postpone the dancing a little too long.

"So without more ado I raise my glass to his Highness, our very much esteemed host, and I ask you, ladies and gentlemen, to be upstanding in joining with me to wish him the happy Christmas he has given to us and also a most happy New Year."

Amid loud applause the Maharaja of Tussore rose to reply:

"Your Highness, ladies and gentlemen, I thank you most warmly. I am sure that the pleasure I have as your host must exceed your pleasure as my guests. For very many years now the fortunes of my State have been closely linked with the mighty British Empire and I rejoice to serve His Majesty the King-Emperor with the utmost devotion. If the crisis should come, little Tussore will throw all its resources into the struggle. I thank you for your good wishes, and to all of you I wish a happy Christmas and a prosperous New Year."

Half an hour later the sound of music in the ballroom of the Palace proclaimed that dancing had begun.

Angela thought what a good dancer John Tucker was as they waltzed to the strains of *Gold and Silver*.

"You want to dance more often, John," she told him.

"It would help to get down my weight, eh?"

"You're not so heavy as all that. Just a bit plumpish."

It occurred to Angela that this was the epithet she had used about John Tucker to the Maharaja, and she looked round quickly to see if the Maharaja was anywhere in sight. She fancied for an instant that she saw his black and gold brocaded jacket behind a column of green marble ahead; but there was no sign of him when they reached it on the way round the ballroom.

"What *are* you going to do, Angela, when this divorce business of yours is wound up?"

"I told you, I shall go to England."

"You hadn't told me so definitely as that," John Tucker said.

And Angela remembered that it was the Maharaja she had told.

"You think you'll be happy in England?" John Tucker went on.

"Why not?"

"You belong to India," he urged.

"Yes, but unfortunately India doesn't belong to me. You know as well as I do what kind of a life I should have in India on alimony from Herbert Winstanley."

"You won't be so wonderfully well off in England."

"John, I find this solicitude just a little boring," she murmured, frowning.

They waltzed for awhile in silence.

"Young MacDonald is looking very sourly at me," John Tucker said at last. "You'll have to give him the next dance."

"So that everybody can feel comfortable, eh? No wonder you're so plump, John."

The waltz stopped and a minute or two later Hector came up to ask Angela if she would give him the next dance.

"Oh, Hector," she laughed when they had made a couple of turns of the ballroom, "you're *not* a very good dancer, are you?"

"I'm more used to foursomes and eightsomes and that sort of thing, you know."

"So I think we ought to sit it out," Angela decided.

Once again as she and Hector were waltzing toward the

great loggia that surrounded the ballroom she caught a glimpse of the Maharaja behind a column of green marble. Soon they found a palm-shaded corner from which the winter air excluded by glass was warmed by pipes. Angela sat back in a comfortable chair and lit a cigarette.

"Look here, Angela," Hector began, "I've told my father I want to marry you and he didn't raise the slightest objection. In fact, he was jolly pleased about it. But he's got it into his head somehow that you won't marry me."

"I'm afraid he's right, Hector."

"But what's the objection to me?" he asked.

"It isn't an objection exactly," she told him. "It's just that I don't love you in the way you have to love somebody you're going to marry. I'm awfully fond of you, Hector, but that isn't enough. If I let you think that I was fonder of you than I was, I'm sorry and you'll have to forgive me. I'm afraid I made use of you to give myself self-confidence at a difficult time."

"I don't understand quite what you mean about self-confidence, but I suppose a chap never can understand what a woman means. All the same, all this autumn you did seem to like my being around and all that sort of thing. And you said you couldn't be engaged because of this King's Proctor wallah. And now apparently that isn't the reason at all."

Exhausted by this long speech, Hector sank back into another chair and lit a cigarette.

"I'm afraid when I heard that Mrs Rose-Ross and all the other mem-sahibs were going into a huddle about you and me and your father was coming out to stop you making an imprudent marriage, that I took a certain amount of pleasure—malicious pleasure if you like—in giving them all a run for their money, but I did always refuse to be engaged to you, and you ought to have realised that meant I didn't intend to marry you. And, Hector, I would never let you make love to me."

"No, but you didn't tell me it was because I was a pain

in the neck. You let me suppose it was because you were frightened of upsetting your divorce."

"But, Hector, you never were a pain in the neck. I was— I still am—very fond of you. I like your simplicity."

"I suppose that means you think I'm a clot."

"No, I do not think you are a clot. I think you're a dear. And it's just because I do think you're such a dear that I wouldn't let you down by marrying you. And if I ever had been tempted to marry you, as soon as I got to know your father I should have resisted that temptation."

"Why, what's the matter with my father?" Hector asked in surprise.

"There's so little the matter with your father that I wouldn't for the world make him unhappy by making a mess of my second marriage. I know that he would welcome me as a daughter-in-law. He has been decent enough to tell me as much. And I wouldn't let him down for anything."

"But you *are* letting him down if he wants you to marry me and you won't do it."

Angela sighed.

"Dear Hector, you aren't very bright, are you?"

"Oh, I know you think I'm a clot," he growled despondently.

"Tell me about that pretty girl you were sitting next to at dinner?"

"Penelope Machell? Well, she's the younger daughter of the Q.M.G. Her sister Enid is here too."

"How old is she?"

"Oh, she's just a kid. She's not twenty yet."

"I was rather flattered when you seemed interested in her. She's awfully like what I was at her age."

Hector took the cigarette from his mouth and leant forward to gaze at Angela.

"Yes, I see what you mean," he admitted. "Extraordinary!"

"I think we ought to go back to the ballroom now,"

Angela said. "I want to tell your father myself that I have had to refuse to marry you, Hector."

"So that's that," he said, exhaling a gusty sigh.

"Yes, I'm afraid that's that, my dear. And in a very short time—oh, such a short time—you'll be wondering how you ever supposed you could possibly have married that woman."

"No, look here, Angela, I'd never call any woman 'that'. It's bad enough calling a woman 'this', but 'that' is frightful. Well, will you tell me one thing. Are you going to marry that chap Tucker?"

"Oh, Hector, just after what you've said about 'that' you're calling poor John Tucker 'that'. But if it gives you any satisfaction, I will tell you that John Tucker has not asked me to marry him."

"But if he does ask you?"

"Hector, please. I've answered your question. I'm not prepared to discuss the theory of a marriage between me and John Tucker. I hate 'isms'."

Hector rose from his chair.

"Yes, I see what you mean. Well, I'll be going back to Tallulaghabad the day after to-morrow. Shall I come and say good-bye to-morrow morning or shall I be a blot on the landscape at Parker's?"

Angela paused for a moment.

"I think I'd rather say good-bye now," she told him. "And, Hector, whatever you think about me in the future I shall always remember you with affection as somebody who behaved decently at a difficult time."

"That's almost exactly what my old house-master said to me when I left Harrow and went to Sandhurst." Hector exhaled another gusty sigh and they walked back along the loggia toward the ballroom.

On the way they came face to face with Kilwhillie, whose face had an expression of stern disapproval.

"Mr Cameron," said Angela, "aren't you going to ask me for a dance?"

"I'm afraid I don't dance nowadays, Mrs Winstanley," Kilwhillie replied with frigid discouragement.

"Then won't you sit it out with me? Hector, you'd better go on or you'll miss your next dance with Penelope Machell."

Hector had not supposed that he was engaged to dance the next dance with Penelope Machell, but Angela spoke so confidently that he at once hurried off to the ballroom.

"I want to tell you something, Mr Cameron, which I think will make it a really merry Christmas for you."

She led the way back to the palm-shaded corner where she had been sitting with Hector. When they were seated she began at once:

"Mr Cameron, I know you came out to India much against your will because Ben Nevis appealed to you to sacrifice your own convenience to the claims of friendship." Kilwhillie was about to speak, but Angela went on quickly. She had, indeed, already made this speech to Kilwhillie several times in fancy and she did not want to forget what she wanted to say in replying to interruptions. "I am sorry to have been the innocent cause of upsetting . . ." oh dear, she had had such a good phrase for what she was sorry for upsetting and now she could not remember what the phrase was ". . . well, it's this way, Mr Cameron," Angela said, surrendering her speech to oblivion. "I may have played with the idea of marrying Hector at first, but I very soon realised that it wouldn't do either for him or for me, and if all the mem-sahibs in Tallulaghabad hadn't been so poisonous I wouldn't have let gossip say that I was going to marry him. And then Ben Nevis was such an angel that I had to make it clear to Hector that it wasn't his father who was persuading me out of the marriage, because I didn't want Hector to think he had a grudge against his father. You know, don't you, that Ben Nevis told me he would be glad for me to marry Hector?"

"He went as far as that, did he?" Kilwhillie muttered, shaking his head.

"Yes, and he told Hector that he would welcome me as a daughter-in-law."

"He really can be most irresponsible for a man of his age," Kilwhillie declared warmly.

"And in spite of it I'm such a designing woman, Mr Cameron, that I have just told Hector I cannot marry him."

Kilwhillie gazed at her in astonishment.

"You have?"

"Firmly and finally. Aren't you relieved?"

"Well, I must confess I am glad to hear it," he admitted.

"Tell me, Mr Cameron, why did you regard the prospect of my marriage to Hector as such a disaster? Was it the divorce or was it something else?" she asked, her dark glowing eyes fixed upon him intently.

"Well, you see, we're very old-fashioned in the Highlands, and Hector will one day occupy an important position in Inverness-shire—a very important and influential position."

"Yes, but there was something more than divorce. Be frank with me, Mr Cameron."

Kilwhillie hesitated.

"You heard that I was Anglo-Indian?" she challenged.

"It was said, yes."

"And it is true to this extent," Angela went on. "My mother's mother was Anglo-Indian. And it may surprise you to hear that I am proud of it. More proud than of having a Cameron grandfather, which I suppose shocks you."

"May I without impertinence ask if you are going to marry Mr John Tucker?" Kilwhillie asked.

"Oh dear, oh dear, you are the second person to ask that question, sitting in that chair, this evening. And I must reply as I replied to Hector just now—Mr Tucker has not asked me to marry him. I suppose you too thought I had waited to unhook Hector until I was sure I had hooked Mr Tucker?"

Kilwhillie pulled hard at his moustache to extricate himself from the embarrassment into which he had been plunged by Mrs Winstanley's guessing what had prompted him to ask her that question.

"I beg your pardon," he said. "The question was extremely impertinent."

"Mr Cameron, can't you and I be friends? I'm sorry I've been such a nuisance to you, but that's over now, isn't it?"

From the ballroom came the strains of *The Merry Widow* waltz.

"I should very much like to ask you to dance with me," Kilwhillie said, "but I'm afraid my dancing days are over."

She knew that this was his way of telling her that the shadow of an unsuitable marriage no longer lay between them. She would have liked to offer him her hand, but she did not think that it would be kind to embarrass him any more.

"I expect you'd like to go back to the ballroom," he suggested.

It was at this moment that the Maharaja of Tussore came into that palm-shaded corner of the loggia. He threw a quick suspicious glance at his two guests.

"I hope I am not intruding upon a private conversation," he said. "I was going to ask Mrs Winstanley if she would give me the pleasure of this dance."

"I shall be honoured, your Highness," said Angela. "Mr Cameron was telling me about life in Scotland, and I'm sure he must be longing to go and reassure his friend Ben Nevis."

"Reassure?" the Maharaja echoed. "Reassure him of what?"

"That life in Scotland is in no danger of being disturbed," Angela answered, with a light laugh.

Captain Gerald Ripwood watched the Maharaja dancing with Angela Winstanley and decided to gamble. He saw that Maisie Lambert was without a partner and asked her to give him this waltz.

"I wondered when you were going to ask me to dance, Gerry," she said with a hint of reproach in her tone.

"I've been longing to ask you," he said squeezing her waist a little tighter. "But I saw that the Maharaja wanted me to get things going in the ballroom and I was being a sort of M.C. I think he appreciated what I was doing. Of course, a military adviser isn't expected to handle the social side, but frankly what I want to put into his mind is the need for a personal assistant and I thought I'd show him how useful I could be."

They waltzed for a minute in silence.

"I think he is awfully keen on your friend Angela Winstanley," Ripwood said. "I noticed him once or twice watching her when she was dancing with other people. And this is the first time he has danced to-night himself."

"I agree with you, Gerry. I do think he is very keen on Angela. But he needn't think he'll get her so easily. In fact, he won't get her at all unless he marries her."

"You're sure of that, eh?" Ripwood asked.

"Absolutely positive."

There was another minute's silence. Then he said suddenly:

"Would you risk it again, Maisie?"

"Would I risk what again?"

"Being engaged to me? I won't let you down a second time."

"Oh, Gerry, but . . . do you love me?"

"I've never loved anybody else," he assured her.

"Oh, Gerry," she meant to breathe in a celestial rapture, but owing to the fact that they were rounding the corner of the ballroom at that moment she had to gulp her ecstasy. "Have you thought much about me since our marriage was broken off?" she asked tremulously.

"Of course I've thought about you."

"But you never wrote to me."

"Well, there isn't very much to write about to a girl whom you were going to marry and didn't, or rather whom you wanted to marry and couldn't. But it's not too late, Maisie."

"It would never be too late if I were absolutely sure you loved me," she said gently.

"Why should I ask you to marry me unless I loved you?" Ripwood asked in the voice of a man much injured by unworthy suspicion.

"But if you couldn't afford to marry me three years ago, how can you afford to marry me now?" she pressed. "I couldn't bear to be a burden to you."

"You'll be a tremendous help to me if . . ." he paused.

"If what?"

"If I pull off this job as personal assistant to Tussore."

"But supposing you don't?"

"We shall always have one another," he said, with that sidelong look in his dark eyes that Maisie had always found irresistible.

"Gerry!" and this time as they were well in the straight of the ballroom floor she did not gulp.

"Hullo," Ripwood said, "the Maharaja and your friend Mrs Winstanley have vanished."

"Gerry, you sound very pleased that they've vanished," Maisie exclaimed in surprise.

"Not at all. I was wondering where you and I could vanish too for a while after this dance. I want to hold you in my arms again."

"You don't think it's just the champagne that makes you want to do that?" Maisie asked doubtfully.

"No, it's you, darling," he murmured, and on that reply he steered them both out of the dance and into the loggia. "We'll go along to my sitting-room," he said. "I'm going to mix you a brandy-Mac."

"Oh, Gerry," she gasped, "not until we're married."

While the military adviser of his Highness was taking Maisie Lambert to his sitting-room and wondering if his

gamble was a rash one, the Maharaja and Angela Winstanley were walking down a colonnade in the heart of the
Palace.

"How quiet it is here away from the music," Angela
murmured. "My heels sound like castanets on this marble
floor."

"I was going to ask you to come to the music-room and
play to me for a little while," the Maharaja said. "But then
I told myself if it was not to be it would be better that I
did not hear you play again."

"If what was not to be?" Angela asked.

"That we shall soon discover for ourselves."

"It all sounds very mysterious," she murmured.

"Not any more mysterious than the unknown always is,"
the Maharaja commented.

They walked on in silence. Angela felt that the sound of
her heart was audible above the click of her heels on the
marble floor. At the end of the colonnade they came to a
heavily carved door. The Maharaja took from the pocket
of his black and gold brocaded jacket a small key with which
he unlocked the great door. It swung open as easily as the
lid of a casket to reveal a small antechamber, the walls of
which were of black marble under a roof of richly carved
and gilded wood. Again the Maharaja put his hand into his
pocket and with another small key—it seemed to be a
golden key—he unlocked a door of fretted teak which led to
what Angela thought was the most luxuriously comfortable
room she had ever seen.

"The view from here is beautiful in the daytime," said
the Maharaja, as he pulled back the cloth of gold curtains
from the wide bow of the window to show the moonlight.
"And this is my desk where I think I am working hard
when I sit at it," he added with a smile. "But I find that
my work is mostly dreams."

Angela looked at the large photographs of two beautiful
Indian women in jewelled frames that stood upon the desk.

"They are both dead," the Maharaja said quietly.

She knew that they must be the Maharanis who had each given him sons and then departed. There was another large photograph of four boys, the eldest of whom might have been fourteen, the youngest not more than five.

"How handsome they all are," she murmured.

The Maharaja drew the curtains and pulled forward a chair for his guest.

"You will have a cigarette?" he asked, and when she had taken from the silver box a slim cigarette, half of which was a cardboard mouthpiece stamped with a gilded monogram, he lit it for her.

"Do you mind if I smoke a cigar?" he asked.

"No, of course not."

"You look startled," he laughed. "But I am not a Sikh, you know."

"I wasn't at all startled." She could hardly explain to the Maharaja that she had been remembering the way John Tucker had asked her if she minded the smoke of a cigar a few nights ago.

"I find that a cigar calms me when I am feeling rather excited," the Maharaja told her. "You are fond of rubies, I think? I noticed on that evening we first met at Rosemount that you were wearing that pendant ruby you are wearing now."

"I thought you were looking at my bracelet. That was a Christmas present from Mr Tucker."

It was as if a shadow passed across the Maharaja's face.

"I will ask you a question. What exactly is the position between you and Mr Tucker? You seemed very interested when you were dancing together."

"Really, Maharaja Sahib, I don't feel called upon to answer such a question," Angela answered coldly. "I think we'll go back to the ballroom."

"I regret that my question offends you. I did not ask it out of idle curiosity. It is important for me to know."

"I really cannot see how Mr Tucker or I can have the slightest importance for you."

"Nevertheless, I must ask that question again because the answer is of very great importance to me. Are you for instance going to marry him when your divorce is finished with or are you perhaps . . ." he hesitated.

"I am not going to marry Mr Tucker," she broke in. "Nor am I Mr Tucker's mistress. Nor has he asked me to be either his wife or his mistress. But since you are so curious about my matrimonial future you had better know that Mr MacDonald did ask me to marry him this very evening . . ."

"And you are going to marry him? But he is a mere boy," the Maharaja exclaimed.

"No, I am not going to marry Mr MacDonald. And now, please, let me go back to the ballroom," Angela said, rising from her chair.

The Maharaja went to his desk and took out from one of the drawers a platinum ring set with three very large rubies.

"Do you like this ring?" he asked.

"It is beautiful."

"It is for you."

"Maharaja Sahib, please don't be so foolish. How could I possibly accept from you a ring of such value?"

"Is it not a custom in England to give what you call an engagement-ring?" he asked, his eyes burning.

"Yes, when people are going to be married," she replied.

"That is why I want you to accept from me this ring."

"I don't understand," Angela said in bewilderment, for although she had played with the idea of being proposed to by the Maharaja, now that it seemed to be happening it was too much like the *Arabian Nights* for her to believe that it was true.

"I am asking you to marry me. I want for myself you and your music. Do not, please, make foolish hesitations. I believe that I attract you."

"Yes, you do attract me," Angela admitted. "You attract me very much."

He moved towards her.

"Wait, wait a moment," she cried. "You know so little

about me. I *must* be sincere with you. There are things you don't realise."

"You have had lovers, I suppose?" He shrugged his shoulders. "I do not think if you marry me that you will want lovers."

"No, I have never had a lover," Angela said earnestly. "And, if I did marry you, you can feel very very sure that I will never have lovers. But you must know other things."

She had sat down again in the deep armchair. The Maharaja's cigar had gone out: he threw it into a golden bowl.

"I am the divorced wife of a bank manager in Jumbulpore."

"That I know."

"My father was a clerk in Campbell, Campbell, Campbell and Co. of Calcutta. His name was Peppercorn."

"That I know."

"My mother was the daughter of another clerk. He was with Macintosh and Macintosh, jute merchants of Calcutta. His name was Cameron."

"That I know."

"But my grandmother was Anglo-Indian," Angela half-whispered.

"That I know also," said the Maharaja.

"Oh, you do?" Angela murmured limply. "You seem to have found out a lot about me."

"I found out all I wanted to know except what you have told me yourself to-night. You have been very honest with me and I shall never forget that. Do you think you will be happy with me?"

"I wouldn't promise to marry you unless I knew that I would be," Angela told him.

"No, I don't think you would. We shall travel a lot in Europe. You will not be in purdah," he laughed.

"And hear lots and lots of music," she sighed to herself.

"Of course. That is why we shall travel in Europe. And now may I put this ring upon your finger?"

Angela rose from her chair and offered him her slim ringless hand.

"It is not too loose?" he asked. "And not too tight?"

"It fits my finger perfectly," she said.

Then he put his arms round her.

"And now we must go back to the ballroom and tell the news," said the Maharaja.

Angela shook her head.

"The news can't be made public for nearly three weeks," she told him. "My divorce will not be final until January 12th."

"What does that matter?"

"It would matter a great deal if the decree nisi were revoked, because then I couldn't marry you. And I want to enjoy the luxury of going on as I am until then. Apparently so unsafe and so uncertain about the future, but knowing that I am safe and certain. It will be like waking up early and turning over to go to sleep again because one hasn't to get up. Do you understand?"

"It is putting rather a strain on my patience," the Maharaja said.

"I know, but it is the wise thing to do and I'm horribly wise really. There are only two people I should like to tell if I may."

"Mr Tucker?" he asked quickly.

Angela laughed.

"No, no, I shan't bother to tell him. But I *would* like to tell Maisie Lambert, because I happen to know that she's trying to make up her mind whether or not to marry your military adviser . . ."

"That's pretty quick work."

"Not really. She and Gerald Ripwood were engaged three years ago, and the marriage was broken off for financial reasons. I think that if she knew I was going to marry you she would feel that Gerald Ripwood might be in a more secure position."

"Well, he seems quite a competent chap. If he puts the

Tussore Lancers in good order I should be tempted to offer him a permanent position here. Is your friend still in love with him?"

"Oh, yes, she's still in love with him."

"Just now I can't help sympathising with people who are very much in love," said the Maharaja, drawing Angela close to him.

"Nor can I," she said, and she gave him her lips.

A clock struck two with a silvery note.

"I never kissed anybody like that before," Angela whispered in a daze of emotion. "I'm so glad I never have. And now could we go along to the music-room for a few minutes? I want to play you the E flat Nocturne. I've a feeling that banal piece of sentiment changed my whole life in an afternoon."

On the way to the music-room the Maharaja asked Angela who was the other person she wanted to tell about their engagement.

"Ben Nevis. But I shall tell him as a secret. I don't want Hector MacDonald to know till it is publicly announced. I shall give up my bungalow in Tallulaghabad and go perhaps to Calcutta for awhile."

"Why on earth to Calcutta?"

"To meditate in luxury on the difference between the past and the future. I shall ask Maisie Lambert to come with me."

When they reached the music-room Angela sat down at the Bechstein to play Chopin's E flat Nocturne.

"You played it differently to-night," the Maharaja told her.

"Not so well?"

"Just as well, but differently."

"I was playing with an emotion that was so utterly sincere that I was unconscious of sentiment and needed no *rubato*," Angela declared. "While I'm away I'm going to practise the Kreutzer Sonata and you must do the same, so that we can play it together when we meet again."

When they came back to the ballroom Hector was dancing again with Penelope Machell, and Angela walked over to where Ben Nevis was talking to Kilwhillie.

"I asked Mr Cameron to sit out a dance with me. Won't you sit out a dance with me, Ben Nevis? I want to tell you something."

"About poor Hector, eh?" the Chieftain woofed.

"And something else too," she said.

They went along the loggia to that palm-shaded corner where she had sat with Hector and Kilwhillie earlier.

"Well, it's been a wonderful evening," said the Chieftain, "except of course for poor old Hector. Extraordinary thing, you know. People accuse me of having no tact. But Hugh Cameron, who's one of the worst people for accusing me of having no tact, actually went up to Hector just now and patted him on the back. Hector turned round as if he'd been bitten. He's never seen Hugh Cameron pat anybody on the back in all his life."

"Wasn't Hugh Cameron trying to be sympathetic?" Angela suggested.

"Not a bit. He said, 'Bravo, Hector, I like that gal you've been dancing with all the evening very much.' It's the last thing he should have said to poor old Hector when he knew you'd just refused him. But he spoke very highly of you. I'm bound to say that for him. 'Yes,' he said, 'I must admit I misjudged Mrs Winstanley. You were right and I was wrong.' 'Well, I always am right,' I said. 'I'm glad you're beginning to realise it at last.'"

"And now I must tell you my secret, dear, dear Ben Nevis. But you must promise me to keep it a secret."

"I find secrets fearfully indigestible, if you know what I mean."

"Well, if you'd rather I didn't tell you I won't," Angela said.

"Is it a permanent secret?" he asked anxiously.

"No, it's only for about three weeks."

"I shall be homeward bound then."

"I'll send you a wireless message to say 'Secret no longer' and then you can tell anybody you like."

"That'll be a great relief," the Chieftain said. "I mean to say, people have nothing else to do on board ship except tell secrets. I was told hundreds of secrets on the *Taj Mahal.* But everybody else seemed to know them so it didn't really worry me. Go ahead, Angela, I'll manage somehow to keep your secret for three weeks."

"The Maharaja of Tussore has proposed to me and I have promised to marry him."

"Good lord!" the Chieftain gasped. "Well, that *is* a secret. I suppose I *shall* be able to keep it, but it'll be like having colic. I shall have to leave Rosemount pretty quickly. I'll find it agony being alone with dear old Banjo."

"Oh, I think the Maharaja of Tussore is going to tell the Maharaja of Bangapatam."

"Well, try and get him to tell Banjo to-night before I drive back with him. Otherwise I might burst in the car or something."

"I will."

"What did you say when Tussore asked you to marry him?"

"I said 'Yes'."

"Well, I think he's a very nice chap, though I was surprised when he missed that panther. I hope he won't shut you up in one of these—what is the word? It's like banana, but I know it isn't banana."

"Zenana you mean. No, I'm not going to be in purdah. The Maharaja is very Western in his outlook."

"Oh, I know. I think he was at Eton. Anyway, I know he was at Sandhurst."

"And we both love music," Angela said.

"Ah, I remember now. He said 'hush' to me when you were playing the piano. I thought it was extraordinary at the time, but of course I didn't know then that he was hoping to marry you."

"But, dear Ben Nevis, please don't think I knew that

then. I was taken completely by surprise to-night. And you *will* keep my secret, won't you? It would be disastrous if anything happened to prevent my divorce from becoming absolute. Moreover, I don't want Mrs Rose-Ross and the rest of the mem-sahibs to say that I only let go of Hector because I had managed to catch a Maharaja."

"Yes, I see I've somehow or other *got* to keep this secret, but do persuade your fiancé to tell Banjo. I should find it a great relief to be able to talk about it to him."

"Wish me happiness, dear Ben Nevis," Angela said. "Look, here is my engagement-ring."

"Good lord, what whoppers! Like three glasses of port. Slahnjervaw, Angela, and I hope you'll be a very happy— now wait, I know this word. A very happy Maharani."

It was five o'clock in the morning when the Christmas party at Tussore broke up.

"You're very quiet, Angela," said John Tucker when he and she and Maisie were driving back to Pippla. "And why wouldn't you dance with me again?"

"I was hearing Maisie's news," said Angela. "Go on, Maisie, you'd better tell John now."

"Gerald Ripwood has asked me to marry him," she said.

"I hope he won't think better of it a second time," said John Tucker. "Well, I suppose you think you know what you're doing, Maisie. And evidently you are a good influence. Now I know why he suddenly paid me back those 200 chips he owed me."

"Oh, yes, I think they're going to be very happy," Angela said.

Then she relapsed into silence again.

When they got back to the hotel John Tucker asked if they would come up to his sitting-room."

"I must go to bed," said Maisie quickly.

"And so must I," said Angela. "It's late, John. Too late," she added, looking at him.

When the girls went upstairs Angela told Maisie to come into her room for a moment.

"You're happy about Gerald Ripwood, aren't you?" she asked.

"Yes, I am. I really am. I can't believe that he'll let me down again."

"No, I can't either," said Angela. "You see, I'm going to marry the Maharaja of Tussore."

"Angela!" Maisie cried. "How too utterly marvellous! Oh, Angela, how glorious!"

"Not quite so loud, Maisie. You'll wake the monkeys. And until my divorce is through this is a secret."

"But can't I tell Gerry? He'll be so thrilled."

Angela hesitated for a moment. If she and Maisie went back to Tallulaghabad the day after to-morrow with John Tucker and faded to all appearance from the scene, might not Gerald Ripwood repent of his proposal and get out of it. It would serve him right, but . . . she looked at Maisie.

"Yes, you can tell Gerry," she said. "He'll know how to be discreet. We're going to tea at Tussore to-morrow. You can tell him then."

"Will you tell John Tucker?" Maisie asked.

"I certainly shan't tell John Tucker. I mean what I say about this being a secret."

"Yes, of course, Angela darling."

"Here is my engagement-ring." She showed it to Maisie.

"Oh, Angela," Maisie breathed in a voice of awe. "I never saw such rubies. They're too marvellous. They make John Tucker's bracelet look like . . ."

"Like a present from a confirmed bachelor," said Angela. "John had his chance, Maisie. I might have said 'Yes' to him that night he arrived. Thank goodness, he shied away at the last moment, because I shall be oh, how much happier as the Maharani of Tussore than as Mrs John Tucker of Scarborough Towers, Tallulaghabad. Go to bed, Maisie."

"Oh, Angela darling, I think I'm almost too happy to go to sleep," Maisie declared in a rapture.

Chapter 18

WESTWARD HO!

"SO you're going to tea with Tussore," John Tucker commented next day when Angela excused herself and Maisie from accompanying him on a drive after lunch. "You seem to have made a great impression in that direction."

"He wanted me to play to him once more before we go back to Tallulaghabad to-morrow. And I want Maisie to have a chance to see Gerry Ripwood again. We shall be back for dinner."

When Captain Ripwood of Bulger's Horse heard from Maisie Lambert the news about Angela Winstanley and the Maharaja he nearly danced round the room in exultation. What a gamble it had been, and the gamble had come off! No more selling of doubtful polo ponies to newly arrived subalterns from England. No more wondering whether that Majority would come in time to save him from a crash. If ever anybody made himself indispensable he would make himself indispensable to His Highness the Maharaja of Tussore (with a salute of 9 guns). The bright blue tunics of the Tussore Lancers should be the model of State troops all through India.

"We'll get married next month, Maisie darling," he declared.

"We might have to wait till February," she said. "I think Angela will want me to be with her until she is married."

"Surely, darling. We must fit in our plans with her plans. That's essential," he affirmed solemnly.

In the music-room Angela and the Maharaja had just played again Beethoven's Spring Sonata.

"And now I'm going to play you Beethoven's beautiful sonata *Les Adieux*."

"It is a favourite of mine too. I have Schnabel's recording of it."

"I shan't play it quite as well as Schnabel," Angela laughed. "But whatever my fingers do, my heart will be playing it."

And she did play it very well.

"*L'absence et la retour*," she murmured. "I shall play it again when I return. And now we must be going back to Pippla."

"But I thought you'd stay on to dinner," the Maharaja protested.

"No, please don't insist on that. You know how much I should love to stay, but I do want to be prudent. There's so much, oh, so much, so much of my future happiness involved. I feel as if I were holding a priceless piece of china in my hands which I might drop and smash. I'll telegraph to you from Calcutta the moment the decree is made absolute and you will say when and where we are to meet. Adieu till then."

He held her in his arms for a last long embrace, and within a few minutes Angela and Maisie were in one of the Maharaja's cars driving back to Pippla.

At Rosemount the Maharaja of Bangapatam had just been defeated in three consecutive sets at table-tennis. The fair stocky muscular Czech professional looked respectfully complacent.

"Your Highness wishes for another set?"

"No, I was up too late last night," the Maharaja replied with a touch of fretfulness. He turned to Ben Nevis, who had been watching the play in a state of wonderment at what some people would do under the impression that they were amusing themselves.

"I shall soon find that the only exercise I can take is tiddly-winks," the Maharaja grumbled.

"You and I are getting older, Banjo. The only consolation is that everybody else is getting older too," said Ben Nevis. "Even quite young people," he added, with the gravity of a sage.

"Come and have a dram of Stag's Breath, Nosy."

"But you don't like whisky."

"No, I'm afraid I don't. I used to try and try when I was up at Christ Church, but it was no use. I couldn't get used to the taste of it at all."

"Terrible," the Chieftain commented in sombre tones. "I mean to say, here are you in your splendid position and yet you've never been able to learn how to appreciate whisky. It shows one can't have everything in this world."

Presently they were sitting in the Maharaja's own sanctum, where Ben Nevis took two powerful drams of Stag's Breath while his host sipped a gimlet in which there was not enough gin to be noticeable.

"I've been wondering when you were going to talk to me about this secret, Banjo," said the Chieftain at last.

"What secret?"

"Why, about Tussore's getting married to Angela Winstanley."

"What?" the Maharaja exclaimed in amazement. "This is the first I've heard of it."

"Good lord," his guest gasped. "Didn't Tussore tell you?"

"He didn't say a word to me about it."

"Well, I know he is going to tell you because Angela Winstanley said she was going to ask him so that I wouldn't find the secret too much of a responsibility. So when he does tell you, for goodness' sake try to pretend you know nothing about it. Yes, they're going to get married as soon as this decree nisi business is settled."

"You know, my dear old friend," said the Maharaja, "I believe Tussore has chosen a good wife for himself."

"Oh, I liked the little woman the moment I met her. I realised Rose-Ross and his wife had got it all wrong and that she had no intention of marrying my boy Hector. I'd have been very glad if she had accepted him. But do remember, Banjo, that this is a secret. I'm the only person Angela has told. Thank goodness, it's not a permanent secret."

"Don't be afraid, Nosy. I shall be very discreet."

"She showed me her engagement-ring. Good lord, I never saw such rubies. They looked like three glasses of port."

"Ah, she likes rubies, eh? I'm glad to know that," said the Maharaja of Bangapatam.

"Well, our happy party's coming to an end, Banjo. I can't tell you how much I've enjoyed myself at Rosemount."

"You'd better come down to Bangapatam and help Croker Bates with his film, Nosy. And I'll give you a chance to shoot a tiger instead of a pig."

"Yes, I should have liked to shoot a tiger," said the Chieftain. "And I'm told the fat is good for rheumatism. I'd like to, but Hugh Cameron and I must be getting back home. I've a letter from Finchampton, who wants us to stay with him in Delhi on our way to Bombay. And we must put in two or three nights with the Rose-Rosses. So I'm afraid we'll have to be off in a couple of days."

"I shall miss you, Nosy. You make me feel much younger than table-tennis does."

"And look here, Banjo. You must come to Glenbogle, you really must. There's a stag I should like you to have a try for. I had an American staying with me this summer, but he couldn't get near it."

"I'm planning to come to England the year after next and, if I do, you shall see me at Glenbogle, Nosy."

"You won't get any ping-pong."

"No, but you shall show me the Loch Ness Monster, Nosy."

After dinner that evening at Parker's Hotel, when Maisie said she must go upstairs to pack for the early start next morning and when Angela was going too, John Tucker asked if he was to be completely deserted for the evening as well as the afternoon.

"If you put it that way, John, I feel I must stay for a little while," Angela said.

"Light up your cigar," she told him with a smile after Maisie had gone upstairs.

"I've been thinking over things quite a lot this afternoon," he began. Then he took two or three reflective puffs.

"And what was the result of all this cogitation?" Angela enquired.

"I'm going to ask you to marry me," he replied.

"I wonder why you thought about it for so long beforehand," Angela said.

"It's pretty obvious, isn't it? I've been asking myself whether I should be wise to surrender the amenities of a bachelor existence for the continuous company of a woman twenty-five years younger than myself."

"That is what Herbert Winstanley asked himself," Angela remarked. "And I'm afraid he regretted that he answered the question in the way he did. Poor Herbert," she suddenly sighed.

"You're surely not regretting that your marriage with him was broken up?"

"No, no. But I think of him opening the bank again to-morrow at Jumbulpore and . . . oh, I just feel sorry about him. I forget now all the irritations of our life together and remember only that when I asked for my freedom he behaved so decently. No, John, I'm not going to marry you."

"You won't?" he exclaimed, obviously much surprised.

She shook her head.

"I wonder why you look so incredulous, John?"

"Somehow I thought the other evening that you were looking for security and I thought that Scarborough Towers must have seemed very secure."

"Yes, all this autumn I have thought how secure it seemed. But I've sometimes thought that about a prison, John. And now be honest. You're relieved, aren't you, that I've said I won't marry you?"

"No, I'm extremely disappointed," he asserted.

"That's only pique. It seemed to you such a tremendous

gesture to ask me to marry you that you can't help being a little piqued by my refusal."

"Perhaps you're right," he admitted. "But why won't you marry me?"

"I've already made the mistake once of marrying a man with whom I was not in love because it offered an easy way out of difficulties. I'm not going to repeat that mistake. You've been kind to me . . . indeed, you've been very kind. So don't hold it against me that I refused to marry you, John. After all, you were a long time making up your mind to ask me. Indeed, I think you only made up your mind to-night because you were annoyed by Maisie and me spending the afternoon at Tussore. Don't look so glum, John. To-morrow morning we go back to Tallulaghabad and I shall be leaving the place at once."

"Leave Tallulaghabad?" he exclaimed. "Where are you going? You've not been mad enough to let Tussore . . ." he stopped.

"To let Tussore make me his mistress? No, John, I've not been so foolish as that. And now don't let's sit here until we get cross with one another. I'm grateful to you for quite a lot. What time do we start?"

"I'd like to get away by nine o'clock if you and Maisie can manage it."

"We shall be ready. Good-night, John."

Hector MacDonald and Duncan Robertson left Pippla an hour before John Tucker's Daimler was on the road, but it passed them before they reached the plains.

"You know, Duncan, when Angela turned me down the night before last," Hector said, "I asked her if she was going to marry John Tucker."

"What did she say?"

"She said he hadn't asked her. But you mark my words, Duncan, he will ask her and I'll bet you twenty chips that she'll accept him."

"What odds?" Duncan enquired.

"I'll lay you twenty chips to ten."

"Not enough. I won't take less than four to one."

"All right. Twenty chips to five," Hector agreed.

"What'll you bet me she doesn't marry Tussore?"

"Marry Tussore?" Hector exclaimed. "Don't be an ass."

"What'll you lay against it?" Duncan pressed.

"I'll lay a hundred chips to one," Hector offered.

"Done," said his fellow subaltern.

"What extraordinary ideas you do have sometimes," Hector said. "I shall feel rather an ass when Angela marries Tucker. I mean to say, after all this fuss about my marrying Angela I shall look a pretty good clot when she marries Tucker, though I expect that would annoy Mother Rose-Ross, because he's rolling in money."

They drove on in silence for a while. Then Hector remarked:

"I was talking to that fellow Ripwood of Bulger's on Christmas night. I thought he'd improved since they were lying next us at Bundlepore."

"Did he try to sell you a pony?" Duncan asked.

"No, he didn't talk about polo. I was asking him what chance there was of seeing some active service on the Frontier. I thought if there was any chance of it I'd try to get attached to one of those Piffer battalions. You know what it is, Duncan, when you've taken a knock over a love-affair like me you feel you want to go and do something. Life in a cantonment looks pretty grim. If I'd married Angela I should have chucked the Army."

Hector spoke little for the rest of the way to Tallulaghabad.

Ben Nevis and Kilwhillie arrived at the Rose-Ross bungalow two days later. Their host at Pippla had insisted upon sending them back to Tallulaghabad in one of his cars. He himself was staying at Rosemount until the New Year, when he was to return to his own State. His other guests stayed on too. The Chieftain had parted from all of them except Mrs Kibbler without regret.

"Now if when you get back to your Highland fastness,

you feel inclined to take up yoga," she had said to him, "do write to me and I shall be only too happy to send you one or two books that are essential to a novice."

"If I take up this yoga business you'll jolly well have to come and teach us all about it at Glenbogle," the Chieftain had assured her warmly.

"Well, who knows?" Mrs Kibbler said. "Don't forget I was a seagull when you were an elephant. Your last self brought you to India. My last self may take me to Scotland."

On this cordial note Ben Nevis and Mrs Kibbler had parted.

Mrs Rose-Ross was not long in managing to get the Chieftain to herself in order to congratulate him.

"*What* a relief it must be to you," she gushed, her faded forget-me-not blue eyes fading almost completely under the stress of sympathetic emotion. "Of course, obviously that young woman has set her cap at this Mr Tucker, and from what I hear she is likely to land him."

Angela's secret was already indigestible enough, even although he had been able to talk about it to his friend Banjo. This unexpected surmise by Mrs Rose-Ross produced acute heartburn.

"I've no reason to suppose that Mrs Winstanley is going to marry Mr Tucker," he said with dignity. "And let me tell you, Mrs Rose-Ross, I should have been very glad if she had seen her way to accepting Hector."

He hoped that this avowal would act like soda-mint and prevent his scoring off Mrs Rose-Ross by telling her whom Angela *was* going to marry. However, it checked Mrs Rose-Ross only for a moment.

"Ah well, that's being kind to Hector. The poor boy must be feeling very mortified to have made his father take this long journey merely to hear that his son has been thrown over for somebody else—and a brewer."

By now heartburn had been succeeded by sharp abdominal cramps caused by the agony of having to keep his secret, and what might have happened if Hector himself had not appeared on the scene and stopped Mrs Rose-Ross's tongue Ben Nevis was never to know.

Yet Hector's arrival was to produce another severe attack of indigestion. Talking to his father in a corner of the room he announced:

"I've just betted Duncan twenty chips to five that Angela will marry John Tucker. And what do you think that ass Duncan said? He said he wouldn't be surprised if Angela married Tussore. Ha-ha-ha! Did I laugh? I should say I did. 'Well, Duncan,' I said, 'I'll lay you a hundred chips to one that she'll never marry Tussore! Of all the fat-headed ideas I ever heard . . .'"

"Hector," his father breathed heavily, "Go and get me another of those idiotic gimlets, will you?"

The sooner he and Hugh Cameron left for Delhi the better. There at any rate he wouldn't be tempted by the Viceroy or Lady Finchampton into telling his secret.

"You're quite all right, sir, are you?" the Younger of Ben Nevis asked when he brought the gimlet.

There was a strained look in his father's choleric blue eyes which he had never seen before.

"I'm perfectly all right," the Chieftain declared. "It's a bit hot in here, that's all. My head's beginning to boil rather."

"I know that feeling, sir," said Hector with a sympathetic growl.

On the following afternoon Ben Nevis told his host and hostess that he was going to call on Mrs Winstanley. The way he said it sounded like the third act in a Pinero play.

"You'll find her bungalow being packed up," Mrs Rose-Ross warned him. "And we can all of us guess what that portends."

"I'll come with you, Donald," Kilwhillie volunteered. "I should like to say good-bye to Mrs Winstanley."

On the way to The Laurels Ben Nevis said, "Look here, Hugh, will you go and say good-bye for me to Mr Tucker and then call in at Angela's on your way back? I want to have a few words with her alone."

"I don't particularly want to go and say good-bye to Mr Tucker," Kilwhillie replied. "But if you think one of us ought to go I'll do so."

"You can leave a couple of cards with P.P.S. or whatever it is you put on them."

"P.P.C.", Kilwhillie corrected.

Ben Nevis found Angela surrounded by boxes.

"Maisie and I are leaving for Calcutta to-morrow morning," she told him.

"The sooner you go the better, my dear. I've been driven nearly mad by all these nincompoops saying you're going to marry Mr Tucker. I've had a fearful time keeping your secret. You don't know what I've gone through."

"Poor Ben Nevis. I am so sorry."

"And you forgot to ask Tussore to tell Banjo the secret, and I let it out to him, thinking he knew. But he promised he would keep it dark. And he was very nice about you. He said he thought Tussore had picked the very wife he ought to have. I was really delighted by the way he took it."

"Oh, I am sorry I forgot about that. But I'm quite sure the Maharaja of Bangapatam will say nothing to anybody except Tussore. And I'm so relieved to hear he took the news so well. How sweet of you, dear Ben Nevis, to come and tell me."

"Hugh Cameron will be here in a minute. He wants to say good-bye. So before he comes I'll just wish you not only a happy New Year but many many happy New Years. Don't forget that wireless message. We'll be on the I.B.C. ship—now what the deuce is it called? Oh, yes, the *Golconda* —Bombay to Liverpool. And I shall send you a wedding-present from Glenbogle."

"Good-bye, dear, dear Ben Nevis, and thank you more than I can say," she said from her heart.

"You've nothing to thank me for," he barked.

"Oh, yes, I have. I should never have met my Maharaja if it hadn't been for you. May I kiss you good-bye?"

And Ben Nevis, blushing crimson with pride, pleasure and embarrassment, was kissed good-bye. Angela's farewell to Kilwhillie was more formal.

The New Year was greeted at the Rose-Rosses' bungalow and the Chieftain's secret again became oppressive when his hostess speculated upon the reason that had made Mrs Winstanley suddenly betake herself to Calcutta.

"But it confirms my suspicions," she said.

"What suspicions?" Ben Nevis asked.

"I still think she is of the country, as we say."

"If you want my opinion, Mrs Rose-Ross, I think it's a pity you aren't all of you a bit more in the country. I can't understand what all this superiority is about. I mean to say, I always try not to feel superior when English people come up to the Highlands. It's jolly difficult sometimes. And then I say to myself, 'Well, after all, we do want to let them our shootings,' and so I treat them like human beings. Mind you, I don't include hikers in that. I look at hikers in the same way as Indians must have looked at us when we started invading them."

Mrs Rose-Ross saw that Ben Nevis resented her attitude toward Mrs Winstanley.

"Poor old thing," she said to her husband, "it's fortunate that Mrs Winstanley decided to accept the brewer's hand. Otherwise, I'm afraid Mrs MacDonald would have received a nasty shock. He's quite gaga about that woman."

As midnight sounded, the Chieftain raised his glass of whisky to all, and then to his heir he growled with emotion:

"Bleerna var ooah, Hector. That's the Gaelic for a happy New Year," he explained to the company. "And now will you excuse me, Mrs Rose-Ross? I'd like to go and first-foot them in the Mess." There he felt that his secret would be safe.

Of the visit to the Finchamptons at Viceroy's House

there is little to relate. It gave immense gratification to Balu Ram and Sher Khan, who both secured sheets of Viceroy's House notepaper on which they asked their masters to write chits commending their services to those who in future required two bearers of superlative honesty, skill and devotion. Sher Khan discovered the embroidered waistcoat of his dreams in New Delhi and, when he showed it to Kilwhillie, enjoyed the felicity of having it presented to him.

"How much was it?"

It says a lot for Kilwhillie as an employer that his bearer by an almost superhuman feat of self-restraint told him only half as much again as he had paid for it.

"I am very sorry when Master go," said Balu Ram when Ben Nevis was tying his jabot for the last dinner at Viceroy's House.

"Well, I shall be very sorry to lose you, Balu. I'd like to take you back to Scotland with me, but I'm writing to His Highness the Maharaja of Tussore to recommend you to him. But wait until the end of the month before you take him the chit I shall write. You'd like to go to Tussore, wouldn't you?"

"Tussore very good place," Balu acknowledged with a twitch of his head.

And the last picture that Ben Nevis carried away with him from India was of Balu Ram standing on the dockside to watch the *Golconda* slowly put out to sea.

"Well, I thoroughly enjoyed our little jaunt, Hugh," he woofed as Bombay began to melt into the haze behind them.

"I've enjoyed it more than I expected I should," Kilwhillie admitted.

"Mind you, I'm looking forward to being at home again," Ben Nevis continued. "I'm longing to see how Mrs Ablewhite gets on with all this stuff I bought in Delhi for curry."

"I didn't know you had been buying stuff for curry."

"Yes, that nice A.D.C. of Finchampton's—what's his

name? Crawford, yes, Crawford's as keen as mustard on curry, and he and I bought all sorts of material for it in Delhi. I think Lindsay-Wolseley is going to have rather an eye-opener."

"Mouth-opener might be a better description," Kilwhillie observed.

"Ha-ha! Jolly good, Hugh," the Chieftain guffawed. "I say, I think India has agreed with you. You're getting a regular wag. I'm glad Tussore managed to get that panther skin down to Delhi in time for you to take it back with you. It was good of him to go to so much trouble. You rather liked him, didn't you?"

"I found him quite agreeable."

"What would you say if I told you that . . . " Ben Nevis pulled himself up. "No, I can't tell you yet."

"Can't tell me what yet?" Kilwhillie asked.

"Ah, that's it. You'll get the surprise of your life when I do tell you."

"I hope you haven't committed yourself to something I know nothing about?" Kilwhillie probed nervously. "I thought you were being unnecessarily insistent that Miss Nutting should come and stay at Glenbogle this summer."

"No, I haven't committed myself to anything. But you're going to be absolutely bowled over before we get to Liverpool."

"I can well believe that," Kilwhillie agreed gloomily.

"Ah, not in the way you mean, Hugh. But don't try and persuade me to tell you now, because I can't."

"I'm not trying to persuade you to tell me anything," Kilwhillie snapped with a touch of petulance.

Ben Nevis was beginning to feel that if Hugh Cameron continued to be so incurious he should have to tell him the secret merely to show him how wrong he had been not to want to hear it. However, he resisted the temptation, and leaving Kilwhillie to his incuriosity he engaged in conversation a bulky weatherbeaten fellow-passenger with a thick dark beard.

An hour or so later he found Kilwhillie lying down in his cabin.

"Oh, look here, Hugh," he protested. "This is ridiculous. The sea is like glass."

"There is a definite swell," Kilwhillie contradicted. "And I am more comfortable lying down."

"But I want you to meet this wallah Witherspoon."

"I don't want to meet anybody with or without a spoon," Kilwhillie snapped. "If I keep to my bunk until we reach Aden I may be able to come up on deck as we go through the Red Sea."

"Witherspoon is his name."

"I don't want to meet him."

"But he's a most interesting wallah. He's been up on the Frontier looking for the Lost Tribes."

"I should have thought that was the business of the soldiers," Kilwhillie observed acidly.

"The Lost Tribes of Israel," Ben Nevis explained. "And apparently he won't have anything to do with them."

"I'm not interested in Mr Witherspoon's racial prejudices," Kilwhillie said.

"But you don't understand, Hugh. The point is that since he went to the Frontier he's more convinced than ever that *we* are the Lost Tribes. He's what they call a British Israelite."

"So is old Mackenzie of Mam."

"Is he?" Ben Nevis exclaimed. "I never knew that. Well, I'm bound to admit that this wallah Witherspoon has made me wonder if we aren't."

"Aren't what?"

"The Lost Tribes. I didn't believe him at first. And when he said that the Saxons were the same as Isaac's sons, I said, 'But I'm not a Sassenach,' and then all of a sudden I remembered MacIsaac."

Major Norman MacIsaac was Mac 'ic Eachainn's Chamberlain.

"I was staggered for a moment, and I think MacIsaac

himself is going to be pretty staggered when I tell him about this."

"I hope you won't add anything more to poor MacIsaac's responsibilities. He has quite enough already," Kilwhillie said severely.

"But what staggered me most of all was when this wallah Witherspoon pointed out that Ben Nevis obviously came from the East."

"I don't know what you're talking about, Donald. But I wish you'd leave me to lie down quietly. If I start trying to understand what you're talking about I shan't be able to concentrate on this swell."

"Witherspoon thinks that Ben Nevis was probably Ben Levi when those Lost Tribes arrived over there."

"And I suppose the Macintoshes were the Maccabees once upon a time," Kilwhillie scoffed. "I never heard such piffle."

"It's all very well for you to laugh, Hugh. But this wallah has given me something to think about. I wish Mrs Kibbler was on board. I'm sure she'd have been interested. And you say old General Mackenzie believes we're the Lost Tribes? Well, he commanded a division in Palestine with Allenby. That's probably where he found out about it. Lindsay-Wolseley, of course, will argue that the Lost Tribes are in Afghanistan, but this wallah Witherspoon won't have any of that. And he's been to Kabul. He's taken a lot of trouble to get at the facts."

It was on the evening before the *Golconda* reached Aden that the Chieftain's interest in British Israelites faded abruptly on receiving a wireless message from Calcutta:

secret no longer wish me happiness love Angela

He came surging into Kilwhillie's cabin with such a rush that Kilwhillie, who had just dressed himself to dine in the saloon for the first time since the *Golconda* sailed from Bombay, thought that the sea was getting up again.

"She's going to, she's going to and I'm really delighted."

"Who is she?"

"Angela. She's going to marry Tussore. As a matter of fact I knew what was going on all the time, but it was a secret and so I couldn't tell everybody else. I couldn't even warn Hector not to lay a hundred chips to one with Duncan Robertson that she wouldn't marry Tussore. And not only that but the silly fellow betted twenty chips to five that she was going to marry Tucker. Well, I'm glad you're dressed, Hugh, because we must drink her health to-night. I shall send her my congratulations by this wireless postage. Extraordinary thing this wireless. I'm jolly glad you're going to have a wireless contraption at Kilwhillie."

"Let me get this clear," said Hugh Cameron. "Am I to understand that Mrs Winstanley is going to marry the Maharaja of Tussore?"

"Yes, he gave her an engagement-ring with three rubies as big as three glasses of port. That's why I knew poor old Hector didn't stand a chance. You were all fussing about his marrying Angela, but I was as calm as the sea is to-night."

"I have to admit, Donald, that this news is a complete surprise to me," Kilwhillie said. "But it gives me pleasure too."

"Of course it's a surprise to you. It'll be a surprise to everybody. I should like to be in Tallulaghabad and hear what Mrs Rose-Ross says to the Colonel when she gets the news. Well, we've had a jolly good time, Hugh, and thanks to my tact and being able to keep this secret Trixie won't have to worry about Hector. I might have had some difficulty in getting it into her head that Angela would be a splendid wife for Hector. Trixie is old-fashioned in many ways. As it is, we've had a glorious time, and thanks to my going East everything has turned out for the best. I must introduce you to Witherspoon to-night. I'm rather tired of this British Israelite business. Yes, from the moment I decided to talk to Winstanley in the train on the way to Liverpool everything has gone right."

EPILOGUE

IN the housekeeper's room at Glenbogle Castle Mrs Ablewhite the cook was talking to Mrs Parsall.

"It would be all against my will, Mrs Parsall, if I was to give notice, but if he is going to rush into my kitchen at any moment and try and teach me how to make curry with a lot of unnatural seeds and what not as nobody's ever seen or heard of, notice I will have to give. It's not in human nature to stand it." Mrs Ablewhite declared.

"It's just that he's a bit excited at getting home," said Mrs Parsall soothingly. "People are like that. They see something abroad that takes their fancy and of course they want to experiment."

"Experiment?" Mrs Ablewhite repeated indignantly. "You've said it, Mrs Parsall. But my kitchen wasn't meant for experiments. Dipped his finger into the curry this morning, he did, like a mischievyous boy. And then what does he say? 'Oh, that curry isn't nearly hot enough yet, Mrs Ablewhite.' 'It's so hot already that it'll take the skin off of anybody's throat,' I said. 'Not in India, Mrs Ablewhite,' he says. 'Begging your pardon, Ben Nevis,' I says, 'but we're in Scotland, not in India,' I says. No, Mrs Parsall, it's no good. I can't stand any more of it. And it's so bad for these Highland girls. Florrie and Maggie were standing there giggling until I could have boxed both their ears. And in fact every time now I give an order they start off giggling again. No, Mrs Parsall, it's not in human nature to stand it. And I'd rather leave."

At this moment Toker came into the housekeeper's room. "Gimlet!" he exclaimed.

"I haven't got a gimlet, Mr Toker," said the housekeeper. "Hasn't Kenny got one in the carpenter's shop?"

"A gimlet, Mrs Parsall," said the butler, "is a drink, not

a tool. Though why they call a good gin drowned in lime-juice a gimlet I haven't an idea. It must have been an uncommonly blunt gimlet which gave its name to such an imitation of an honest drink. Well, I hope Ben Nevis doesn't go to America, that's all. Or he'll be drowning good whisky in Coca-Cola and calling it a screwdriver."

"Mrs Ablewhite has been a bit upset about the curry, Mr Toker."

"I wish Mrs Ablewhite could have seen Colonel Lindsay-Wolseley's face at lunch," said the butler. "I'm bound to say it wasn't entirely her curry, because Ben Nevis made me chop up three of these chillies and put them in the Colonel's helping. Oh dear, oh dear! Well, the curry was pretty hot to start with . . ."

"Thanks to his interference," Mrs Ablewhite put in, with dignified resentment.

"But what the poor Colonel went through with those chillies was beyond anything I ever saw at a luncheon-table since I started as second footman with old Lady Nuneaton. I saw the Colonel put his hand up to his throat. I think he thought his collar had caught fire. And then his forehead came out in a regular pool of perspiration and he gulped down a glass of claret and looked round at me with the look of a poor trout gasping away on a river bank."

"Tut-tut-tut-tut," Mrs Ablewhite clicked, "how terrible for the poor man! Well, that settles it, Mrs Parsall, I'll have to leave you. I am not going to have my good name as a cook dragged in the mud just to humour his lordship's Indian fal-de-lals."

Toker held up his hand.

"It'll pass in a day or two, Mrs Ablewhite," he declared impressively. "He's excited to be back home again, and full of his trip to India. Goodness me, I was expecting him to pop a turban on my head at any minute. But it'll pass. Before another week's out he'll be asking me what disgusting concoction I think I'm giving him, and when I tell him it's a gimlet he'll look at me as if I'd stuck it into him. And I shan't take any notice at all. I shall just remove the gimlet and put the decanter of Glenbogle's Pride in front of him. Yes, it'll pass, Mrs Ablewhite. It'll pass like everything else in this world. He won't know he's ever been east of Inverness in another week or two. And if you could hear what he says about your wonderful cooking you'd never have the heart to leave us."

"Well, that's as may be, Mr Toker," said Mrs Ablewhite, but when she went back to her kitchen Mrs Parsall turned to the butler gratefully.

"Thank you, Mr Toker. I think you mollified her."